ONE:
Empire

Alexander J Beld

CONTENTS

ACKNOWLEDGMENTS

Thanks to everyone who supported and helped me complete this story

CHAPTER ONE

Cold, blue light from the sun reaches down through the ocean and cuts through the darkness behind my eyelids, waking me up. It leaks in through my doorway and I gaze back out at it through the window nearest me. I've never actually seen the sun, even though we live somewhere around the 27th level of a tower that scrapes the sky and cuts clouds. The water has been above my level since before I was born. Back inside everything in here is dark and wet. Somewhere a pipe is leaking and a number of people cough uncontrollably. I hold back my own cough and look up through a hole in the blanket draped over our cube. The source of the leak is likely impossible to find and it can't be fixed anymore than I can stop my coughing. This whole level is falling apart and has been for years. My body is following close behind. My joints always ache my chest has started to feel tight over the past few weeks.

Everything lacks color in the darkness of the morning, even the people. As they walk past they seem more like skeletons to me, paled from the lack of sun and shriveled by the absence of food. They barely fill their clothes, which are just as poor in appearance. They are covered with holes and tears that have been delicately sewn back together. But in the early morning light, it all takes on the light blue color. Hints of white light shimmer through as waves lap against the side of the tower. The rhythm of each wave breaking against the tower is something I don't notice when going about my day, but when I wake up early like this I try to listen to it, the heartbeat of my private thoughts.

I usually wander back to the same ideas. How surviving is such a simple existence, which is all there really is to living in the People's Towers. It's the point of every day, of every person's life down here. There isn't much more to each day than making it to the next one. And from what people say down here, those on the top floor of this tower don't have it much better. If they ever find the means to, they leave immediately. Because of this the government rarely has reason to come down here. No one at this level has the means or the energy to cause trouble. We are a waste of resources, but some of the more hopeful people down here believe that things will get better if we wait. I disagree.

They believe strongly in the power of Empire and how the government says we are the last remaining people on the planet ever since the water rose. They say where other cities toppled, we stood strong, when others starved, we found food and how others failed, we succeeded. People believe it needs to be bad for things to work and that we were part of the team, making it all happen. I've never seen it that way. How could I trust a government I've never seen at work? All I've ever seen besides the filthy water and sloppy food that comes down the pipes are a few posters and the patrollers every couple years. Of course, everyone hears other things from work at the assembly lines, or patrollers as they pass by, but the posters almost always tell the same story.

Before I get too riled up I decide it's time to start with my day. My family's cube fits eight people in enough space for three. Someone's feet are in my face. Judging by the size and marks on the bottom it's most likely Dakota. My sisters are almost stacked on each other and my younger brothers are lying across me, one of them is using my stomach as a pillow. A space is open where my mom was until she left for her production shift an hour before sun up.

I quietly move my brothers and roll over to where she had been earlier and try to rest for a few minutes. The inch wide walls that surround us barely feel like a home. People say that one person would work in this little space on a screen. It would be amazing to have that much space. We used to have Lily and June, my youngest sisters, sleep on the desk until they got too heavy and it finally gave out. We hung a blanket over the top and across the doorway for some privacy, yet the sound of our neighbors softly snoring in the next cube over still penetrates the wall.

In another few minutes I'm up and walking toward the level's market. Markets are illegal in Empire, but the patrol almost never makes it all the way down to levels under the Deadline. If the water were to break through even one window, Empire could easily lose three or four patrollers over a few pieces of contraband. So, they let us have it.

There is barely enough light to see the trash and filth that has been flushed down by the people living above us and avoid stepping on it as I pass through the row of cubes. The trash tubes stop just below our ceiling and they plop strange liquids and unusable scraps onto the floor. We installed drains below them but they clog constantly. I pass the showers and debate trying to clean up, but it's just as likely that I'll be covered in someone else's piss, so I move on. Besides, I have no desire to undress in front of everyone since someone has stolen the curtains again. I stop for food even though I'm not hungry. There isn't a line yet and I don't want to spend half my day waiting like everyone else.

I snag a bowl and the puller for today gives me a large serving of slop as he pulls down on the lever that releases the nutrient injected food we are given. Every floor has the option to eat one bowl for free each day. Only people on the bottom levels take up the offer on a daily basis. I spoon the thick goo into my mouth and tongue it around to crush the balls of vitamin powder that didn't get mixed in the whole way. It slides down my throat slowly as I fill my mouth, wanting to move on quickly. I throw the bowl down onto the table and move on with my cheeks ready to blow. On the other side of the food table, the walls are freshly marked with new propaganda posters from Empire and ONE Industries. The bright paper shines in the midst of the dirt-smeared walls. They might as well save time and use the same poster. ONE makes everything we use and wear. They also supply Empire with all of their weapons, uniforms and tools.

The new slogan on ONE's posters says, YOU ONLY NEED ONE. The Empire poster has ONE's symbol on its lower right corner and reads, ONE SAVIOR, ONE LEADER, ONE PEOPLE, FOREVER. What would really be nice is two loaves of bread, a warm shower and some new clothes. It still seems silly to me when ONE sends their

posters down here, since there isn't a single person who can buy from

them on this level. Still, each month a stack comes down still hot from

being printed. Many of the other citizens down here are all too happy to

slap them up on the wall. It's hard to resist the urge to rip them down and

silently continue on to the market.

At this early hour the scavengers are still setting up their tables

in the small market, laying out their recent finds. Hopefully this means

the items I'm looking for will be here today. My mom always gives a

few bits of metal and a couple ONE tokens to purchase supplies for the

family, both are generally accepted down here.

"Hey kid what'll it be today?" a scavenger prods.

"I got something for you." another says as I pass through.

All the scavengers know me. Even though the area is cramped,

it's packed with a number of tables and each salty scavenger yells over

the other to be heard. They so badly want to be the ones to have me in

front of their table. I'm only the second person to arrive and they are

hungry to sell what they risk their lives for. As a child it was hard to

ignore their promises of good parts, but now it's easy to decide for

myself which parts look best. After bargaining with some scraps for a few minutes I have enough to keep my filter going for a couple months. If you can't filter water, drinking is out of the question. On the bottom levels like this, most of the water we get has already been used to clean off several other people or used to flush out drains. It's more bodily fluid than water, which is why filter parts are most of what can be found at this market. And they work hard, turning a gritty, black goop into a barely hazy liquid. The parts wear down quickly. After trading for a few other pieces of necessities I force my way through the gathering crowd over to Sal.

"Well kid, I found something you might like," he says in his low, scratchy voice. He is old but strong. His worn skin sags over his defined muscles.

My eyes light up as he pulls out a tattered book from the dry times. He grins as he hands it to me. "Where did you find this one?" I almost scream the words at him. It's a hardcover but the name of the book is too worn to read. There was another book back in the cube that Sal had found about a year ago, but most of the pages are missing. "Are all the pages there?" I feel like I'm yelling now.

"Most of them anyway, maybe you can do some mixing and matching and get one whole book, eh?" Sal says with a wink.

I scan the pages of the book rapidly and turn it over several times. My hands quiver with excitement and I don't even bother to tell him that you can't mix pages from two different books. He probably can't read much other than the posters. My other novel has a picture of a black tower. Just as ominous as Empire Tower, always seeming to watch and lean over me. It has always filled me with a sense of dread. At first the book was frightening to me, more for what might be behind the cover than its illegal quality. It was all too similar to the symbol of the government that has always been looming over us. Every poster and painting contained some form of a black spike rising from the ocean. Some people loved it, usually placing a hand on the image to show some kind of respect. My family is one that has seen the tower for its real purpose. Not to care for us or keep the peace, but to keep us exactly where we are. I'm afraid to openly talk to my mother about these feelings and ideas. If the wrong person were to overhear our conversations, my whole family could be down in the water by the end of the day.

Most people don't know how bad we have it, or maybe it's easier to go on by pretending we don't bathe in the dirt of every person that lives above us. But mostly, people believe the government propaganda that tells them we would be nothing if it weren't for Empire. Yet the government is the reason two patrollers are dragging away my neighbors right now and why I've just pocketed my metal scraps and Sal is handing me the book inside of a bag. I'll bring back the bag tomorrow with the scraps inside. We are all caught off guard by the quiet and unannounced arrival of Empire's law enforcement. Usually they come down the lift and the bell let's us know they're coming. Today they must have come in through the stairs.

People start to quickly spill out of the market and scavengers cover up most of their contraband. Fortunately for us the patrol doesn't care about us right now. They are just looking for people strong enough to scrap for materials and to repair support beams to keep the towers standing. If they've come all the way down here they will also have to fill their quota for rebel captures whether or not they actually find one. This also makes it hard for the rebels to recruit anyone when the patrollers only leave the young and weak behind.

"Go back to your cube kid. It's going to be a long day," Sal says as he shoos me away.

I just nod at Sal and walk back as quickly as I can while still appearing calm. I hide the book in the floor, knowing it might not come out for a few days. The patrol was down in force, which meant there had most likely been some kind of rebel attack. At least they would say that was the reason. Down here you never knew the truth. Judging by the amount of patrollers down here the rebels had been incredibly successful in their real or made up endeavors. They hadn't come down this far in over two years and many of us were out of practice. Our neighbors were taken away for contraband like my book. They would be back in a month or so if they didn't die while scrapping for materials on the surface of the old dry world, now the bottom of the ocean. You couldn't pay most starving men to do the work Empire needed, so it became a punishment. Only half of them would return and those who did would be happy to only be missing a few fingers. From what I had heard most people that go in the water are eaten by sharks or white squids that the scavengers call skulls. The rest drown from accidents or faulty oxygen equipment. I wonder how an old guy like Sal makes it back every day. Then again he only scraps in the lower levels of towers where predators are less likely to find you.

My family starts moving some of our belongings into the freshly emptied cube next to us before someone else can. If the previous owners ever came back we would give it up, but it wasn't likely that we would have to. As we're finishing the move a patroller approaches us and demands that we drop everything. We step out of our cubes and line up as best as we can. He is much younger than most other patrollers. He might have been a year or two older than myself, somewhere around twenty. He has freckles and a large nose. Orange hair pokes out of the red beret that is folded over his forehead and his grey jumpsuit hangs loosely on his small frame.

"What is this!" his voice cracks as he holds up a piece of scrap metal.

"It's just spare parts," I cautiously reply.

"It's contraband and a secondary form of currency. If you were worth anything you would be picking up scrap with the rest of this filth," he screeches and spits on me as he does.

He pockets the metal. He'll use it for himself, probably to buy a seat to the next execution or hoop event. The patrollers and their families aren't paid, but they are given everything they need. They tend to steal so they can spend time pretending to be just as wealthy as top floor citizens. Of course, no one would ever persecute someone like him. That would require an explanation too difficult for people down here to swallow, not that we would ever hear of it anyway. My attention and the young patroller's are turned towards a scuffle that has started up a few cubes away. I quickly give my sister several remaining pieces of scrap to hide in her baggy pants and slowly follow the patroller as he runs to the scene

"Hold him down!" screams one patroller as a small man squirms underneath him.

"Please," the man screams into the floor. "I didn't do anything. I never hurt anyone. Someone help me, please. My kids."

No one comes out of the crowd to help him. No one ever does. Before he can get out another word two more patrollers jump on him and the man finally tires out. Patrollers are well fed, making it hard for people like us to fight them off. Their weight alone is enough to usually bring us to the ground. They probably picked him for his short hair. According to the patrollers, rebels cut their hair, so most people usually leave it long. His had probably just got knotted up and he had to slice it off. It was just bad timing.

The freckled patroller stands at a distance staring until the one that first tackled the man calls out to him. "Alright kid it's your time to show us what you're made of." He says with a grin. "See how many licks he can take before he pops."

Without a word the shaking patroller pulls out his club and approaches the man that has now returned to his struggling, but with much more wild and aimless flailing. Many others within earshot have now been drawn to the commotion. Heads sporadically pop out over the top of cubes and some of the more courageous residents of the level have joined me. When the young patroller sees this he hesitates for a second as he raises the red stick above his head. After some encouragement from the senior patroller he drops it like a hammer into the back of the man's head. The reaction throughout the level is mixed as several people cheer, while others look away in disgust

"Give him his licks!" one man shouts.

And this releases a barrage of insults at the man who is about to die. "Get that bag of bones," shouts an equally slender man.

"Rebel scum!" shouts a woman standing next to me. I try to push back through the crowd, but they've gathered too tightly and I'm stuck with my front row view. The patroller feeds off of the energy of the mob, continually striking harder. I cringe at the sight of skin splitting, but I don't find myself able to close my eyes the whole way. The fear and excitement I feel all at once is a disgusting reaction to the situation, as inhuman as a thrashing shark. When the man's head finally cracks the shouting climaxes and then falls into a hush. Splattered with blood, the patroller sways with glazed over eyes. He spins around to look at the crowd that has gathered until his eyes fall on me, blood is splashed across his face and his gaze begins to focus around me.

"You!" he yells while pointing his club at me. It drips from its new paint job. "Contrabander! I'm not done with you."

"We have our quota," his superior says. "Let him be Patrick, he just wanted a show like the rest of us. There's no point, he's just a kid."

I mutter something along the lines of an agreement before pushing through the quickly dissipating crowd and running back to my cube. The heavy fall of boots drowns out the slapping of my bare feet on the wet concrete. I run past my cube without hesitating. Alison's worried look follows me as I brush past her. She doesn't call out to me. We both know it's better for me to be the only one who has their attention.

"I'm going to break your feet bottom feeder!" Patrick bellows from behind me. "You'll be sliding on your belly like you were meant to when I'm done."

His club flies past my head, spraying blood onto my face before colliding with the jaw of a man resting against the outside of his cube. He falls to the floor clutching his face. The rest of the people watching or milling around duck for the nearest cube as I rush past them. I speed up as I turn the corner and slip on a pile of brown slime. I don't care to think of what it was. Instead I scramble to my feet and sprint a few more steps before realizing the boots aren't stomping after me anymore. I go to my knees and crawl back to peer around the corner to see what has happened. Patrick's superior has him by the neck and is quietly saying something in his ear. His face goes pale as he is thrown to the ground. As Patrick crawls to get his club the senior patroller kicks him and the whole group of them laugh as his face lands in a dark puddle. He looks up and glares at me through the sludge smeared across his face. His fellow patrollers continue to harass him with insults and laughter as he wipes himself off.

"I'd say we've just about broken the rookie in," one of the patrollers cries through his laughter.

After the laughter dies down the patrollers collect their gear and herd all the offenders to the lift. Ten people in total, most of them are being marched to their death. Somewhere down in the bleak depths of the submerged city they will die scared and alone. All for whatever harmless item, device or substance they had. The dead man, the first victim, is left there as a reminder not to join the rebellion, even though he most likely wasn't a rebel himself. Once the doors to the lift shut, a collective sigh of relief can be heard through the entire floor and everyone goes about their business as though the patrol was never there. Even those who cheered for the man's death seem in higher spirits, they too have something to hide. The hypocritical supporters may some day suffer the wrath of their so-called savior. I wish it had been some of them.

No matter who you are, you can't grumble about today, not even the family of the dead man dares to appear upset about his brutal beating. Many of us were willing to inform on anyone who even hints at disliking the government. No one ever gets anything for it, except for the supposed fulfillment of coming closer to true Oneness. Some families have feuded through sharing false information to send those they disliked below. Generally, it's a good idea to only speak out of necessity. This practice has kept patroller's out of our hair for years, until today.

It may have been awhile since we've seen patrollers, but death was something we experienced often. Disease comes through almost as often as starvation. We live two people to a few square feet and even with the amount of death we see down here it seems like there are even more children all the time. My family alone stands strong at three boys, four girls, and my mother. Our father died three years ago, we don't know how, we just know that he never came back from his fishing post. He could have fallen into the water or simply been forced to go below. It may have been that supplies were short and arrests had been made simply to force more people into working. It was not outside of

possibility, he was a strong man. Even when we were starving he seemed

to be able to move towers for us if only he tried hard enough.

"Sam are they gone?" my sister Alison asks from behind me.

"Yes," I whisper.

She is followed by two of our younger sisters, each one holding

onto a bit of her shirt. You could tell that they had been crying by the

clean skin, trailing from their eyes to their chins. Lily's stuffed toy is

held closely to her chest and her blonde hair is tangled in it. Alison's

green eyes glare at me while she ushers Lily and June back to our new

cube.

"What were you thinking? If you had been taken away what

would we do? We would all be dead in a week!" She hisses it so our

siblings can't hear her.

I don't say anything, instead I just stare down at my feet. Her

anger makes me feel ashamed, but angry myself at the same time. Even

though I want to yell at her and tell her that we were all dead anyway and

that our lives are worthless because we will never do better than just

enough to live, I don't. It's a lost battle already. It's better to keep it all to myself like I always have. It would ruin any hope that my brothers and sisters still hold on to. And Alison is right, without me they would all die much more quickly. Even though it feels like something I have little control over. Instead of dwelling on the image of my life being choked from me in front of my family, I walk past Alison and pull open the hatch that holds all of our apparent contraband.

"I'm not going anywhere," I finally state, cracking open my new book.

It sags in my hands and I quickly relax them, taking care to turn to the first page. It still hasn't dried out the whole way. I sit down on a blanket while my brothers and sisters huddle around me. I taught myself how to read over the years, though not very well. To my family it doesn't matter, we could spend days on a single chapter. It is one of our only forms of entertainment and it keeps everyone from running around and getting into trouble. As I read, their excitement causes them to miss parts and I constantly reread paragraphs, to the dismay of whoever was paying attention at the time. Small hands reach out to the pages and poke at certain words. I describe the meanings as well as I know how. Every word enchants them. This is the closest thing they will ever have to an education, but I am proud that it's coming from me.

It also keeps their minds off of the events from today and none of them will run off to find the body only a few steps from us. Some of them are still young enough that they can't remember the last time a patrol was down here and keeping them sheltered from the pain of this world for a few more years is an ever-present thought. After I finally work my way through a few pages our mother returns from the ONE factory lines. Her dark hair is greasy and it randomly attaches itself to her face, giving her a savage appearance. Her panicked eyes complete the look.

"Is everyone OK? Is everyone still here?" she charges into the first cube. "Where are the rest!?"

Word spread quickly about patrollers taking people. Fresh captures are generally walked past the assembly lines to be geared up and briefly trained. It's a fair assumption that she recognized the people from our level. To her relief she turns to see the rest of my brothers and sisters come around the corner. All at once she looks tired and content, her shoulders sag as she slouches down into a pile of blankets. She looks up at me through her slick hair and pulls a loaf of bread out of her bag with her withered hands. I don't bother asking how she had managed to afford it. I just take it and divvy it out. We eat all of it and still go to bed hungry.

The next morning I wake up to the sound of my stomach and several smaller ones growling. If I didn't find a way to bring in more scrap metal or tokens I might have to try scavenging with Sal to keep my family from starving. My mother hasn't eaten anything but slop for two days. She looks thinner all the time. And most days the rest of us only had enough to nibble on after our one bowl. Some days Alison and I would skip our meal so everyone else could eat more. Lily rolls over and looks at me with her big blue eyes, "Is there any more bread?" she whispers. "My tummy is so rumbly, it's hard to sleep."

I brush the hair out of her face and softly reply, "If you go back to bed I'll get you some more when you wake up." She smiles at me before closing her eyes and rolling back over. Of all my brothers and sisters, lying to her was the most painful. It's mainly because she believes me so completely every time I lie and tell her things will get better. When they don't, she doesn't have any less faith in my promises. I'm not sure I will ever be telling the truth when I say that it will get better, but if we make it one more year I can apply to work again and we can at least keep ourselves from starving for a little longer if they give me a job this time.

A hand gently grabs my shoulder and squeezes. "Sam they're back." Alison reaches over me and points down toward the lift. The slate metal doors are slowly opening up and the patrollers from yesterday are stepping out. Panic washes over me as I realize we still have our books and toys out. They never make it down here this early and I've never even heard of them coming down this far twice in a week. Patrick is leading the group and they are coming straight toward us. I give them one look and grab my new book before taking off. Without hesitating or yelling, the group of patrollers follows.

"Sam wait!" Alison calls after me.

I turn the corner and make my way for the market. If I am lucky I can lose them in the confusion of the setup. I turn back to make sure all of them are chasing me. It doesn't matter what happens to me as long as they leave everyone else alone. Just don't slip, I tell myself while rounding a corner. Two of the patrollers aren't so lucky as they run through a patch of sludge. They lose their footing and slide into a window. Fortunately it was one of the few that had been reinforced on this level. Still, everyone goes quiet for a moment, watching the window just to be sure we aren't all about to die. The metal support sheets shudder, but the glass shows no sign of cracking.

"Watch it guys," one of them stammers. "We don't need another flood-in like Carnegie Tower yesterday."

And the chase is back on. I dive through a group of scavengers setting up and duck behind some crates. I lay flat on the ground trying to slow my breathing. My shirt is soaked through my heart pounds against the floor. A few minutes pass by before I have the courage to take a peek. Four of them are still pushing through the scavengers and their tables asking where I had gone. No one will give me up outright. People generally like to inform in secret. To snitch on me in a crowd would paint a target on whoever would be stupid enough to do it. Instead of asking about my location Patrick has thrown Sal up against the wall and has his club across his throat.

"What did the kid even do huh?" Sal chokes out. "You freckled little shit, if you weren't wearing that uniform I'd shove this stick up your scrawny little ass."

"Suit yourself you salty old bastard," Patrick laughs back. "You know punishment is served at our discretion down here."

Patrick pulls the stick back from Sal's throat and swings back to hit him. Before he delivers the blow I come out from behind the crates and yell "Patrick!" I couldn't let someone else take the beating for me, though not for the same reason everyone kept quiet about where I was hiding. I care about the man and I doubt I'd be able to face him the next time I found myself on the other side of his table, so, I start running again.

"Grab that kid before he disappears again." Patrick spits through gritted teeth.

Who's really in charge here? I wonder as I look back to see Sal on his knees, shuddering from each cough as he recovers from the brief chokehold. The determined face of Patrick speeds towards me through the other faces that stare on. It's all the incentive needed to keep moving and scanning for a place to hide, but I've already run out of places to go on this level. It's not possible to keep running laps all day. Even in the crowd there's no hiding, they part at the sight of me coming towards them. As I reach the next row of cubes a sharp pain explodes in the back of my head. I stumble and before I can get my feet back under me I tumble over, ending up crumpled against a window. All five patrollers are now standing around me in a semicircle and they're all holding their clubs except for Patrick.

"Guess you aren't such a bad shot with that thing after all," one of them says as they hand Patrick their own club. "You earned this one boy."

He eagerly takes the club, slowly walking up to me tapping the palm of his hand with the red stick. He stands over me with a grin on his freckled face. I wonder how many times he'd gotten to do this since yesterday morning. Patrollers had always scared me, but I never thought that I would be killed by one for having a book.

"I'm a lot better at this than the last time you saw me bottom feeder." Patrick says as he raises the club above his head the first time. He hits me hard enough for my head to smacks against the glass. The thud echoes through the level. Someone gasps, causing Patrick to pause and look behind him before he hits me again and then I realize everyone is watching in silence, just like the day before. He hits me a few more times and with each blow my head thuds against the window. His hat falls off in the midst of the savage beating, revealing his orange, fiery hair. It becomes difficult to keep count of the blows. Eventually one of the other patrollers grabs his arm and stops him.

"Kid, stop playing with your food, either kill him or let's get out of here," One of them says.

A drop of water rolls down my forehead. I tilt my head back and see a crack in the window growing towards the ceiling. I try to say something to the patrollers but my face hurts too much to move my mouth. My jaw is locked shut, but feels loose at the same time and my face burns. The window makes a crunching noise as the cracks spread across the glass. The patrollers still haven't noticed. Patrick comes in for one more swing when a piece of glass pops out of the window. It grazes his cheek and for a long moment no one moves or says a word. I slowly start to get up, being careful not to touch the glass and one of the patrollers even helps to pull me away from the window.

"Let's get out of here before we really do have another Carnegie Tower incident" the captain says. "We don't need to die for bottom feeders."

"Should we evacuate the level through the lift?" Another patroller suggests. He is careful to ask quietly as they all continue to huddle around me.

The captain responds by running toward the lift, pushing everyone out of his way as he crashes through the crowd. Patrick and the rest follow through the bewildered citizens without even looking back at me. As I run for my family's cubes I take one look back at the window. Water is now pouring through a gaping hole at this point. There isn't much time to get everyone to the stairs before the window is completely broken through.

I stumble into the crowd and start to push people out of the way as they just stand watching the water pour in. Get out of here! Get out of my way! I scream inside my head. My still swelling jaw won't budge. No one reacts to my frantic movements. They stare blankly at the water with open mouths. I continue shoving my way through the crowd until I see Lily curled up against a cube. The few people smart enough to run step over her. A few feet come within inches of her face and she only curls up tighter. I force myself against the current of people and pull her up. I throw her on my back and start moving. Dozens of faces run past me, trying to recognize them in the confusion is impossible. There is no way to know where the rest of my family is. All I can do is hope that we all meet on the other side of the door.

"What's happening!" Lily screams over and over in my ear.

Her screams are drowned out by my thoughts of escaping the level. I shove past the people that have gathered in the row of cubes, attempting to collect their personal belongings. I can't understand why blankets and rags are so important. Two women fall as they trip over a blanket trailing on the floor at their feet. People start to crash into each other and shout for loved ones as they cross paths, all running for different parts of the level. Those that had stared before start to shout, but the rushing water quickly drowns their voices out. A sudden surge pulls cubes out of the floor, wiping them away with people still in them. As I get closer to the stairwell my mother's head appears above the crowd. I hope she has everyone else with her. If not, it's too late to go back. She reaches the door just as a wave of water comes through. It picks up several people, swirling them around with the garbage. They are pinned against the far windows, but the glass holds for the moment. Blood smears across the windows from the people who hit the glass too hard before washing away in the foamy water that swells against the glass. At that moment I briefly pause to look for Sal. A few minutes ago he was ready to take a beating for me. I hope that I'll get the chance to thank him, for everything.

I'm lucky enough to slide behind a column just in time. Lily is clinging to my front now. I can't tell if she's stopped crying or if the water is has gotten that loud. I lean into the column and hook one arm around while waiting for the initial rush of water to slow. When it finishes I wade my way to the door. Alison is at the window of the door. She's pounding on it and yelling for me to hurry even though I can't hear her over the sound of the water. Another rush comes through, as the windows on the other side finally break open. This gets me running through the water, lifting my legs high in an attempt to run and dive for the door with Lily still clinging to my neck. Alison opens the door and the rush of water pushes me through, slamming me face first into the far wall. All I can manage is to land on my side and wrap my arms around Lily. As everything fades away, all I can hear is her screaming for me.

CHAPTER TWO

I start coming to, part way up the stairs as we near the next level. Several hands are on me, carrying me up the stairwell. The worried faces of my mother and Alison glance through the arms of those helping me up the steps. This is my first time in the stairwell. The railings are mostly yellow, but splotches of grey show where the paint has been chipped and scratched. The walls are clean and have fresh propaganda painted across them. The same slogans appear with several paintings of Empire Tower. Each one has its own a working light, they glow hot white. The heat coming off them comes through my wet clothes and warms my skin. The propaganda isn't surprising to me, but I can't figure out why we couldn't ever be given warm lights like these ones. It's also surprising that the patrollers didn't stay to make sure none of us got out.

It is against Empire law to travel up a level without payment and proper paperwork, so I've never had a reason to use it. I once tried to sneak in when I was much younger, but my dad caught me moments before I could slide through the doorway. I had only caught a glimpse of the stairs. Mostly, people going to work at ONE use the stairs so they can get to the water level and board the ferry. People can travel downward, but the stairwell is filled with water just below our level. I'm sure it's starting to fill up higher now that our level has flooded in.

When I start to squirm the men from my floor put me down on my feet. I try to walk on my own and fall into Alison. She almost falls over under my weight. "Come on big brother we're almost to the next level, you can go back to napping when we get there," she says.

Lily is still crying somewhere behind me. I chuckle in an attempt to show that I'm OK and pain shoots through my entire face and neck. Alison puts my arm around her shoulder and helps me up the last few steps. I make half an effort to look around and I see ten people around us. Every one of them is only another wet shape to me as my eyes struggle to focus, but none of them are the right height to be my brother Philip or sister Kat. Alison and she must have realized who I was looking for.

"They didn't make it Sam. They were on the other side of the level. We could only grab June and Dakota. You got Lily out," Alison wipes away a tear with her free hand. She never cries and she's doing her best to hold it in now.

I don't even try to acknowledge what she said. I just let my head hang down so I can't catch my mother's eye. Does she think this was my fault? I can't help considering it myself. If I hadn't caught the patrollers' attention yesterday all of this might have been avoided. I already miss everyone I knew down there, especially my family and I feel awful thinking about how much easier it would be to eat without them. Just as I'm starting to beat myself up a lanky man from the group pushes past us. His clothes almost fall off him and his ribcage shows through the holes in his shirt. He walks up to the door to open it. He pulls slowly on the handle, nothing happens so he pulls with two hands until it pops off. The guts of the lock fly out after it. He almost topples over until a stubby woman I don't know shoves him against the wall.

"It was a push you idiot," she spits in his face. "Now we're stuck in this shit hole, there's no way we can sneak in two floors up."

"Get off me Kara we don't have time for your complaining," he says while poking her in the chest. "We can still find a way in."

Just as Kara is about to get back in his face, Alison squeezes herself between both of them and bangs on the door. It shudders with each blow and rust comes off the hinges. Time and salty air have almost

turned the door into red sand. The two instantly forget about their

argument and stare at her with disbelief. The man grabs her by the

shoulder and pulls her around.

She looks up at them with confusion, "What? We need to get in

right?"

The two of them are about to turn their anger on her until the

door scrapes open. A tiny, balding man with broken glasses leans out

from behind the door. He looks around at us searching for words to say,

his mouth hanging open as he soaks us in. After some stuttering he

finally finds something to say.

"It's illegal to let lower people into higher levels, what do you

want bottom dwellers?" he asks.

All at once Alison, Kara, and the man start yelling reasons why

the small gate keeper should let us through the door. He starts to close it

as I fall to my hands and knees, spitting out blood and a loose tooth. A

woman must have been standing behind him because suddenly he's on

the ground and she's holding the door open all the way. She takes one

look at me and waves us in.

"How badly is he hurt?" she asks.

"Well it looks like he got beat to hell by a patroller and he tried to finish the job by head butting a wall," Kara explains.

"Let's hurry, get the young hero inside," the woman lets out a sigh to make her sarcasm more apparent. "Everyone might as well come in with him, we're breaking the law no matter how many come through the door."

While I'm still coughing a couple pairs of hands pick me up by my armpits and drag me through the doorway. The feet of the woman and the small man lead us on. I can hear voices, they sound far away and I'm not sure what's being said. We walk down a row of empty cubes until we reach three empty ones. They take me to the one in the middle and set me down on a blanket. Alison comes in with another rolled up and puts it under my head. My mother just sits in the corner and stares at me with her expressionless, gaunt face. My vision goes in and out as I struggle to keep my head up. Every time I pull up it lolls to one side or the other. I blink a few more times in an attempt to focus my eyes, but I fail to stay conscious.

I wake up expecting a head digging into my stomach and a shoulder in my side. Instead the morning greets me with a throbbing head and shooting pain all the way down my back. I try to sit up until a firm hand presses down on my chest. I can't see who is holding me down because my eyes are swollen shut. The hand moves from my chest, running its fingers through my hair. It calms me and convinces me to lie back down. Dread slowly comes over me as I start to remember what brought me here. The urge to thrash and scream builds up in me, but all my body can manage is to tense up. Whoever has been running their hand through my hair must have noticed.

"It's OK. Why don't we try to sit up now," the voice whispers.

It's a girl and at first it seems like it might be Alison or my mother, but she sounds nothing like neither of them. Her voice is much more calming than my mom's and not nearly as harsh as Alison's. If anything it's soothing to me, it helps to fade away all my other concerns. She helps me sit up against the wall and puts a couple blankets behind me to lean on. At first the pain is nauseating and I try to slouch back to the floor, but without her help it's hard to even wiggle. She hands me a mug of warm liquid and I drink it without question. As the mug empties she starts to sound further away. I don't want her to leave so I reach out for her. She takes my hand and puts my arm down across my body. At the same time she takes the mug back from me and lays me back onto the floor. As she leaves she speaks to me one more time.

"I'll let everyone know you woke up, most of us didn't think you would make it. Get some more rest, the drink will help you stay asleep," She says.

I fall asleep as her footsteps fade. The dreams start with Philip and Kat being washed away by the water and in the next dream skulls and sharks are eating them as they claw at the ceiling. The worst is when they stare at me blankly asking where I was when the water came in. They float in the water above the cubes. Their bodies are already decaying. Bits of bone and muscle poke out through their skin and their eyes don't move. Instead they float lazily, looking down. They reach for me and pull at my clothes, biting my ears as they continue to ask where I was and plead for me to save them. It's hard to know if the drink caused this or not. This probably won't be the last time my dreams are like this. The comfort of sleep has now been taken from me.

I wake up in a cold sweat, coughing. My eyes are still swollen shut, but it is easy to tell that it's night because all I can hear is the constant drip of water and muffled coughing I'm so accustomed to. I feel around the cube to see if anyone is there with me, eventually I find my mother sitting in the corner. She wakes up when I grab her foot.

"Sam is everything OK?" she grumbles.

It's still difficult to move my jaw much so I nod my head hoping she'll able to see. She gently caresses my face, feeling all of the lumps and bruises. It hurts a little but I don't stop her. After a moment I move closer to her, leaning against the wall with her. She lets me rest my head on her shoulder and she holds me for a long time. We sit there listening to each other breathing. Eventually she shifts her weight and sighs, preparing to say something.

"I'm sorry I couldn't get Philip and Kat," she cries. "I…" her words break into uncontrollable sobs.

Without speaking or seeing it's hard to do anything to try and comfort her. I manage sit up taller than her so I can more easily reach an arm around her. After a moment her hand grasps for mine and I squeeze it tightly. She grabs it even harder in response and when she starts to cry she pulls me in closer. I'm careful to keep my face clear of her head and shoulders. She sobs into my chest until she's exhausted. We fall asleep that way despite the pain it causes me to sit up. In the morning my shirt still feels wet from her tears. I wonder if she had woken up later in the night or had been crying in her sleep.

One of my eyes finally opens and it's bright enough to finally take a look around our new home. After unwrapping my mother's arms from around me I find my feet with the help of the wall and take a look over the top of the new cube. The level doesn't look any different than the last one. Just rows and rows of cubes littered with trash and exhausted people. Everything seems just as dull and tired. My mom looks more exhausted and frail than usual. It's hard not to wonder if she had been eating or going to work while I've been sleeping or if she has been here with me the whole time. Most likely she just cried here, never even getting up to eat. No one would miss her at the factory. People died or fell ill all the time. If anything the floor leader wouldn't report her missing and just pocket the extra tokens until she started coming back to work.

My legs are heavy. Standing up on my own for the first time in days isn't easy. Even though the pain is still there, shooting down my back, it's manageable. Light hits my face as my head clears the top of the cube. A ball of fire hangs in the sky outside one of the windows, the sun. Now I finally know what color it really is, yellow. This is the first time I'm really seeing it. The actual color had always been a mystery to me, only ever seeing it through the surface of the ocean. It hurts to look directly at it, but the warmth on my face is refreshing. It breaks through the cold from the level below. Something I had been so accustomed to.

The surface of the ocean shimmers as yellow and blue mix. Waves lazily roll up against the bottom of the windows. Each one sprays water up and across the glass, leaving beads to roll back down and shine in the rays of the sun. It looks too beautiful to only be seen from the inside.

Before leaving my cube for a closer look, a girl blocks my way by standing in the doorway. She's breathing heavily and taking me in with large brown eyes. We both stand there for a moment just looking at each other. She's about my age, shorter, and has long dark hair. Just as I'm about to ask her if she was the one who had taken care of me, she confirms my assumption.

"I saw you stand up from the other side of the level. You've been sleeping for more than a week but you should still should be laying down Sam," she states. "I've been taking care of you and your mom, I'm happy to see you finally standing on your own, but you really shouldn't be up at all yet. Why are you up?"

I nod at her rapid comments in a lazy attempt to say thank you and shrug in response to the last part. Before I can even finish a step to try and move past her, she puts her arm up to block my way. "You're not going anywhere yet," she almost yells in surprise at my attempt to leave. "You still need rest and several patrollers came looking for you and any other lower level dwellers that might be here illegally. It took us forever to convince them that no one made it out. If they saw your face too many questions would be asked. And that scrawny one with the freckles is vicious. I don't want to have to talk to him again."

We stand there for a second trying to read each other and after a moment I decide she won't try to stop me. I push her arm out of the way and start walking past her toward the windows. After several steps she's at my side, grabbing my arm. At first it seems like she is trying to stop me. Instead she helps me stay on my feet as we approach the glass. She whispers quietly into my ear. "I could have stopped you, you know."

I take my eyes away from the surface for a moment and give her a look.

"I'm much stronger than I look, Sam," she continues.

My first attempt at speaking in days comes out as a croak. My throat is dried out and feels ripped. The inside of my mouth sticks to itself from a lack of fluids, but that doesn't stop my face from flushing red with embarrassment. My second attempt is more successful. "I would like to see you try," finally crawls out. My face throbs with every word. She just looks at me and smiles. We stand there quietly for a moment until the silence starts to feel strange. Not wanting to strain myself I softly whisper to her. "Who…?" Before the question is finished she put two fingers on my mouth, silencing me. She lets go of my arm and steps back. We both continue staring through the glass for a time. I cough to break the silence and she finally says something.

"My name is Azalea," she says. "My mom and I try to take care of people on this level and several others. It's been harder lately with the patrollers down here so often. They keep hurting more and more people every time they visit so we've been running out of energy and supplies. They've also made it against Empire law to 'tend to potential rebel members or sympathizers,' she mimics a deep male voice. "It seems like everyone who isn't a patroller is somehow connected to the rebels these days. It took a lot to hide you from them, especially when they were making daily visits down here."

I give her a worried look and she laughs at me saying, "Don't worry, we only buried you in trash twice. No one wanted to do anything to actually risk their own life for you though."

I take a whiff of myself and find myself smelling fresher than ever. I let out an exhausted sigh and feel my shoulders slouch. Hanging my head I turn around making my way back to bed. Azalea grabs onto me once again after I stumble. She walks me back, and helps to lay me down on the pile of blankets. I want her to stay longer, but I'm tired and there isn't anything else to say that makes sense, especially to someone I just met. It would be nice to know more about her, maybe because she cared for me, but it could be more than that. It could be the same reason her voice was so soothing to me before. The feeling is so bizarre to have after just meeting her. The thoughts flutter through my head as she pulls a blanket up to my chest and leaves. It all passes before I've even made a decision to speak up.

She pauses at the door and says, "Maybe tomorrow I can spend the day showing you around, normally it wouldn't take long but you walk like an old man."

Normally there would have been a response with some kind of sass, but I just gaze up at her instead. She looks like she's smiling as she leaves the doorway. I hope that she is. In the morning she wakes me up by shaking my shoulder. I sit up as she plops down, next to me.

"You ready to get moving?" she says giving my shoulder a flick.

I mumble out a tired yes and take a look around the cube at the same time. My mother is gone. She must have finally started going back to the factory. I move to get up and Azalea is standing before I can get to my knees. She pulls me up the rest of the way, almost on her own.

Feeling so small in someone else's arms is odd to me. Is my body suddenly that frail now, or is she as strong as she claims?

We make our way out of the cube. With both eyes open and more light to see, this level looks far worse off than my own. Everything seems better when you can't see all of it I guess. Azalea guides me as we walk. It's difficult to keep my eyes from bouncing from object to person to object. Most everything is the same, except small details are more noticeable and it's easier to tell people apart, which reminds me of the woman who let me and everyone else in.

"Where is the woman that let everyone from below in?" I ask Azalea.

"Oh, that would be my mom, she left for one of the other towers a couple days ago to help out there." She replies. "She makes rounds by working at the factory and taking the ferry to a different tower. She has a fake entry ID for almost all of them now. We probably won't see her for about week at this point."

"Oh," is all I can say as I look at the ceiling for the first time. It's covered in several colors of mold. Liquid drops down into puddles that I don't notice until I step in one. It becomes apparent where all the puddles and dripping had been coming from on my level. Dark and gloomy has been traded for bright and disgusting.

Azalea stops and glares at me, "Yeah ceiling's moldy, get over it. Recently hit in the head or not, it's still rude to just say oh and barely acknowledge that I just answered your question."

I slowly take my eyes off the ceiling and look at her apologetically. Just then a drop of discolored, warm water hits me square in the forehead. She smirks at me as I wipe it away and look up at a damp collection of red mold. Azalea yanks me along. We make our way around the corner to the market. It's small like the one below was, just a few tables with boxes of supplies stacked on and around them. The people of Empire don't have a lot of space but we all use it well. It feels less congested than usual. After a closer look around it becomes obvious that there are less people here. There must have been half as many people on this level as there were on mine.

"Where is everyone?" I ask Azalea.

She looks at me, confused for a second, "What do you mean? We've lost 20 or so people to the patrollers and gained the 10 people from your floor. So this is close to how it always is on this level."

I look at her in disbelief and keep walking. How could there be twice as many people living one floor below and why didn't they ever help us? Were we that forgettable? I want to yell at every person that complains up here. Living below them in much more cramped and dirtier conditions than these people my whole life should give me the right. They've made our water even filthier for years. How could it be this much better one level up? I know it isn't their fault so I stifle my anger and try to push the thoughts out of my mind. Still, I feel myself thinking, *you call that sick?* as one man complains about a cough. And my calm is almost broken when a woman announces that her bread she just bought is moldy as she starts to pinch off the surrounding bits. My eyes follow each crumb that falls to the floor, only to be trampled on by her and others. We push through the other market goers and pass her on our way to the market tables filled with old weathered items and I remember the book Sal had given me.

"Oh, how could I have forgotten it…" I whisper to myself.

"What?" Azalea shakes my arm after I don't respond. "What did you forget?" she asks again with a more concerned tone.

"I lost a book in the flood," I reply after a moment. "One of the people lost down there had just given it to me. I never even had the chance to pay him for it and I'll probably never find another book now."

Azalea doesn't say anything she just looks around as her hands grip onto my arm more tightly and a disturbed look appears on her face. "I suppose you're right," I say. "Maybe that shouldn't be my main concern right now and I probably can find another eventually."

She whips her head around to face me. Her eyes on fire as she yells, "How can you be so concerned about some stupid story book when you just lost so much of your family and friends?"

I don't respond. I shake myself loose from her hands and walk away from her without turning back. I know what I have lost. It was everything and everyone that I knew. The familiarity of my home, my friends and two of my siblings, it's all gone. She can judge me if she wants to, but I have the right to miss every piece of my life that was lost below. She calls after me, but doesn't get a response. I get to my cube lay down exhausted and just cry for a long time, hoping no one will bother me for the rest of the day. Everything feels tight and it becomes hard to breathe. The loss of my siblings and my only friend, Sal, sets in and I don't know what to do.

CHAPTER THREE

The next day I force myself up early. It's become easier to pull myself up to my feet, but the temptation to lie still for several more hours tries to call me back to sleep. My curiosity manages to fight off the desire and I begin to explore the other side of the floor. I shuffle around taking in everything at my own pace. Without being distracted by Azalea and now that both my eyes can open past a squint I find that there is much more to see than the sun and water. It's interesting to see other towers instead of seemingly endless water and I find myself going in circles trying to memorize each of them, as if they might not be there by tomorrow. Across the way, in the gaps between towers, crews of fisherman and construction workers hang from small cranes and support struts that dangle or reach below the surface off the side of the towers.

The construction crews cut at metal with their torches or fuse pieces together. Sparks soar into the air and crash down into the water sending up small clouds of steam. As the crews make the cranes longer and sturdier throughout the day the fisherman slowly follow to get further away from the towers. I have seen their hooks before and some of the fish they have caught. It always seemed so easy whenever fish, even sharks were pulled so quickly into the air. Once they had them out, the real struggle began. The fishermen sweat more than the construction crewmembers beside them. Their dark clothes and thick fishing vests can't be making it any easier. They must be weighed down by whatever they have in all those pockets on their vests. The thin shirt and light, breezy pants of the work crews look much more comfortable.

There are hundreds in uniform, out there fishing or working on the dozens of towers. I never knew how tall some of these buildings were. Most of the close ones reach high above my line of sight and cast a shadow across the water. Even the ones standing far off look impressive. The most interesting part of the view is what looks like a frame being built for a new tower. Beams of metal reach up on either side, bending at the top. It looked like a whole tower had once been there and was now being peeled back.

I press my face against the glass to get a closer look and notice two towers that have been connected by tubes of glass and people are actually walking across. The walkway shines in the light of the sun, revealing only shadows of the people inside. Dozens of feet march back and forth. The sun creates a glare and blots out everything but the pairs of feet as it crawls higher into the sky. I lean in and look up at a whole other world I didn't know was there. More people than can be counted are walking around from tower to tower in these clear tubes. I had thought that the Empire ferry system or the underwater rail tubes transported everyone. Most likely, the glass tubes are for top-level citizens so they don't have to use the ferry with dirty people like me.

"Checking out the sky bridge system?" Kara asks as she comes up beside me. "I guess they're building them to connect all the towers, of course only the top levels and work crews get to use them."

"You know I never realized how many towers were really a part of Empire," I say. "Do you know which one is the Empire Tower?"

Kara looks at me like I'm volunteering to scavenge, "You're kidding me right? It's the one with the pointy top that's taller than the rest. What else would it be?"

My face flushes red at her comments. It did really make a lot of sense that the tallest would be Empire Tower, considering height mattered more than money. Just as I'm about to say something in my defense Alison speaks up from behind us, "Cut him some slack, you only know more than him because he was out cold for a few days."

"So that one there," I say pointing, in an attempt to move past a potential squabble.

The tower casts a shadow that stretches ominously over the rest. It really does look like a spear rising out of the water and it almost seems to shine. Instead of black as it always appears to be in the posters, it's pale, even in comparison to bottom dwellers like myself.

"Yes," both Alison and Kara spurt out at the same time as though saying it first meant that they knew better. They both make the same grumpy face at each other when I tell them I'm going to take a look around. They know that I'm trying to get away from their bickering and it obvious they each think the other is at fault. Their shared disgruntled appearance tells me they are obviously upset, not only by me leaving, but being left together. Alison looks like a smaller version of Kara at this point. Both have their arms crossed over and the scowl on their tired faces favors the same side. At least now she has a role model. I walk away without even giving them a wave.

Even though I have already seen most of the level it feels good to be walking around on my own and getting a real feel for it. It would have been nice to look at the tubes and towers a bit longer, but talking to them didn't seem appealing. And it also helps to get to know a place by going unnoticed and you can't do that next to explosive people like Alison and Kara, or by being helped around. For some time I stand at the edge of the ferry platform. At times I watch people walk by behind me in the reflection of the windows and when no one comes by I take in the waves and the sun as it inches across the sky. After awhile my legs begin to ache and I give them some relief by leaning against the doors to the platform. They are closed and won't open until the ferry returns from ONE and a card scans the lock, which means no one can go outside. Still I rattle them by applying some pressure on the door just to see if it will give. Of course, it doesn't, but the outside is something I've wanted to experience for some time. Before he passed, my father would tell me about the sun and how hot it was and that a constant salty breeze was more refreshing than any drink or shower. He always told me that it made his work worth it and I wanted to feel that. The feeling of it being worth it more so than the breeze, that feeling of worth has escaped me for some time. Even taking care of my family no longer felt all that productive.

The thought reminds me how upset I still am about Azalea's

judgment of me the day before. Most of the people I've known all my

life are now gone, but it doesn't mean that I also didn't care about one of

the few real possessions I had. The book had meant a lot to me. To me, it

represented my hate for Empire and ONE, love for my family and

knowledge. It was my rebellion, however small. There was no schooling

to speak of in the People's Towers. My ability to read, even slowly,

might help me in the years to come. Without something to practice with I

couldn't get better and being able to read more than a simple propaganda

poster is important to me. More than that, I want to be able to make an

opinion, to think. The mind is the one safe haven a person could have in

Empire if they worked for it. Even if no one ever heard my ideas, they

were still there and they belonged to me. During bad nights, when my

hunger was more than an ache, the desire to read one more inspiring line

could help pass the pain and bring me to my feet in the morning.

In the middle of my thoughts I reach the far end of the level, not

noticing until I almost bump into the corner. Instead of walking along the

next side I stop and look out at the new view. There is nothing but water

on the horizon. The emptiness of the ocean was amazing, but it poses the

question. *Was anything else out there?* Maybe other pockets of towers or

even dry land, Sal always told me there were, and some people had even

gone looking for it. No one ever heard of someone coming back so most of us didn't believe anything was out there. Leaving Empire is illegal, but no one was ever stopped. For the government it was one less mouth crying out in hunger and a little more space for everyone else. Just as I am about to turn back and go to my cube Azalea surprises me.

"You know if you stare out there long enough you'll go blind," she says.

I turn to face her and she's staring at her feet. She seems much smaller than the day before, almost like she's trying not to be seen. I notice my fists are clenched and I relax them to seem less angry. When my body relaxes she takes it as an invitation to speak.

"I'm sorry about the day before," she mutters and kicks at her own feet. She isn't used to apologizing by the way her face has flushed. "Even though I don't have much I've never lost any of it. I might have been too harsh on you."

Similar to her I'm not used to this whole apology business and I don't know how to respond. No one, besides my family had ever apologized to me before and it was even more surprising that a stranger was apologizing to me now. I barely knew her, she had taken care of me and now she's apologizing when I owe her for my well being.

"No you were right," I finally say.

"You're a stupid boy," she mutters without looking up. "Take a win when a lady gives you one."

I pause for a second and I start to laugh at her. She looks up at me and smirks, shoving me in response. I have never been happier to be pushed by someone. Talking to girls was foreign to me and when they are sad or crying it's even harder to find the right words. It was a relief that she was acting more like a boy again.

"You're a real jerk you know?" She says. "Apologies don't come easy down here and you don't take mine seriously?"

I just laugh again and this time she laughs with me. She wraps around me with a suddenness that makes it feel unnecessary, my face burns red with a mixture of embarrassment and delight. For what feels like a day nothing else happens. She looks up at me with confused before I finally hug her back. The hug is one of the warmer than the lights in the stairs or sun coming in through the window.

"You're really bad at this aren't you?" she says into my chest.

I don't say anything and she seems to take it as a yes. She lets go of me and grabs my hand leading me back toward my cube. Halfway there she turns around.

"I asked one of the scavengers if he knew where books could be found," she tells me. "He said it would be expensive to buy any that he finds."

"I don't have anything to give," I say.

"That's OK I can get it for you," she says. "You'll just owe me."

I don't ask her how she can pay for it. It's well known how most girls who don't work pay for things in Empire. The thought of it makes my stomach feel like its ready to jump out of my body. I tell her not to bother and leave it at that. There are few men who wouldn't do the same if anyone would take them up on their offer. People always find a way to get what they need. At a loss for words I tell Azalea I have to go find my brother and sisters. In truth I hadn't seen most of them since we had arrived on this level. They were probably told to leave me alone while I rested and without both Alison and myself to watch them they had likely been left on their own most of the time we had here. Eventually I find Dakota sitting behind a crate peeking over the top. I sit down next to him and don't say a word until he notices me.

"Shhhh," he puts a small finger to his pursed lips. "Lily and June are lookers."

They are playing fish in a barrel, a game with one person hiding and everyone else trying to find them. If they find him together the game is over, but if June or Lily find him separately they will hide with him until the last one finds them. So I quietly slide closer to Dakota and make myself as small as possible so that they won't see me either. It's nice to see them still having fun in the aftermath of a loss. We wait in almost complete silence, except for Dakota's giggling that becomes less controllable as each minute passes. He can never keep it in for long when we play this game. He manages to stifle it for a few minutes until a commotion starts on the other end of the level and we completely forget about hiding. I look up over the cubes in hopes of seeing my sisters crashing through the level to find their brother and instead, a large black square in a cage is lowering down from the ceiling. It lights up the inside of the level with a scramble of white and grey. A scratchy hum follows and those closest cover their ears and shy away.

"What's it?" Dakota asks, tugging on my shirt. "Let me up. Let me up. I want to see."

I crouch down to one knee and he jumps onto my shoulders so he can see above the crowd. He is heavy, but this way I won't have to explain what's going on while trying to figure it out myself. He's even heavier than just a few months ago and my shoulders already ache under the weight. I already want to put him back down, but for something like this I'll make an exception. The square is made of glass except much more reflective than windows. Dakota's small head now towers over the gathering crowd. I watch him with a pleasing sense of curiosity as he makes faces at the screen. Everyone on the level slowly pushes in to get a front row view of the massive hunk of glass now that they're used to the noise. Dakota and I are frozen, staring, even when Lily and June find us. They yell, "found you!" collectively only to join us in gawking at the unusual object. They both climb up onto the crates Dakota was just hiding behind to get a better view. I hold the crates steady with one hand while still holding onto Dakota with the other.

I peel my eyes away for a second to look for Azalea to see if she can tell me what might be happening. She comes from behind us around the corner of a cube, briskly walking towards the box hanging from the ceiling and myself.

"What's happening Azalea?" I ask, trying to keep my voice and siblings balanced.

"I'm not sure," she says while staring past me. "Some patrollers and ONE techs came down the day before you came up and they spent a whole day putting that thing in the ceiling. They wouldn't talk to anyone and this is the first time it's done anything."

Before we can guess what it might be, the screen turns black and goes silent for a moment. The crowd voices a general disappointment before an image flicks on the box. The left side of it is distorted from cracks that travel down the left side. The image is of a man. He is thicker than any person down here and his forehead glistens with sweat. He's also wearing a dark red jacket over a bright blue shirt. The clothes don't even look real. They shine and look as though they would flow over his body if he were to move. When the man starts to move and talk I almost drop Dakota. His clothes do in fact move with him in a way that is surprisingly graceful. The people closest to the box fall over each other, scrambling over one another until their curiosity takes over their surprise. The man's voice is muffled by the excited voices of the crowd, so we all move closer. As I push through the crowd of people the voice coming from the screen starts to fade in. Everyone else follows and we weave a path through the gawking faces.

"...ollowing the recent events of the Empire Tube bombing orchestrated by the rebels, the government has decided that any travel to or from our government's capitol will be restricted to those with government positions and those who are invited."

I look to Azalea for answers and she just shrugs, neither of us knows exactly what all this means. We can't say whether or not any bombs actually went off, or which tube might have been attacked. I've also never heard of anyone being invited anywhere by the government, unless it was to the ocean floor. Since we can't disagree with the man, we just keep watching.

"As a result, a new set of laws has been passed and is being implemented in every tower as of tonight," the man pauses for a second looking straight out at us while he wipes his forehead with a white cloth before continuing. "Any unauthorized travel to or near the Empire Tower will result in immediate termination, any person found on a level they do not or appear not to belong to will serve a two year scavenging sentence. Any person found with items known to be used for currency other than government issued tokens will serve a one-year scavenging sentence. Any person found with contraband will be arrested and questioned as a rebel and any person heard speaking in an ill manner in regard to our government will be publicly beaten," again he pauses, shuffling his papers before letting out a purposefully drawn out sigh.

"It is unfortunate that the traitorous group of rebels has forced our caring government into such a corner. They even had the nerve to try and release a statement that blames the bombing on the government and ONE. Fortunately we managed to stop their pathetic attempt at taking over our network. Our great government would never waste time, resources or lives. The very thought of it is absurd. So not only are they violent monsters, they are liars. No person that believes in our great union would ever question the Empire or Chancellor Carnegie. Without Carnegie there would be no food, each tower would fend for itself and there would be chaos across the board," the man starts to turn red in the face as he wildly gestures with one hand while crumpling his paper with the other. His hair becomes disheveled as his voice continues to rise and the top button of his shirt comes undone.

"We are all one, we have one savior and one leader, forever," with that he leans back in his chair and sweeps the sweaty hair off his forehead, takes a deep breath and a look back out toward us. "Our core values, our Empire and people's values are exactly what the rebels want to destroy, that's all they desire and if they get what they want they will destroy all that they can't take and there will be nothing left for the people. This is why we need a leader like Carnegie. We also need each other in the days to come. Stay vigilant and stay proud. This is Astor

Bertelsmann and as always I am your voice, the go between for you, the people and our great leadership." The screen cuts out and a single white rectangle appears on the center of the dark screen before it starts sliding back up into the ceiling.

Afterward most of the crowd stands there not sure where to go or what to say, a few cheer or clap one or two times before realizing they haven't been joined. After a few more moments those who remained silent move off in groups and start chattering quietly, while the unquestioning supporters talk excitedly about the rebel criminals and who might be a conspirator. I put Dakota down before we go back to Lily and June, who had given up on getting closer when the yelling had started. They all look confused and frightened. They huddle up together on the floor, fearful of whatever had just happened. They need an explanation and I have nothing that could begin to comfort them. The sight of Alison appearing out of the crowd is a comfort to me. Lately I've counted on her to calm our siblings down. She kneels down to the three of them and gives them a smile.

"Hey guys. That was pretty weird wasn't it?" she says almost laughing. "Sometimes important people argue and do silly things and they yell about it. But no one is mad at you guys though and none of that stuff matters anyway. So why don't we all go back to playing fish in a barrel. Sam can hide first."

Suddenly they're all excited and smiling again. I don't think I would ever have been able to find the right words for this situation, much less swing their moods so quickly. I'm still trying to understand it all myself. It's shocking that Alison has gotten so good at lying. I almost believe the casual air that she has about herself. For me it had always been much easier to lie about the simple things like food and water. Alison had caught me in a lie about a year ago when I couldn't back it with logic and since then she's been trying to do better in hopes of our siblings staying ignorant as long as they could. At this point she might even be able to convince me if she tried and I find myself feeling jealous at her ease of it. When our eyes lock as she playfully covers Dakota's, we tell each other that we are anything but optimistic. I wish we could be as ignorant as these three. Right now she's is telling me how worried she is, mainly about mom or me being taken away. Without a word said between us she can tell that I'm thinking the same thing. Sadly there isn't much we can do, so I hurry off to start the game.

I find a spot between a mess of pipes and a window and huddle down. I'm careful not to lean against the pipes as wisps of steam come out of the seams. Sitting against the glass, I manage to find a spot where it's possible to look out the through a space in the pipes without being seen easily. Dakota and Lily pass by several times without taking notice. They take so long I doze off, until being nudged awake. My body jerks in response almost sending me into the pipes. Unsurprisingly Azalea is sitting next to me.

"Hey stop snoring, we're hiding," she says with a sassy tone.

"Sorry," I say rubbing my face as I try to pull myself out of the haze of sleep.

"I'm only kidding with you," she giggles and nudges me again. "Sleep if you want. It may be awhile yet."

This time I nudge her back and she falls over and pulls me down with her. Now we're both laughing on the ground next to each other. Before I can get up she grabs me by the front of the shirt, pulls me towards her and kisses me. It hits me with a wave of warmth and suddenly the world fades away. If I weren't already on the floor I would have fallen. I lunge into the kiss and grab the side of her face running my fingers through her dark, soft hair. I reach another hand around her hip until a familiar obnoxious cough breaks the through the moment.

"If you guys wanted to spend some time alone together you could just say so," Alison says from behind all my other sisters and Dakota in tow.

Dakota and my sisters all start to laugh and run off as we get to our feet. Alison stays behind with a wide grin on her face. A smile stretches across my own face, mostly out of excitement with a hint of embarrassment. Azalea stands next to me, her tan face burns a pale red I didn't think it could.

"Sam, just make sure we don't add any more to the litter, OK?" Alison says as she pats me on the shoulder and walks away.

"I'll see you tomorrow," Azalea blurts out as she scurries off.

I'm so shocked from the whole experience that I feel like I'm floating as I head back to my own cube. I take my time weaving through the maze of cubes and people. For the rest of today there is nothing that feels urgent or necessary. I lie down and think about her until falling asleep.

The next morning Azalea shakes me awake. She's in the middle of saying something, too important to wait for me to wake up the whole way. I reach for her face, but realize the seriousness when she quickly swats my hand away.

"My mom isn't back when she should be," she says. "I think they've taken her."

"Who took her, why?" I say, trying to cover all my questions in a sentence.

"Patrollers must have caught her tending to someone or in a random search or somehow," she says through stifled sobs. "If they searched her they would have found all her passes!"

"Maybe she's late," I offer and get up off my back. "If they're searching people the tube or ferry could be behind schedule."

"No they have her," she whispers and starts to wail. I throw a hand over her mouth and shush her. She tries to pull my hand away, but she's too hysterical to fight. Without saying it out loud she knows I'm telling her that she can't be upset about her mom being taken. Her outburst would grab too much attention and could easily get her reported as a sympathizer, especially if it was true.

After a few tears she quiets herself and I reluctantly remove my hand from over her mouth. A few tears spill off her jaw and into her lap. Everything in me screams to cry and worry and be angry along with her.

Maybe someday if things change, but today we hold back everything except fear.

As Azalea finally calms herself the static that signaled the first appearance of the screen starts again and the color flushes from her face. She paws at my arm to keep me from leaving and croaks at me as she fights back the tears as they start welling up in her eyes again. Still, I leave. The need to know is too much for me, though I know knowing is what she fears. Azalea buries her face in the bed of blankets as I leave her there.

Most of the level is getting up to see what will be said this time as the static becomes louder. It momentarily becomes unbearable before it switches over to Astor's round head. Less sweaty this time, his face is caked in some kind of powder. His cloth has left his hand and is neatly folded in the breast pocket of a loud, yellow jacket, which is just as shiny as the last one.

"Today I am proud to say that we have made a fatal strike against those that attempted to ruin us," he says with grin that shows off his double chin. "Today we have found the perpetrators in our midst. Though most of the vile men and women died in our attempts to capture them we have at least managed to take one. She claims to be peaceful, only having a desire to help. Yet this cannot be true, for what help can she offer that we do not already give. She is a coward and a liar, part of the small band of rebels that we seek to eradicate from our civilization."

The view sweeps away from Astor and closes in around a figure through a window and on top of a neighboring tower. Two men in black uniforms stand next to the woman with a bag over her face. Astor's voice falls away as I try to see behind the cloth. When it is pulled up, Astor goes on about proper justice and healing wounds as one. When her face is revealed and it is Azalea's mom, the level bursts out in an uproar. Several men shout that they had always known, while others defend her with examples of lives saved. Some of those lives might even belong to those who now accuse her. In response to the bickering the screen lets out a high-pitched whine. Arguments come to a halt, with only a handful still glaring at each other instead of watching the screen.

"As we know her crimes are real, there is no need for a trial and she will not be named or remembered," Astor continues. A few cheers come from the front. "Her sentence is death and we have decided that this historic moment should be viewed by all. This is the last day of rebellion."

As he finishes, Azalea's mom is shoved from the top of the

tower. The cameras follow her descent until she splashes into the water.

"I saw her hit, just over there," someone yells from the far side of the level. The crowd pushes over each other to get closer to the windows. The screen stays focused on the image of a woman floating face down, water already turning purple around her. It disgusts me how intrigued everyone is by it, though I can't deny that something new like this seems to have broken even the most defeated looking people out of their trance. Some, who normally only get up to eat are now eagerly pressed against the glass with their noses squished against it. Excited breathing fogs the windows and people have to wipe the glass clear with their sleeves.

Azalea staggers past me, taking me by surprise as she staggers toward the screen that now shows a shark chewing on what was once her mom. She doesn't notice when I call her name or grab her shoulder. She just brushes me off. And when the sharks drag the body under, Azalea falls to the floor. I pick her up quickly. Behind me Astor begins to tell us what real justice is. He explains that any more attempts at rebellion will be met with equal aggression and that soon, any remnants of oppressors will be eliminated. It is important that that she gets back to the cube before anyone can see. Alison sees us coming and helps me lay her down on some blankets. In the distance people continue to cheer on the feeding sharks.

"Do the people on this level know they are related?" Alison asks me.

"What can we do either way?" I ask in return. "Hopefully today will be enough excitement and they will forget about her."

"There has to be something more we can do for her," Alison says excitedly. "She's your girlfriend and she saved your life."

"I'm leaving," come the soft words from Azalea. When we don't move out of her way she becomes upset. "Let me up! I have to go now!" Tears start to stream down her face.

"Where are you going?" I ask as I pull her to her feet.

"Up," she says more calmly, though the tears keep coming. "I have the papers for it. If I leave now I can disappear, I know people who can help me."

"Goodbye," Alison says to her with a hug. "I'll miss you."

My sister's sudden acceptance of this decision shocks me into silence. She would never let me do something like this on my own.

Though I guess there isn't anyone keeping Azalea here anymore, except for me. It would be nice to be selfish and tell her we can hide her somewhere, but that would never work. At least if she's alive there's a chance I'll see her again.

While I struggle with the idea, Azalea returns the sentiment to Alison before walking away. I join her and together we walk to the stairwell. As we reach the door, people are just starting to leave the windows to return to the daily tasks, or lack there of. The calm that has been restored almost lets me believe that she can stay. Though I know better, the way things are going people will begin to expect more and if they don't get it they'll look for it. Azalea would likely be next on the list if she were to stay here.

"It really does seem like I could stay," she says as she opens the door. "They're calm now, but they will get hungry again. Don't get hurt anymore."

Then she's gone. I shout goodbye up the stairs over the sound of her feet falling on each step. She keeps running and doesn't say anything. Another person passes out of my life. At least this one isn't dead yet. It gives me hope, but even that doesn't keep me feeling whole.

CHAPTER FOUR

The events of the day before have come and gone too quickly for them to feel real. Instead of dwelling on it I'm wandering through the market and staring at useless junk. All the items of worth have cleared out over the past two days, even though the patrollers haven't made their way through yet. I'm just about to give up on the market as a whole when I notice a sack that has been left unattended next to a crate. I peel back the top of it and find a stack of books and for a moment any thoughts of heartache are washed away. They are all in incredible shape compared to mine. Still, mold pocks the surface of the covers and the bottom of the bag is damp from the water held by the pages.

I hesitate to pull one out. I try to tell myself that it's too much trouble as my hand slides across the top of the bag. It's not worth years of scavenger service I say in my head. Yet, my hand digs in deeper and wraps around the spines of the top two books. I pull them out, neither has a legible name on the cover. I gently peel through the pages of the first one and instantly place it back in the bag as I find it of no interest. Paging through the second book I find myself unable to stop. The second page rips while I'm turning it, causing me to slow down and consider returning it to its proper place, but only for a moment. I must have been reading for some time before noticing the large figure standing over me. A tall bearded man with bulging forearms interlaced across his chest is looking down at me. His light brown hair covers most of his face, but his deep brown eyes pierce through the mess to find me.

"That's my bag young man," he says barely above a whisper. To me it feels like a roar.

I put the book down on top of the bag, starting to shake as I do. When I try to walk away as he grabs my shoulder. His hand encompasses my shoulder, the warmth spreads through me, but the power in the grasp freezes me. He pulls me back and sits me down on the crate in front of him. He gets down on his haunches before speaking again.

"Do you know how to read or are you just a thief?" he says in a much less menacing tone than before.

"I just wanted to see what books you had," I squeak out a

whisper.

"So a reader who may have become a thief if he liked what he saw?" he replies. When he doesn't get an answer he continues, "Was there one you found to your liking?"

I nod.

"Which would that be?" he says with a hint of excitement as his eyes light up.

"The one I was holding," I tell him.

He remains quiet for a moment before speaking, "I'm not supposed to and you were most likely going to steal from me, however, I like you still. Maybe because you didn't try to lie, but I can't really say."

Instead of the one from the bag he grabs a book from the inside of his jacket. He releases it and it falls into my lap. I don't even try to catch it and a cloud of dust flies off the cover into my face. I've never seen something so dry. The dust blurs my vision and I sneeze several times. The giant of a man chuckles, it thuds out of his chest with each laugh. He couldn't be quiet if he tried.

"Don't get caught with that," he says, picking up his bag. "The penalty is much too high in these volatile times."

He starts to lumber away, hiding the bag in his equally large jacket. In my head his footsteps are much louder than is possible. For some reason I follow him until I'm running to catch up. As I get close he turns to face me.

"Don't follow me," he states, waving his hand at me

"I just want to know…" I'm cut off by a shout before finishing my question.

"You two, the giant and the kid stay there," a voice from behind me, bellows.

"Alright it's time to go," the giant manages to say so only I can hear. "You should come with me unless you have the urge to work in the depths of the ocean for the next year or more."

"What do you mean, where can we go?" I ask as the large man grabs me by the shirt and tosses me towards the stairwell door. My feet leave the ground for a moment and my shirt is ripped. The sudden jolt jostles my senses, but I land on my feet and start running with him on my heels. After a few steps he is past me. I safely assume that the man who yelled is a patroller and that it is quite possible that there are more on the level, currently coming after us. As we near the door a patroller skids to a halt as he bursts through a row of cubes. He raises his hand, signals for us to stop as he reaches for his baton. The giant does not slow and swings his colossal arm into the patrollers face in stride. The result of that single punch is unbelievable. The patroller's jaw is twisted and dangling. His eyes have rolled back into his head and he is on his knees. A muffled croak escapes his barely moving mouth as his limp body sways back and forth to the ground. My apparent accomplice reaches the door in the meantime. He is holding it open and yelling for me to hurry.

"Young man you need to move now," his deep voice booms through the air.

The patroller has finished falling to the floor, but another is already coming my way. The whole level is watching now, as people look from over the top of cubes and lean over each other to get a better look without getting closer. I try to find Azalea only to realize she's already gone. My family is somewhere, but I'm moving too quickly to see any faces and there isn't any time to stop. I am halfway between the patroller and the door to the stairs. My feet pounding on the floor as they carry me faster.

A patroller tackles me to the ground right at the doorway. The giant reaches through the door in an attempt to save me. Before he can, my foot is already buried in the face of the patroller. He doesn't stop fighting until his teeth start to fall out. Looking down my leg I barely recognize the patroller's face. It's been flattened by my foot, the realization causes me to pause after he let's go and my would be savior drags me through the door.

"Well, that went well for a poor situation," he says to me as I pull out the tooth and get to my feet. "Well little thief, you're going to be sticking with me for now. I would venture to guess that it isn't safe for you to return, especially after you rearranged a patrollers face. So Empire's most wanted, what name will they not be calling you by when you take the plunge?"

"Sam," I tell him, before realizing how insensitive yet true the question was.

"Well Sam, I'm Bartholomew, but those who know me well call me Bear and since we'll be spending at least some time together I suggest you call me that," he says to me in an almost formal manner.

Bear is the most bizarre name I've ever heard. He reaches his hand out towards me to shake it and I put my hand out to grab it, as the door swings open. One last patroller is trying to force his way through the door. He squeezes his shoulder through until he can reach into the stairwell. He waves his club at us, as Bear smashes the door into the man's chest, releasing a loud crunching noise that echoes through the stairs and begins to sound wet as Bear continues to lean his weight into it. Blood dribbles out of the patroller's mouth as he falls to the ground gasping for air. He reaches towards his crumpled chest, but his arms start to shake in rebellion, as he gets close they completely give out.

"Almost forgot about that last one," Bear gruffly says to me, with a somewhat hidden look of alarm on his face.

There most likely aren't many people that cause him real worry. With a sigh he leaves the dying man and starts down the stairs towards my old level and the water that now stands a little higher in the stairwell. I follow him without comment, a mixture of awe and fear guide me. We take a few steps into the water and come upon a set of O2 gear. The equipment familiar to me, but it's usually rustier. Either way I've never used it before and the thought of starting now is already causing a shortness of breath. Bear snags up one of the large metal tanks and a large slender tube. There is also a bag that appears to be made out of some sort of hard cloth. Water is beading and rolling off of it. It must be extremely valuable if it can't get wet. Bear grabs the bag and pulls out two black balls that turn out to be a suit of pants and shirts all in one. He lays them down and starts undressing.

"Take your clothes off," he commands. "You'll never fit in yours with them on."

I follow his instructions without question and move quickly. The back of the suit has a zipper on it. I unzip it and slide my legs in. The suit has a slimy feel to it and suctions to my skin as my legs make their way through each hole. It's a struggle the rest of the way into the wetsuit and before I think to, Bear is already zipping up the back. As he gets to the top the sudden force of the pull takes me to the tips of my toes for a moment. He grabs me by the shoulder and spins me around. The sudden movements and the pace of the situation have me in a daze. I give Bear a blank stare with my mouth wide as he holds out another O2 tank for me to take. It's much smaller than the other and just has one small rubber piece at the top of it for me to breathe through.

"You'll be needing this to breath in a minute," he says.

"I don't understand," I reply. It's obvious to me that this is to breathe with. The idea of going into the water just seems ridiculous. Or maybe I'm just pretending so he'll take us another way.

"We have to go underwater to get where we are going," he says quickly. "More patrollers will be coming so we don't have much time. Put the rubber piece in your mouth and breathe in. When you breathe out take the piece out of your mouth."

I begin to ask him how I will see as he shoves me down the stairs into the water. Water fills my eyes and mouth, causing me to scramble around in the water. A large splash follows as Bear flies in after me. He grabs me and pulls me up to the surface.

"Cool it," he yells, spraying water into my face. His beard and hair sag and latch onto his face. "Relax or you won't have enough oxygen to make it. Open your eyes and follow me, it will sting at first but I'm sure you can suck it up." He pulls goggles over his face as he yells his instructions.

With that he ducks back below the surface and starts to swim down the stairs. I go down after him, trying to suck on the mouthpiece and breath back in, when it doesn't seem to work I breath in and out, harder and faster. I can't see, I'm drowning and it isn't working. Air, I need real air. When I break through the surface the relief is instant, but a new panic sets in as Bear keeps moving.

I try again, going more slowly and opening my eyes. The water is cloudy and there isn't much for visibility. The water burns my eyes burn as I search for Bear. His shadowy figure is already half way through the door to my level. He has to slide the door all the way open so he can fit his massive body through. I hesitate to follow. People I knew and loved could still be in there. I must have paused too long because Bear comes back and urgently waves me through the door.

I inch around the corner, following him and doing my best to keep my eyes on his back and feet. Swimming over what remains of the cubes gives me a new perspective on the living situation for the people of Empire. I make the mistake of looking in one or two of them and realize how tiny our lives are. Many of the undersized homes that survived have become cushy graves for those who hadn't escaped. The decaying, lifeless bodies are still clinging to blankets and other useless items. Vulture fish peck at the peeling, rippled flesh of my neighbors. The eyes are already gone from every face I see and the hollowed sockets seem to follow me no matter where I move. Here and there a few floating corpses do the same. Their skeletal limbs now held up by their bloated stomachs. The fish move in waves from body to body, gently bringing them down as they pop the stomachs and gorge themselves.

I begin to understand now, why they had gone back for the blankets, scraps of food and bits of metal. These few items was all that we had down here. It was sad that they died for things so insignificant on their own, yet I feel even worse knowing that for many people, these simple items had kept them alive. Now their corpses were keeping the fish fed. It would have been better if it had all been washed away.

Distracted by the graveyard feeding frenzy, I bump into Bear. He turns to me and pushes me down into a cube with one arm, propelling himself down with the other. He keeps his head just above the top of the cube scanning back and forth. I try to join him and he pushes me down again. We each take a seat on either side of the old inhabitants of the cube. The hair of the former resident stands on end and slowly ripples with the water. Most of the skin has been removed from the face, giving them the look of a crazed skeleton. After a moment Bear finds a spot closer to me, next to our new friend. I can't tell for certain, but it appears that his head is hanging and his shoulders are slumped. I prod him and give him a questioning look. He responds by using his hands to make what looks like a squid, which tells me one is near by. Scavengers call them skulls because their mostly white bodies and long gangly tentacles that have the appearance of gnarled teeth. They also have two distinct black marks on the body. I'd seen them through the windows a few times, but never too close. Everyone would hide in fear of the ghostly squids attacking and breaking through the glass. Most people claim the dark spots are the eyes, but anyone who has been close enough to really know is most likely dead. From what Sal had told me, they would kill even when they weren't hungry. According to him their only motive was to kill.

I look at Bear again and all he gives me is a shrug as if to say, *I have no idea.* We both know that we don't have long to think this through. I take a pull from the canister, the bubbles float up to the ceiling and collect there. I start to think of everything that had been left behind here. Family, my book, the people I knew and Sal were all lost here. Then I remember something about Sal that could help us. He had always bragged about the spear gun he owned. He said it worked better because it was from the dry time, that probably wasn't true, but it did work. Sal always said it couldn't kill much in terms of skulls or sharks, but most anything would think twice after taking a spear to the face.

I tap Bear on the shoulder. He had gone back to peeking over the top of the cube. The skull was still out there and at this point it must know we're in here. Bear finally lets me peek over to see it gently coast by the outside of the window frames. Each tentacle lazily grazes the side of the building as it turns each corner. When he finally gives me his attention I make a gesture like shooting a gun. He puts his hand to his forehead like he is shading his eyes looking back and forth as if to say "where?" I point towards the market and give him the same shrug he gave me moments before.

Bear floats down all the way to the floor and begins to do a mixture of swimming and crawling. I follow behind, slinking across the floor in hopes of avoiding attention. My stomach and legs drag along the ground raising a slight dust trail in my wake. Twice, I have to push myself up and over half skeletons. I do my best not to disturb them. As we come up on the former market area Bear stops and reaches a hand back signaling for me not to move. As he peers around the corner a shadow glides above us. I instinctively roll over and see the tentacles of the skull disappear over the top of a cube. A set of pink circles with black spikes poking through fill the diamond shaped tips of each tentacle. My body sinks into the floor. It would be nice if I could fall right through. I frantically grab at Bear's foot to get his attention and point towards where it went. He nods and swims into what once was the market. I wait for a moment, watching where the tentacles had disappeared, half expecting the whole body to come charging back to snag me. But something tells me it's still waiting for a proper moment to end the hunt.

Bear waits for me to collect myself so I can lead the way to the gun. We reach Sal's old area and start moving the tumble of crates and tables that now lay there. There's nothing useful in any of them. Bear is still keeping watch in the direction we last saw the skull. I throw a crate out of frustration, as much as one can be underwater, and I sink back to the floor. My knee hits the ground first, instead of stopping with a thud it squishes into the floor and a cloud of dust and bubbles form a square beneath it. I point out the soft spot in the floor to Bear. He produces a long knife from a belt on his hip. With ease he pops the square out of the floor. It crumbles, sending more dust and bubbles up into the water. As the dust clears a wave of relief washes over me as I see the already loaded gun and four harpoons to go with it. It seems to be in working condition, but then again I've never used one. I hold it out for Bear to take from me. He already has the other four harpoons attached to his belt. As he takes it something slides around my leg and squeezes down around my ankle. Suddenly I'm being pulled toward the nearest window. My eyes bulge and bubbles fly up in front of my face as I start to thrash my legs. The idea of being ripped up and chewed has become all too real. I'm still holding onto the gun and Bear tries to pull the gun and myself back in. He slowly loses ground as our bodies push a table and several crates out of the way.

As we near the edge of the level Bear tries to wedge his body in front of a metal beam that had been used to reinforce the windows. His

chest and shoulder slam into it and it immediately starts to bend, even

underwater the metal groans. Bear's eyes widen, a cloud of bubbles flies

from his mouth as he struggles. Once I start to go over the edge he just

lets go of the gun. All that to just give up? I have too much time to think

about that and my quickly arriving death as the tentacle lazily pulls me

down to the next level and through another window. The skull knew that

it had captured its prize. As I am pulled further down, nearing my death I

start to calm down despite my anger at the situation. I didn't even want

to be on this level ever again, much less underwater. All I wanted was to

read a book and now I'm about to be eaten by a ball of arms. I have to at

least poke out an eye. I want this thing to work for it.

The skull reaches out a second tentacle and begins pulling me

more quickly toward the head and the two large black dots. I start

wondering where the mouth is until the answer kills my curiosity, as the

remaining tentacles spread and reveal a mouth that looks like two sharp

fingernails, one overlapping the other. It sends a cold ripple down my

spine as the image of it clipping off parts of me fills my head. Next to the

mouth are two small fidgety eyes. They take a moment to lock onto me. I

ready the harpoon gun as I'm drawn closer. The harpoon won't fire when

I pull the trigger. I madly search the gun with my fingers for any sign of a switch. As I get near enough I start to kick wildly at the eyes in an attempt to free myself. The skull only tightens its grip and something pinches me in several spots around my ankles. I give up on the idea of shooting the gun and get ready to stuff it in its mouth. Just as I do the squid starts to flail and releases me. My first thought is to get away. Until Bear appears at the top of the skull's head I know I have to stay.

He has his knife in one hand and a harpoon in the other. Both are lodged inside the head of the now squirming skull. I hurry to get the gun working so that I can join in the fight. Bear can't die in my place. Finally my fingers find a notch near the back of the gun. It slides forward and a green strip of paint appears where it once was. I pull up on the squirming skull aiming near the base of the head to avoid my, twice now, savior. The harpoon soars leaving a small trail of bubbles behind it. A cloud of dark red mist instantly sprouts from the point of impact. The skull tries to run away with Bear still riding it, it crashes into columns and crushes a whole cube. Just before I lose sight of them Bear lets go of his knife, kicks off from the top of its head and swims back toward me. He gets close enough that his smile can be seen behind the big piece of rubber in his mouth. Between breaths I smile back at him. It was exhilarating to have faced a living nightmare, only to walk away with a few scratches. Bear pats me on the shoulder and points out the window I was dragged in through.

We casually swim out into the open water and we start down the side of the building. Shadows of giants, hidden by the ocean fill my view. There still isn't much visibility, but it's easy to see that there are buildings everywhere. There is almost no space between them. I try to count them as we spiral down and around the building until we reach the opposite side. There we find a large, yellow tube with two small fan-like blades on either side. It's latched to the side of the tower. Bear easily removes it and with the press of a button. The fans start to move and give off a humming noise. He motions for me to grab onto one of three handles and without warning we're off at a speed I didn't know was possible. We cruise past towers and other smaller ones that are completely bizarre. Many don't have the straight edges I've come to expect from most towers. A fair number have fallen apart or landed on neighboring ones. The fact that we are heading down becomes apparent as the base of the towers and their support beams come into view.

Below us, lights blink on and off throughout the grid pattern of the ocean floor and I realize that they're torches and we're over the scavenger work yards. Their tearing apart large metal frames that lay randomly between the towers. Another torch lights up and a giant pole fall over and raise a cloud of dust. As we float on we pass more than one hundred flames that blink on and off across the grid. All of them cutting metal or welding it onto the support beams that surround each tower. The daily ritual of diving into the depths is a frightening prospect to me. Just this one day has been enough.

We sink down lower, almost to the ground and have to follow the paths of the old world to avoid small and large towers alike. The scavengers don't pay any attention to us as we quietly pass, just overhead. We enter a clearing and aim for the ground. Skeletons of something that look like the veins in the back of my hands line the open space. As we near a building we shoot into the cover of a shadow. Bear turns off the tube a few feet above the ocean floor and our momentum takes us the rest of the way down. As we land Bear momentarily releases the big yellow tube and pulls out one of the remaining harpoons. He digs it into a barely noticeable metal circle and pries it open almost as easily as Sal's secret compartment. It pops up and it swings on the hinge of the other side, creaking as Bear pushes it the rest of the way. He shoves the tube in first before he pulls himself in feet first. He disappears into the darkness and I follow after him with a sense of dread filling up inside of me again. Once I'm in Bear's arm reaches past me towards the light and closes the way in.

When it closes every shred of light is closed out, until a green light radiates through the dark. Bear is holding a glowing tube making it possible to see the upper half of his body. He gives me thumbs up before swimming to an even bigger metal door. The light reveals concentric circles of metal protruding from the wall. A dozen metal rods weave through the door to hold each piece together. He pounds on the door between two of the rods with everything he has and it lets out a resounding bong. We wait for a moment, not moving until something starts sucking me down to the floor. I flail in the water in an attempt to stay near the top. Bear laughs at me as he holds onto the wall. I hit the bottom of the floor and the water rushes past me. The realization that the water is draining out of the room calms me down. The water continues to recede until there is nothing left but a puddle beneath me. I toss my O2 canister to the ground and pull myself up by the door. My wet hair sticks to my brow and gets stuck in my eyes. In the pale green light Bear is still quietly laughing to himself. I'm about to ask why it's so dark until a harsh white light comes from a small bulb in the ceiling.

"You're going to be seeing a lot of new things in a moment," Bear tells me as my eyes slowly adjust. "Give me your oxygen tank and try not to act too amazed." I pick it up from where I had tossed it and shove it into Bear's chest. He might be frightening, but I hope I've at least earned a playful shove at this point. He chuckles and keeps talking. "Hobbes was right for once about taking extra gear, Jack will never hear the end of it now," he says to himself before speaking to me again. "Now listen, I wasn't supposed to bring you down here, but since you know the way here now you can't necessarily leave either. We can't risk you telling someone. Just try not to sound stupid or say anything that may be upsetting."

I just give him a nod and try to keep my breathing steady. I'm just now understanding the full extent of my underwater excursion. Though my real concern lies with the well being of everyone who hasn't made it out of the towers. Who knew what could happen now, any overly emotional behavior could easily draw too much attention. And I didn't know if anyone in my family knew what happened and what about Azalea? There were probably wanted flyers with my face on them already flying around. Maybe they would show my face on the screens that drop down from the ceiling and Astor would claim I was somehow the last dirty rebel ruining Empire all on my own. I also felt incredibly tired. My body sags and my heart pathetically beats on after more than an hour of nearly dying.

The door hisses and booms, as it slowly rolls open. A second door moves in the opposite direction bringing me back into the present. The sudden light that fills the room from behind the door is much worse than the single bulb above me, it's blinding. With my hand shielding my eyes I can make out the shapes of three people standing at the edge of the chamber.

"Who's your friend, Bear?" a stern voice asks.

"Jack, the kid got caught standing next to me while trying to trade with some of our books we have multiples of," Bear says with a defensive tone in his voice. "The patrollers were after me just as much as him. With how things are now, I couldn't..."

He is rudely cut off by the wave of a hand. The hand most likely belongs to Jack. He walks into the chamber and stops just in front of me. My heart flutters out of beat for a moment, too tired to fully drum on the inside of my chest. The feeling causes my legs to tremble, threatening to give out at any point, but I stand as tall as I can and look into straight into what I hope are Jack's eyes. As I adjust to the light I realize he doesn't appear as old as I had thought he would have to be able to command authority over someone like Bear, especially in such a harsh manner. He has a good amount of stubble and his hair is cut close, a rare sight in Empire. With one hand on his hip he leans over me and pokes me in the chest with a thick finger.

"Give me one good reason to let you in," he growls under his breath. "I want to know why I shouldn't throw you back out into the water without an air tank. We don't like surprise visits from new people right now." And with that he pushes my tired body to the ground with just his pointer finger. I land hard and let out a cry. Bear instinctively reaches to help me up only stopping when Jack glares at him. Still he comes to my defense.

"The kid is tougher and less scared than we could have ever been at his age," Bear says standing unusually straight. "He may seem small even to you but he took out a patroller and helped me fight off a skull on our way here. He has guts when he needs to. We could train him, he could be something we desperately need."

"And what is it that we need so badly? Another saint? No, we don't need someone who will sacrifice their self, only to be given up by the people they helped. We need more useful bodies. I'll believe this one can be of use when it passes advanced training," Jack says marching back and forth. "Take him to your brother, he's skipping basic. And until he passes he's on parole under the threat of being thrown out the airlock."

He marches off without another word. Bear finally helps me up and dusts me off. The two other figures remain. I walk further into the light and focus on the other two figures now that Jack is out of my face. They turn out to be an old man with a long white cloak and glasses and a beautiful, very pregnant redhead.

"Don't worry about him," the man with the glasses says with a dry sarcasm as he rubs his chin. "He's had a lot to worry about lately. We can't take many chances with people these days." Without introducing himself he turns on his heel and walks off speedily.

"So I'll just leave the books here Hobbes," Bear calls after him while pulling his cloth bag out of the waterproof one. "Has there been another argument between the two of them?" Bear asks the woman.

"Two actually," she sighs. Her freckled nose scrunches up with distaste. "The first about changing our tactics from out of sight to outright violent and the second started when Hobbes tried to apologize for the first fight. And since no one else thought it might be important to ask, what's the name of the newest rescue?"

She looks at me and carefully shifts her body to face me. I stare for a moment until Bear slaps me on the back.

"I'm Sam," I manage to spurt out.

"Well Sam, I'm Madison and Jack happens to be my husband, like Hobbes said, don't worry too much about Jack and know that if Bear trusts you then the rest of us do. Jack just has a lot to worry about, we're in a delicate time," she says. "We've recently had a loss and it has worn on Jack. It's not an excuse, but I hope that it may provide you some comfort to know that the anger is not your doing," she turns her attention to Bear. "Bear why don't you give him a tour before you take him down for training and stop by to see Hobbes. Leaving those books there will only create more arguments the way those men have been the past few days."

Bear responds by picking up the books along with his gear. Madison reaches out her hand for me to shake just as Bear had earlier. I grasp it firmly and she grabs mine even harder, shaking it thoroughly with both hands. She smiles even though her face looks tired and sad. Neither Bear nor I move until she leaves the room herself. Eventually Bear turns to me and hands me his waterproof bag.

"Hold this," he says. "We're going to take a tour but it's going to be done quickly. Also, remember what I said earlier. Try not to do anything to get noticed, the newer you seem the less welcome this place will be today. Some down here are just as worked up about recent events as Jack is. There have been a slew of killings of people thought to be related to rebels, some of the guesses have been right."

"So is that why Jack is so worked up?" I ask.

"We'll talk with Hobbes about it," he says avoiding the question.

CHAPTER FIVE

I sling the bag over my shoulder as we start down the long hall that lies ahead of us. A number of people putting gear together similar to Bear's, sit along the wall. Several of them give him a nod or a wave as we walk past. The hall is wide enough that we can move through them with ease, but it still feels cramped without windows. Several of the men and women stand up and tap a closed fist over their hearts. Bear gives them a silent nod in return. As we reach the end of the hallway a man holds the door open for us, managing to give Bear the same signal before we pass through. We both let out a tired thank you, as we do.

The next room is much darker. It's made up of large stone walls and columns. The high ceilings are made of the same grey stone. The only light comes from an opening at the top of two large connected stairways that form a u-shape. Large arches surround the space and on the far wall, three of the arches are filled with more stone. Water leaks

through small gaps in a steady stream. Below, a pump churns as it pushes

the water out through a corroded metal wall. *Do not touch* is painted

across it in white. A generator coughs and spits exhaust just to the side.

Drops of water that land on it hiss and vapor lazily rises up from it. I

can't help but to step in several large puddles as we make our way to the

stairs. Small cracks reach out from the center of the ceiling and water

drips off everything. Giant strips of metal are bolted over the larger

cracks, but water still seeps in through the corners. We take the closer set

of stairs passing a few more people who look ready to head out. I

stumble over some cables near the top of the stairs as my feet start to

drag.

"You're really in for it if you're already fatigued," Bear

mumbles. " Though I am sorry about your current situation Sam, you'll

need to remain tough. Also, it may be of comfort for you to know that

some of those men and women who are leaving will eventually be

looking out for your family. They'll be moved to another tower in time.

However, they may end up below the deadline. But that is the price to

survive Empire these days, avoid one cause of death only to find

another."

I sit at the top of the stairs to catch my breath. "Thanks Bear," I say. "There's one other person."

"Azalea," he says, cutting me off. "She's with us. She's very fond of you and she's Jack's sister," his eyebrows raise when he sees the shock in my face "So yes that does answer the question as to why Jack is so upset, that was also his mother. Many others down here have recently lost family in a similar manner or to the slave labor they call scavenging. That is why some don't like the sight of new faces right now, they are fearful of spies. But in regards to your feelings towards Azalea, there isn't any need to worry. He didn't know you existed until you walked through his front door. Otherwise you would already be out the airlock. I on the other hand have been informed of just how fond she is of you. And I will say she is like a sister to many so be careful with her. And to answer the curious look on your face, no I did not bring you down here for her. I only realized who you were after I learned your name. A coincidence, though it is hard to say whether it will be a fortunate one or not. Also, yes Azalea will return here shortly."

"I don't notice the resemblance between Jack and her," is the first thing I think to say to Bear. "But I'm glad she didn't think it was a good idea to be sent down here. Her brother is the opposite of her. It's hard to believe they came from the same woman."

"You have all rights to be upset with Jack and the situation you're now in," Bear says taking a seat next to me. "And to be fair no one sees a resemblance between them anymore. They're many years apart and have had different lives. There is not much else to say about it. However, if she likes you as much as I believe she does, it won't be too long before she will make a point to contact you in some way, even while you are in training. Now, if you have caught and calmed your breath maybe I can begin to show you your new home."

I suck down one more gulp of air before pulling myself up by the railing. My legs wobble as they take on the weight of my body again. Bear takes me through the opening and into another hallway. I allow myself to relax when we aren't confronted with another set of stairs and I try to take in my surroundings. The yellowed walls are lined with more signs of decay. Everything may all be crumbling, but this place still makes me feel wealthier than the chancellor. I bump into Bear as he stops at a door.

"I told you to keep it together," he grumbles. "They're just walls and ceilings, close your damn mouth."

He pulls out a small metal object and slides it into a knob on the door. He turns the piece of metal the door clicks and he pushes it open. I stand there confused. Bear looks at me like I'm a lost child.

"Key, door handle, lock," he says, waving his hands with sarcastic grace. "Now that it's open can you do the rest?"

I scowl at him and charge into the room. The place is filled with disorganized junk. Stacks of papers, maps and gear sit in the middle of the room and line the walls. An obvious path is laid out from one side of the room to the other. It looks like there is a place to sleep on the far side of the room, but it would be hard to reach without knocking something over.

"What is all this?" I ask.

"These are my quarters, which were given to me along with my last promotion," he says.

"It looks like you've been here awhile," I say.

"About a year," he says as his face flushes red. "I have something for you in here. I think you've been needing this."

He opens a cabinet and starts to push various jars and containers to either side. Eventually he produces a large loaf of bread from somewhere in the back.

"Eat it, it's real bread," he says. "It's a little past its good days but I'm sure you've eaten worse."

I pull off a large piece and shove it in my mouth. After the first taste I know I've never eaten something this good. Half the loaf is gone before Bear stops me. He rips a piece off for himself and places it on a shelf next to him.

"We should get into some dry clothes now," he says handing me some. "These are my brothers. He is closer to your size."

It's struggle to get out of my wet suit. The material peels off slowly and even pinches me at points. Before I am even halfway out of the suit Bear has made a full change. He helps me out of mine by pulling the legs off as I sit back. He almost picks me up off the ground as he does. While he waits he balls up the rest of the bread and quickly pops it into his mouth.

"Time to move on," he says through the bread.

As we leave he locks the door. With an outreached arm he shows me the way we are headed. This time we head down the hall with me leading the way. He does a good job of making it seem like I'm leading the way by staying a few steps back. That or he's trying to keep himself from being associated with me. We go all the way to the far end of the hall and I pause waiting for direction even though we can only go left. Bear bumps the back of my knee and it almost gives out. I take it as a sign to keep moving.

"The next door on the right," he eventually says to me.

On the other side and there is a small, dark room followed by another door. Through it is a brightly lit, white room and Hobbes wearing goggles, sitting at a table littered with wires and large pieces of metal. His grey hair stands out in the midst of all the white, giving it a darker appearance. Blue sparks fly up from the table as he prods something in the pile of metal with a slender metal tool.

"Are you here to give me those new additions or did you leave them down below?" he asks without looking up from the table.

"Yeah we managed to bring them the rest of the way," Bear says. "Give the books to Hobbes, Sam."

I reach across the table to hand them over. Hobbes still doesn't look up. He simply states, "There is fine." So I drop them on the table with a large thud. Most of the metal and equipment on the table rattles as a result.

"So Bear," he says. Finally looking up at us as he pushes his work into the rest of the chaos. "Has Jack's wife told you to come and mediate in hopes of negotiating peace? I've already tried to apologize and I will not be going back to embarrass myself again. Enough is enough with his erratic behavior and aggressive mood. I don't care if he's lost loved ones. Who hasn't? Even if he was the only one it is no excuse to be so abrasive and willing to risk lives for the sake of vengeance."

"I couldn't begin to try this time Hobbes," he says. "I don't even know the full extent of the arguments the two of you have had over the past few days. My only advice this time is to leave him alone so that maybe Madison and time can calm him. The two of you do not agree often. And it seems now that you can't even accept apologies between one another."

Hobbes slams his fist into the table. This time some of the odds and ends fall off and clatter on the floor. "That man has never apologized once in his life," Hobbes yelled. "His brain would probably melt if he even considered that he might be wrong. He is becoming an overgrown child with too much authority. This was my home to give to the people we bring here and now he acts as though it was his bloodline that saved this place so long ago," He pauses a moment before speaking again. "I'm sorry Bear I know you don't ask to be put in the middle of this, but you have the misfortune of somehow being liked by both Jack and I. As improbable as that may be..." he trails off.

"I'd rather both of you hated me if it meant you could get along, considering I'm the one who is rarely here," Bear says trying to lighten the mood with a gentle smile. "In other news we have this would be book thief that I am showing around. Is there anything interesting to show him down here? Just to warn you I have already shown him keys and locks, so you will to find something much more sophisticated."

Hobbes laughs, his furrowed brow breaks momentarily, "This might do the trick. Young man, I'm sure you are aware of some of the tools and weapons ONE has made. Either way here is something that may intrigue you. I have been tinkering with it for the past few months. Take several steps back please."

He pulls out a chrome stick from the pocket of his white coat. Bear takes two large steps back. At the same time he puts a hand on my chest and pulls me back with him. I watch with anticipation as Hobbes twists each end of the object and more starts to extend out of the top. At first it grows slowly, then it shoots out and stops with a quiet click. After that, nothing happens.

"You made a stick?" I blurt out as Bear attempts to hide a chuckle.

"No it's meant to be much more than that," Hobbes says with a defeated tone. "When it finishes extending it is supposed to be encompassed by a flame so hot that it can cut through or melt almost anything."

As he says this, a blue light flares up from the stick creating a large whooshing sound and extinguishes almost as quickly. Hobbes fumbles it before he twists the handle and it recedes back into itself. Once it is finished he casts it into the pile of junk instead of putting it back in his pocket.

"Do you think sometimes your tech doesn't work because of the way you beat on it?" Bear suggests. "What is this one to be called anyway?"

"I have dubbed it the hot stick," Hobbes voice trembles with frustration. "I thought it was working, but it seems that the power source is too small. I've attempted to use super compressed oxyhydrogen or create a battery to do something similar to the arc welders most scavengers use. Neither was sufficient so I tried to emulate the electromagnetism used for ONE's underwater rail system. It would seem that all I have found is another way that it won't work."

"I'm surprised you managed to come up with such a clever name while figuring out all the rest of that," I say jokingly.

At first Bear smirks at the comment, but masks it after Hobbes glares at the both of us. An awkward shrug in response only earns a more hostile look from Hobbes.

"I didn't mean to offend," I finally offer.

Hobbes stifles his anger and says, "Yes I do struggle with the names, but that's why Bear and his brother do the final naming after they test it."

"Will this one ever be ready for that stage?" Bear inquires.

"I was hoping that I had already finished," Hobbes says while picking it back up. "Hopefully soon." He regards it with more care before dropping it into his pocket.

Bear nods his head and starts moving toward the door. Before leaving I try to wave goodbye to Hobbes. He doesn't see because he's already back to prodding at something on his table and the sparks start to fly again. Bear takes us down the hallway two doors further and we enter one on the right. This time the room has high ceilings and rows of standing shelves. My nose and eyes instantly feel dried out from the stale air. I quickly forget everything outside of this room after I see that every shelf is filled with books. There are even piles stacked along the walls, reaching far above my head. All of the books are in better condition than anything else you could find in Empire. They are brightly colored and only a few seem to be missing their covers.

Bear steps into the room and throws out his arms to his sides, "This is my job as of late," he says. "I locate books throughout Empire and I bring them to one of five rooms like this and on my days off I help Hobbes organize them and sometimes I even spare a moment to read. Hobbes cares for them, ensuring that they don't fall to pieces. You may take a look, just don't knock anything over or Hobbes might actually get that hot stick working just so it can be used on you."

I drift past Bear, scanning the shelves as I pass between them. Some of the words are too difficult for me to understand or even pronounce. There are some that are familiar though. One called The Animal Encyclopedia catches my eye. Most of the animals appear alien to me. Most of the fish are easily recognized, but the names are strange. The animals covered in hair are even stranger. When I come across one called a grizzly bear I quickly see why someone down here would have decided to call Bartholomew, Bear. According to the book both are massive, hairy and the thought of being attacked by either frightens me.

"If you find the *w* section you will find the one my brother is named after," Bear says. "It's spelled W O L F."

I turn to the book over and thumb through to that section find a picture of a much more vicious appearing animal, even though the book tells me it is much smaller. Its lips are peeled back and long menacing teeth are exposed. The word WOLVES is printed across the top of the page.

"I've decided I don't want to meet your brother anymore," I say, returning the book.

"He isn't so bad," Bear says. "Just don't upset him."

He winks at me and shows me back out into the hall. I take a look back into the room, looking at all the books waiting to be read. Bear gives me an understanding smile as we leave the way we came. He leads me toward the center of the building and we arrive at what has a similar appearance to the lifts in the towers. It is much more crude than the sliding metal doors and fully enclosed carriage. The shaft looks more like

Bear ripped out a hole in the wall and used his own hands to dig down into the darkness. The carriage itself is a mixture of odds and ends, giving it a flimsy look and feel. The idea of getting into it is far from appealing. I find myself wanting a tour of a bathroom or some stairs.

"If this works anything like Hobbes stick I'm not getting in," I proclaim.

"Do you want me to make you?" Bear asks with a smirk.

I don't reply and he opens the gate to the lift with his hand instead of a button. It clanks open and momentarily sticks, twice. We step in and Bear slides it shut, the gate and everything else shudders in response. I've never been in a lift and I had hoped I would never have to be. To me it seemed insane to travel inside of something that moved you. This is much worse than anything imaginable. Bear presses a button that glows in response. The metal death trap clangs and drops several feet before it is caught by something and begins a slow, descent. As we lower, the box we are in gets darker until my eyes are level with the floor. A dim light flickers on at the top of the cage. The front of the lift is still open as we travel down, eventually the wall turns darker, wet and jagged. I reach out to touch it and Bear snatches my arm before I do.

"Leave all that you wish to keep inside the lift," he says in a strange, almost singing voice.

As we continue to slowly travel downward the lift starts to gently sway from side to side as it shoots down faster and jerks when it slows. I lean into the side of the lift to keep myself from falling over. Bear lets out a grunt of disapproval and slams the back wall of the lift several times until returns to its slow, even pace. Feeling sick I slide down to the floor forcing my stomach to keep its last, small meal. The cold metal of the lift comforts me as I place my face against the wall and doze off for a second before it comes to a sudden, jostling stop.

Two rough hands pull me up and out of the lift, waking me up. The owner of the hands can't quite lift me off the ground so my feet drag as he pulls me into himself. I find myself being stared down by a furry, smiling face with wild eyes. This must be Wolf.

"Feeling a little sick there slick?" he says letting go of me.

His smile fades into a look of disappointment when he doesn't get a coherent response. He drops me and gives Bear a look before covering the side of his mouth with one hand. "Is this kid Jack's idea of some sick joke?" Wolf yells jamming a thumb out towards me with his other hand.

Bear stares his brother down. "He didn't ask to be here so don't go on harassing him, Nathaniel," Bear growls. "Still, Jack wants him here and he isn't allowed back up until you say he's ready. And though he may be small give him some credit. He didn't back down when we had to fight off a skull on our way here."

"Couldn't swim away fast enough runt?" Wolf addresses me again. "Also, Bear don't call me that in front of the recruits."

Even though my gut is still settling from the trip down I manage to stand up as rigidly as Bear had to Jack. Wolf's dark eyes stare into mine. Our eyes lock for a second, before he lunges at me. I brace for the impact and turn my head and close my eyes. He stops just short of my face. All I could think of was having my head beat against a window. At least I didn't cry out or fall over.

"Didn't even touch him," he says, giving me no credit. His slender hips rock back and forth as he saunters away with pride.

Bear pushes me forward to follow. I look back to him for some kind of comfort or advice, instead he just points towards his brother and motions for me to keep following. After several steps I realize I'm walking alone. At the same time the lift clangs into place and start its journey up. I don't look back at Bear. Wolf doesn't need the satisfaction or another reason to cut me down. I don't know if I could ever live up to his standards. And maybe that's why Jack put me here. There are only two ways to leave this place. The quickest is out of the airlock without an oxygen tank and the other is gaining Wolf and Jack's approval. I'm not sure which option I prefer. The first will be easy, but I'll be dead. The other seems like it's going to be shit. At the same time it doesn't seem likely that Bear or anyone else would let me die, if they have any say over the matter. I hope they do.

CHAPTER SIX

Wolf leads me to a rusted out box with small windows. I assume that it's some kind of living space. On the way we pass a mess of pillars, platforms and nets. A large flattened area, indented a few feet into the ground takes up a large portion of the space. Other than that there is just empty hollowed out cave. As we get closer to the box a face appears in one of the windows. When it disappears thirteen other boys pour out of the doorway.

"They'll help you get settled in," Wolf tells me as he walks off towards a much smaller box.

When I reach the others they don't speak or move out of my way to let me in. I try to squeeze past and the tallest boy wraps a leg around mine and pushes me over. I crash down on the damp rock and hit my jaw on a sharp edge. Blood dribbles off my face and mixes with the cold air.

"Hey!" one of them yells. "Why'd you do that?"

"This runt hasn't even been to basic," My attacker says. "Anyone of us could have stopped me. I did it slow too. He didn't even try to counter me. Do you think you can just pass through?" he says to me. "You must have some wealthy sympathizer parents. They probably paid your way here."

"No," I say in a way that even sounds like a yes to me.

"We had to earn our way," he continues, ignoring my denial. "We're recruits, you're just a runt."

"I didn't ask to be here," I try to explain. "Why would anyone?"

"No, you probably begged until you peed yourself," another boy says. "Right Robert?" he says to the apparent leader.

"Screw it," Robert says. "Let's show him the inside. It's nothing Ritzy like you're probably used to."

They let me in, but don't actually show me anything. I look around myself, careful not to get too close to anyone else. Two rows of stained cots are set up along each side. And at the far end there is a shower station, which actually has curtains. There is one empty cot and it is covered in a thick layer of red dust. Above it is a small, crumbling hole. Robert passes by me and jumps. Even more flakes of rust fall down and land in my hair. I shake it off before taking a shower. Some of the other recruits steal my soap and towel. This being my first shower with clean water, I don't really care. The slightly heated water washes away everything my trip down to the base didn't. I put my clothes back onto my still wet body and finally get to sleep.

After the first week of training I'm already starting to consider breaking a rule that would count as a violation of my probation. The training isn't as difficult as it was made out to be, but the cruel treatment from the recruits here is unbearable. They all are under the impression that I want to be here and that I was somehow given a pass on all the previous training that they have gone through. By day two they had taken everything but my essential gear. I am finally used to sleeping on the cold floor with nothing between it and my bare skin, using my clothes as a pillow. If only they knew that this was just barely worse than my daily life. The chilling floor soothes the bruises they left along my back and ribs when they stole my cot. Most nights I race to fall asleep before being tortured by the feeling of small squirming bugs rolling across my skin. I do my best not to cry out in the middle of the night. I don't want them to enjoy my suffering. I want my cot back, but I can't fight all of them on my own. Most nights I fall asleep watching Robert, hoping he falls asleep before me. He's a full head taller than the rest of us and no one challenges his authority. Everyone else is most likely just happy to be left alone.

After the first day I had been so tired I fell asleep without taking off my newly issued boots. Before I could do as much as yell in surprise from being shaken awake, my cot had been pulled out from beneath me and I was kicked with rebel issued boots from every direction until a rib cracked and the feeling left my legs. Robert now sleeps on both cots pushed together. When Wolf saw he said nothing and I was still expected to make it through the full day of training. My legs lagged in response to my thoughts all day. I was happy enough to have a floor to lie on when the day was done.

Now, a week later we have our first break. The schedule we were given is seven days of training for eight hours and one day of rest. All week I've dreaded this day. I have a feeling if I don't do something today there won't be much rest for me. With no source of entertainment down here my situation will only be worse on days like this. I wake up before anyone else and creep into the shower room without waking anyone up.

A few days ago I had already decided that today will be the first time things don't go Robert's way, even it if it does mean breaking one of Wolf's rules. I don't even want to see his flat dumb face. It looks like it was bashed in with a frying pan when he was a baby and I'm repulsed by it and the awful stink that he carries with him. By the time I start to get dressed some of the others are starting to stir. I lie down and pretend to use my boots as a pillow. One of them, Paul, kicks me in the shin as he and Dylan head to the showers themselves.

"Wake up runt," he says.

Dylan laughs at this and sneers at me as I pretend to wake up. Paul flashes a look of concern that confuses me. On the first day he had tried to defend me for a moment, but ever since then he's been one of the worst. It makes me wonder if he was trying to deprive me of sleep or give me a chance to get out. Once they leave the room I'm up with my pack already filled and out the door before anyone else has had a chance to stir. The small metal shack in the underground facility is apparently made out of tubes from dry times. If so, it's no wonder they're falling apart, they have to be a few hundred years old. I'm glad to be the first one out of that box. Only the two shacks and the training course resemble anything that could be called a facility. The rest is a large cave with black ceilings that go as high as five levels at some points. The air is wet and cool, constantly chilling me. Still, it's calming, unlike the stifling air in the book room or rank smells from bottom levels of a tower. I inhale deeply, trying to collect my nerves as I look up at the rafters that crisscross along the top of the cave. My plan is to find a quiet hidden place in the shadows to read the book Bear had sent down to me the day before.

I dart my way through the obstacle course and shooting range, ducking behind barrels and cement blocks or anything else large enough to hide me. If someone were to make their way outside all they might see is a flash of my shadow cast along the wall. It's a good head start, but there isn't time to relax yet. If they see me there is no chance of me going unnoticed. Taking the long way around has been safer, though Wolf's shack is still ahead. He said we have the day to ourselves. Still, I am unsure of what he would say about my actions.

I sprint through the last patch of open space and throw myself into the darkness behind Wolf's living quarters. Every second counts now. Most of the morning has already passed and there is still ground left to cover. It takes a moment to catch my breath after hitting the ground. I made it so it doesn't even matter that I just landed in a muddy puddle. If anything it will make it harder for me to be seen while I climb. The only thing that worries me is the book. The pack is waterproof. Hopefully all the movement hasn't bent the cover or ripped any pages. There was also a note inside, written by Bear.

"I shouldn't have sent this to you so be careful with it," it read. "Send it up in the laundry once you have read the last words. Hobbes is already upset enough as it is that I have 'misplaced' this book. He made a real threat for the first time in his life. If it were to suddenly return in pieces I think he would have a heart attack. Also, Azalea has returned. She informed me that she looks forward to seeing you again and hopes things go well for you down there."

The book held a number of stories from a number of people. In part of the note he had scribbled some information on the book. He had called it an anthology. He knew that most nights I would only have a short time to read, which is probably why he sent me a book of many short stories. I wish I could thank him for it, but I have nothing to write with and I wouldn't be seeing him for some time.

"Careful," Wolf's voice comes from nowhere as I get to my feet.

I almost fall back into the puddle as I jump in surprise. His tattered boots are poking out from behind his shack, rocking on their heels. As I follow his legs upwards I realize he's sitting. He is smoking his pipe and each time he inhales the red glow lights up his face. It's the first time he doesn't seem angered or disapproving of me. The way he said careful is similar to how Bear would have if he were reading his note to me and if anything Wolf smiled when he said it. Though, it's hard to tell through his beard and the pipe resting on his lower lip. His chair creaks each time he leans back and then forward again.

"Careful of what?" I ask.

He responds with a puff of his pipe as his face fades back into the shadow, a cloud of thin smoke leaks out into the small ray of light that has managed to pierce through the darkness between us. Without a sound his legs recede and quite suddenly I am alone again. I pause for a moment and wonder what exactly the answer to my question should have been. It doesn't have anything to do with the climb itself. If he found that too dangerous he would have stopped me right out. Considering how the first week went I'm certain Wolf will make it clear by the end of the day. Wolf loves to deal in mystery. He gives us ambiguous instructions, mainly to see if we are smart enough to solve our own problems. When we fail he is quick to show us how we could have succeeded had we deciphered his instructions better.

Once I'm in the shadow of his shack the journey to the wall of the cave is quick. I am climbing up the rock face moments after my warning, which still baffles me. It isn't difficult to climb the rock, but it takes some time. When I reach the beams I have to take a break. I sit on one of the metal rods and lean against the wall. The cold stone cools my sweaty head and back. It takes a few minutes to gain control of my breathing before moving on. If they see me, this spot will not be far enough away. I crawl on my hands and knees across the framework and concentrate on my balance while trying to move quickly at the same time. My pack slides from side to side on my back. I straddle the beam below me and take a moment to tighten. When there comes a point at which two beams come close to each other I set up a hammock I stole from the supply room late last night.

The book cracks as it opens and for a moment I fear that the spine might be crumbling. After it doesn't I go on reading and continue for several hours before taking a break to readjust and eat some of the food from my pack. I reach for my canteen to take a swig when Roberts voice comes echoing throughout the cave.

"All right where the hell is that damn runt!" Robert screeches.

I almost drop my canteen in fright, fumbling it for a moment before regaining control. The hammock sways slightly from my movements and the fabric strains as it tightens around the metal supports. I hunker down pulling my pack over me in attempt to make myself as small as possible.

"There's no way," I whisper to myself. Saying it over and over as Robert becomes more frantic. His voice becomes shrill as he yells out towards his small band of bullies. I take a peek over my hammock to watch him.

"How hard can it be?" he spits out. "Have you forgotten how to use your eyes?!"

He grabs Paul, who is nearest to him, and throws him to the ground. Paul grumbles as he adjusts his shirt, but still gets up quickly to search for me. Robert hits another recruit in the head with the back of his hand and his knuckles crack against the skull. Why does everyone let him lead so brutally? He is bigger than the rest of us but there are so many of us and just him. As he goes to lash out a second time I yell down to him. "Did you forget you also have eyes?"

Everyone pauses, looking for the source of my voice. It becomes so quiet that Robert's heavy breathing can be heard from up here. After a few moments pass I speak up again. "If you want me so badly Robert come get me yourself," I taunt. I even wave down to him from my lofty position, hoping it makes him even angrier. He becomes so upset that he visibly starts to shake. He stops when he finally finds me.

"Come down here, now," he spits.

"Why would I do that?" I say. "Whenever you want to come get me I'll still be here."

I make a show of grabbing my book and reading, wiggling down into the hammock to get comfortable. I peer over the edge of the book and get an overwhelming sense of joy, as his face burns red. He runs to the wall I scaled earlier and starts to scramble up. He falls before reaching ten feet, landing hard on his back.

"Coward!" he belts out.

"I climbed it," I say without looking away from my book. "Can't you?"

After that he starts to climb wildly up the wall. When it becomes apparent that he will reach the top I start to pack up and bury the book below everything else to keep it safe. As he starts to crawl along the supports I make my move to the opposite end and don't bother looking back until I hear a collective gasp from everyone below, followed by a small cry from Robert. An almost inaudible help escapes his lips as he hangs from a beam with one hand and flails aimlessly with the other.

I remove my pack and clip it to the nearest support beam, quickly running hunched over with my hands inches above the beam, ready to catch myself the moment I slip. As I reach him I can see a couple tears rolling down the side of his face. They cut a path through the dirt that has accumulated there before dropping fifty feet below. He mouths *please* at me as though actually saying it might cause him to lose his grip. The benefits of letting him fall pass through my mind as I wrap my legs around the metal, hook my ankles together and grab his hand. He's heavy and pulling him up strains every muscle. His legs start to flail as his shoulders clear the beam. When I finally get him high enough, he manages to pull himself up the rest of the way and his midsection flops onto the beam. We both sit there breathing heavily, Robert staring down at the obstacle course below. He's still sobbing, taking in staggered mouthfuls of air.

I turn away from him to retrieve my pack. His comfort isn't of any concern to me and I don't want to look at his sobbing face all day. I take my time moving to where my pack is waiting for me. The thought of letting him fall still feels like it would have been a valid option. As I reach my pack Paul cries out from below, "Look out Sam."

Before it's possible to react two enclosed fists crash down on the side of my head. As I fall I grab one of the straps of my bag. Lights flash in my eyes and any noise sounds drowned out and far away. A constant hum has taken over the inside of my skull. Robert stands above me with a vicious grin across his face. Confused I reach up toward him. He swats my hand away and spits at my face.

"You're dead now," he says quietly. "You should have let me fall."

With the same hand that had reached out for help I grab the laces of one of his boots and pull. The move was complete instinct and before I realize what's happened, Robert is wobbling and his body involuntarily leans toward me and then away. He tries to pull back with his leg as he leans back, but instead of freeing himself he spills off the other side. He falls and his weight helps me pull myself back up. My fingers are still intertwined in the laces, but they snap and slide out of my grasp just as I start to pull him up again. Robert doesn't make a noise as he falls. All he does is stare back up toward me while he falls, keeping eye contact until he dives headfirst into a platform from the training course about ten feet off the ground. It made the fall shorter and softer than a fall all the way to the rock. Still, he's stopped with a sickening crunch and blood quickly pools underneath him.

I make it down to the ground with my pack and head towards the small group that has already huddled around my would be killer. As I climb up to the group they open up the circle that has formed and I look down at what I've done. Robert lays there sprawled out in his own blood. His eyelids blink as he wildly scans the group. His face has lost all color. Upon seeing me he begins to struggle in an attempt to talk. All that comes out of his mouth is a gathering of red bubbles. They pop as he continues to noiselessly open and close his mouth like a baitfish. His breathing continually slows and starts to sound wet.

No one moves, instead we watch him desperately suck down air and spit up blood. When I look at the faces around me I'm surprised to see a mixture of disgust and intrigue. My feelings on the situation are neutral. My delight of having survived is washed out by my repulsion of the cost. I don't understand why he had to come after me with such blind hate, but once he did I was no longer able to look at him as a person. Then again maybe I had stopped the first time he struck me. He was an enemy from the first day and I had done nothing to bring it on. Today he seemed more like a tyrant and a coward. Maybe his death was the only way to stop him.

"Shame," Wolf's voice cuts through the silence.

"Does anyone know why I'm not helping poor Robert?" he asks making eye contact with everyone except me.

No one responds. Robert sloppily exhales in fright and tries to move, only managing to flop. His eyes fill with fear and the knowledge of what's coming.

"If you remember I told all of you that any fighting would be overlooked, but I also made it clear that anything to risk the completion of this training or the life of a fellow recruit would be heavily penalized and that penalty would be left for me to decide. In this case Robert attempted to terminate Sam's life prior to his completion of my training program. And so I have decided that Robert, who had the audacity to not die from what he hoped would have killed Sam, should now be removed from training."

As he finishes this last sentence he stomps down on Robert's neck. From underneath Wolf's boot, Robert's throat snaps with a wet crunch. Wolf makes sure the deed is done with the twist of his boot heel. Robert flounders, his arms shoot out and wriggle in an attempt to stop

Wolf, but they settle back to his sides before they can achieve anything. Paul retches at the sight of the compressed neck and several others look ready to do the same. Wolf, without taking his eyes off Robert speaks up again.

"From here on out there are no days off. It gets harder now as it has become obvious all of you have had too much free time." he turns to me and whispers, "Come with me Sam."

I can smell the metallic scent of blood as he brushes past me. Everyone else gapes at me, or Robert. Eventually one by one they all leave and go back to the shack. "Now." Wolf says from below. I climb down and catch up with him as he continues to walk toward his shack.

I don't say anything as we trudge up the slight incline. Wolf takes the two steps that lead to his door in one stride and pulls it open for me. I try to glance at his face to see if it can tell me anything, but it looks as uncaring as ever. I sidestep him as he stops and shuffle in through the doorway. His shack is much more organized than Bear's room and well lit. The cot is in the furthest corner from the door with an old water damaged trunk at the foot. The next day's clothes have already been laid out on top next to a fresh pair of polished boots. An exercise mat takes up a good portion of the floor. And a desk is tidily pushed into the corner adjacent from his cot. He motions for me to sit at the desk with a wave of his hand.

"I want to stand if that's OK, sir," I say with my heels together and my back as stiff as a board.

"Suit yourself kid," he says with a hint of a smile.

The smile is unexpected and it throws me off. Yelling, being hit or even being told I had broken one of the few rules Wolf had and would soon be joining Robert seemed more appropriate. This is the first time he's smiled since the day I came down here and he had made me flinch.

"What did I tell you at the beginning of this day?" he asks while stuffing his pipe.

"You said 'careful'."

"Exactly, and from your lack of response I take it you have no idea what that really meant at the time. Are you aware of what it means now?"

I search his face for the answer, but his smile is gone and his face is back to his less caring demeanor. He sucks on his pipe while trying to get it lit. When he finally manages to he blows the smoke in my face and I cough uncomfortably.

"What do you want from me?" I eventually ask.

"I think you do really know the answer, but I'll walk you through it if you insist on playing the fool," he says. "Let's start by having you tell me what happened today."

"You already know," I say. Normally this kind of answer would try his patience, but I feel like he is too busy trying to test mine.

"Tell me again, I like to hear stories when I smoke," he says this with an eagerness that disturbs me.

"I planned this day out all week," I explain. "I was ready to leave the shack before anyone was really awake. I made it out here and we know what happened after. I climbed up to the rafters and hid all day until Robert came after me."

"You seem to have left something out," Wolf says with a new grin breaking through his beard. "Why did Robert come after you?"

"I yelled at him," I say.

"Why?" Wolf presses.

"He hit the others because he couldn't find me and I didn't want other people to be hurt on my account," I finally say.

"So you were worried about other people, people that had been hurting you since you came here. Even better, you saved the life of their ringleader, for a moment. Who returned the favor by trying to kill you."

"Well I ended up killing him in the end," I lose eye contact with Wolf as I say this.

He does not respond right away. He gently places his pipe on the desk, smoke still wafting out, and gets out of his chair. As he stands before me he claps both hands on my shoulders.

"You did what you had to and he was doing what he wanted to do," he says with a tenderness I didn't know he could muster. "Maybe you wanted it a little, but that doesn't change the fact that only one of you was coming down alive. You weren't careful like I asked. You should be dead. You're luckier than I thought. I wanted you to be careful for you, plain and simple. Instead you cared for your enemy first, as though his life was important to you. What you need to learn from this day is that you always take care of you first, because if you die now you can't be useful later. In the field you don't help others unless they will be of use to you later. And you especially don't help those who aren't for our cause. I don't want you to see anyone in the field as people when you leave here. They are either a tool or an obstacle and you only help when it doesn't put you in harms way."

"I don't know if I can do that," I whisper. "That doesn't seem right sir. I feel like we should be fighting so people don't have to be that way."

"No wonder Bear took you in," he says. "I pity both of you. And if that's the case you will have to continue to be careful. The balance between all you young men may be upset now. Except now, you appear to the rest as more than another recruit, maybe even a man. You took down the one person everyone feared. They could see you as something great, the boy who took down a giant. Fear can be a great tool, but not for a team. Let's just hope you don't have to kill again until after your training is over."

Shocked by all this I open and close my mouth several times, not sure what to say. Wolf finds humor in this and chuckles, patting me on the shoulder.

"What? Did you think I would be mad that you finally defended yourself? No, I was wondering how long this would take, if it would ever happen. With you being a low level dweller I thought you would take it all the way to the end of training or even let Robert kill you like the limp fish I thought you were. You surprised me. You aren't like the rest of those sad broken people. So no, you did not break any of my rules if that's what you had originally thought, but your training is far from over."

When I get back the first thing I do is take back my cot and any other prizes Robert has claimed from me. No one tries to stop me or even looks at me. The rest of the day continues this way. None of them speak and the day drags on without incident. By the time the lights go out everyone has already been asleep for sometime. Except for me. I don't sleep all night. The sound of the other's snoring reminds me terribly too much of Robert's sickening attempts to draw air into his lungs. Still, morning comes too quickly. Wolf pounds on the door as usual. The sign for us to get ready as he prepares the facility for today's training session. For me it is a morning like no other. I don't have to wait to shower in fear of being humiliated. I'm not harassed and no one says a word to me. It is a lonely feeling. I get dressed and I'm the first to the range where Wolf stands waiting.

Paul shuffles in next to me moments later. We don't say anything to each other even after he gives me a nod I say nothing. We silently wait for the rest to show up. As the last of them file in Wolf begins.

"Today is the day many of you have been waiting for," he says removing his pulse gun from its holster. "We are going to learn to shoot," he pauses as some let out an excited gasp. "Shut it, all of you. You're not children and this won't be playtime, so listen. The first rule of the shooting range is, any person who even pretends to aim their weapon away from the targets will be shot. Whether or not it's an accident, no one will be getting shot at my range. Except by me."

He turns from us and takes a stance with his legs spread, shoulders squared down the range and fires. A flash of blue lights up along the barrel and the revolving battery of the hazard yellow pistol. Right as the gun spins up the crackle of electricity sets my hair on end and I can feel a cloud of heat settle over me as the pulse leaves the barrel of the gun. The feeling of the shot going off jolts me as the bolt of plasma collides with its mark. Looking down toward the concrete block that serves as the target, the result is stunning. The white circular spot of paint is now a mostly black, crumbling chunk of block. A large piece falls to the ground that was once the center and it has been pushed back at least half an inch. Wolf turned back to us with his gun raised up next to his face. The mid-section still slowly winding down.

"Who knows anything about these?" he asks.

Paul slowly raises his hand up above his head. Wolf nods at him, telling him to say what he has to say. "I know that they are all made by ONE and that the core, which powers the gun, is supposed to last at least one hundred years," the words pour out of his mouth quickly and nervously.

Wolf looks at Paul in a disapproving manner and leans toward him gesturing with both arms out wide as if to say, *so, what else?* Paul stares back blankly with nothing to say. Wolf's face takes on an even more dissatisfied appearance mixed with borderline boredom. Just as his face starts to melt into frustration I speak up.

"Well the part that spins, I think that's the core and the spinning charges the gun. That creates the projectile. The electricity contains the plasma as it moves through the air."

"Good guess," Wolf spits. "Go on, if you can."

"I can't," I say flatly.

"Well at least the two of you know something," he sighs. "Or you're at least brave enough to speak up. This weapon creates a small ball of lightning when the magnetic confinement cylinder reaches its full revolution speed as you press down on the trigger. It only takes a drop of plasma mixed with the electricity that the magnet creates when it spins. Instead of lightning in a bottle it acts more like a bottle made of lightning. The electricity running through the ball of plasma allows it to expand only enough to become a deadly projectile of significant force, both in kinetic and heat energy. Any questions?"

He leaves us wordless as I resist the urge to stare at my feet. Sweat starts to bead on my forehead as the silence continues. Without a response Wolf begins pacing from one end of the group to the other, eyeing up Paul and myself as he does. After a moment he pauses in front of us both and glares down at us. We stare back and give him nothing. Wolf breaks eye contact and points us toward a table on the far side of the range.

"Grab one each and hit the target. If you're successful you will both be taking charge of teaching everyone else how to turn them on," he commands. "Then I will take over from there."

We rush towards the table saying nothing to each other as we approach it, already panting. Just yesterday Paul was my enemy now he's just another recruit. I'll have to talk to him now if we end up teaching together, however briefly. For now we move together with only our footsteps to break the silence. When we reach the table we both hesitate to touch the guns. I pick the first one up. This seems to pull Paul out of a trance as he quickly takes one for himself as if it might get away. He fumbles it on the table for a moment before regaining his composure.

"Don't break my guns," Wolf snarls.

Paul pales at the sound of Wolf's agitated voice. I nudge him with my elbow and nod to the line Wolf had stood up to when he fired the first shot. He follows me and we both take a stance like Wolf's, aim and pull the trigger. Nothing happens as my finger continues to squeeze harder. The group behind us murmurs nervously in response. Paul keeps pulling with the same result. I bring the gun in with both hands and inspect it. It seems like a simple weapon. Point and shoot should be the all there is to it. Then I remember the harpoon gun and notice a small knob at the top left of the handle. Below it is a small red dot. I push up on it without response, but when I push down it slides. It covers the dot and reveals another, deep black. The core hums to life in response.

"How?" Paul asks looking over my shoulder.

I reach over and flick his switch into place. He grins with approval and thanks. He winks at me as he gets back into his stance. With both cores slowly whirring they crackle back and forth. The hair on my hand stands up and when I put my finger on the trigger a small shock shoots through my fingertip. The core speeds up in response and I feel my body tense as I hesitate to pull it the whole way back. Just as I am about to, Paul fires off three rapid shots causing me to look away and my shot goes wild, sending rock in all directions behind the targets. Some of the recruits cover their heads and I almost drop the gun in surprise of the power. My hand is sweating. I can't tell if it was from the heat or my nerves.

Paul unloads several more shots, each one hitting dead center. His face, a mixture of delight and ferocity. The only other person I've seen act that way is Patrick, the guy that tried to lodge a stick in my skull. Paul's face frightens me. Realizing that I still haven't hit the target I push him and Patrick out of my mind and take three somewhat successful shots. They at least keep Wolf from yelling. As we finish, both Paul and I turn to the rest of the recruits. There is a mix of excitement and worry on their faces. I try to hide my own worry and put on a face that only seems thrilled with the experience. If everyone is afraid to use the guns we could be here through the night, until Wolf is certain we are proficient.

"Nice work you two, Sam you could use some more practice though," Wolf says. "Unfortunately a call just came down and you're to meet my brother at the top of the lift. Paul, take charge of the lesson. And remember no games and no shooting until I say so."

Wolf leads me to the lift and starts it up and it crashes to a stop at our feet. As I pull open the gate Wolf taps me on the shoulder.

"Kid I have to say in a short time you have managed to completely change my opinion of you. My brother and I do not agree often, but maybe I'm starting to see what he sees," he says.

"Thanks."

I step into the lift and force the gate closed. Before it starts back up, Wolf is already heading back to the range. The trip up doesn't make me nearly as queasy as the one down did. When I reach the top Bear is already there, waiting for me. He opens up the gate before the lift comes to a complete stop. As I step out into the hall I have to shield my eyes from the light.

"Here take these," Bear says.

He hands me glasses with dark glass in the frames, they say *sorry for partying* along the side. As I slide them over my eyes the relief is instant.

"I called you up here," Bear speaks again. "But the person who wants to see you is Hobbes. Jack declined Hobbes' request to pull you from training so I placed one. Let's hope we don't run into anyone important on the way."

This turns out to be no problem as we take the short walk from the lift to Hobbes. I still remember how to get there and find myself speeding ahead of Bear. I reach the door first and let myself into the hallway and wait at the door to the Hobbes' workshop.

"You raced ahead to wait?" Bear scrutinizes me. "Next time have some patience or have the balls to open a door."

This comment sounds more like Wolf the past week than the Bear that brought me here. He reaches past me and opens the door, pushing me through with his other arm.

"When you finish I'll be in the book room," he says.

I wave him away and keep walking into the room. The door shuts with a bang that echoes through the hushed room. I walk up to the table Hobbes was at last time I had been here, there is no sign of him. Last time I had been so nervous I hadn't taken my eyes off of the old man with glasses. The room was not as white and clean as it had seemed before. Grease stains were splattered across each of the walls and a few had even reached the ceiling. The lights had burn marks splotched on them and a good number of them were cracked or broken.

I remove my eyes from the walls and ceiling and start fumbling through the various gadgets on the table. None of it appears to be completely put together. I pick up a small, polished disk. It has a light colored metal on one side and contains a number of cogs inside the other. Next to it lies a small white piece, outlined in numbers. Two small arrows reach out from the center and generally point towards eleven. The two are different lengths and widths. The longer and thinner one is slightly closer to twelve, leaving eleven behind.

"When you're quite done with it could you put down my five hundred year old watch?" Hobbes voice comes out of the open air.

I drop the gadget onto the table with a surprising thud and several of the cogs bounce out. My attempts to catch them fail as they land among a pile of spare parts. Suddenly the wall to my left shimmers and falls to the floor like a blanket. As it crumples to the floor it turns transparent, but continues to glisten in the light. At the same time Hobbes is revealed and when the shiny sheet settles he steps over it. His face shakes slightly as he holds back his frustration, but its change to a deeper shade of red gives him away as he approaches me.

"If I didn't think you had promise I'd be sending you back down to that hole Wolf loves to fool around in," he whispers in a way that still feels like a shout.

I begin to apologize and he waves me off. He stands next to me and grabs onto a pair of tweezers, expertly guiding them through the chaos of his worktable. He plucks out the parts that escaped and sets them back into place. With a sigh he sets the tweezers down and takes a seat on the stool next to me. He swivels around for a while, staring at the ceiling with a vacant look. I shuffle my feet awkwardly until he remembers that I'm there.

"So you're wondering why I'm staring at this damn ceiling and what the hell you're supposed to be doing here, right?" he finally asks. Before I can answer he continues, "I know how things have been going for you down below and I know that you are a very curious and potentially smart person. It also helps that Bear has, for some reason, taken a special interest in you. On top of all that, I get a passive aggressive joy, knowing that Jack despises you. If I can help you and you can help me, all the while in defiance of Jack, we all win, except for Jack of course. All these are reasons why you have been brought here, though none of them will be the reason why you stay. Curious you may be, but I need more than that and I need more than potential. I am a man of science and logic so I need certainty and reason." He removes his glasses and lets out another long sigh while he rubs his eyes. "Excuse me, but I haven't slept lately. I have several projects going on at once, as you might be able to tell with the current state of my workstation. What I want to find out about you is one simple fact. Do you have anything of value in that brain of yours? This isn't to say I don't necessarily care about you as a person, but if you're dumber than a box of rocks I could care less about how curious you are and I will simply send you back to be molded into an unquestioning, soldier. So you will take a test and if you meet my expectations we will proceed."

As he finishes he crosses his legs and motions for me to take a seat on another stool. He reaches across the table spilling parts and tools onto the floor and produces a stained stack of paper and a pencil. There are several questions on each page. The letters A through D have been crossed out and rewritten several times. A fresh set of letters has been written above the center of each possible answer.

"There are three hundred total questions and you have two hours to answer as many as you can,' he explains. "Not only do I want to see if your brain is worth more than telling your mouth to suck in air, I want to see how you handle pressure. The last time I administered this test over two hundred of the questions were answered. While you work I am going to work as well, so I won't have time to answer silly questions. Good luck."

Hobbes stands up and fishes a small timer out from his pocket and places it to my left. It is already ticking. It shows that one hour and fifty-seven minutes remain. He must have started it as soon as he handed me the test. A feeling of dread sets in as I start to rapidly read through the first question only to realize I miss half the words when I try. The test continues on in a painfully slow manner for me. With just over an hour left I'm only at question seventy. And as I struggle through each question Hobbes hammers and drills away at scraps with no clear sense of doing actual work. At one point he catches a glare from me and simply smiles back through his plastic facemask as sparks fly off a metal sheet.

With ten minutes left I have managed to make it to question one hundred thirty. With ten seconds left I furiously fill in the answer circle for question one hundred forty four. The buzzer goes off and I throw down the pencil and slouch down onto the table disgusted with my own performance. I don't even lift my head as Hobbes tosses down his tools and walks over to me. He slides the test out from underneath my limp arms and slowly flips through each page. He hums as each scratchy turn of a page cuts more deeply into my confidence. Some time later I feel myself being shaken awake and lift my head to a stern looking Hobbes. He reaches over to me and brushes my face as several small screws and various small parts fall off my cheek. Then shuffles the test on his crossed over legs and clears his throat.

"So one hundred and forty four," he says to himself. "You have managed to surprise me after all. You did better than I thought, especially with the kind of racket I was stirring up not ten feet away."

I beam at this input and find myself feeling good for the first time since I came here, but Hobbes swiftly crushes that feeling.

"But just so you don't become too sure of yourself I should tell you this test is meant for a child. But that is the only test I could give you considering you were a bottom dweller and most likely had no education. How did you learn to read anyway?"

"I taught myself," I say with a hint of pride returning to me.

"Well I suppose if we had started there the test could have been avoided," he says with a weak smile.

I drop my head back down to the table and close my eyes.

Hobbes chuckles to himself for a moment before telling me to get off the stool.

"I have some things to show you and since this may be the only time I can show you for awhile, you're going to need to take some notes."

He hands me a small, hardcover book along with another pencil. The inside of it is almost blank. The inside cover, however, has a faded message written on it. *Keep writing...you're getting good,* it reads. I safely assume the message was meant for someone else. Hobbes leads me out of his workspace taking me through a door opposite the one I came through. Inside it there is a small room with a ladder. I fumble with the book as I attempt to follow up to the hatch. It fits about halfway into the pocket of my jacket and I catch up to Hobbes as he steps into the room above.

The room is much darker than any other I had been to yet, but I can sense how filled it is. It's a struggle to avoid the slew of cords that run across the floor. I stand next to Hobbes as he sits in front of a screen similar to the one that dropped from the ceiling at the people's tower. He presses a few buttons on a small board below the screen. A new image pops up. It is a small building and of course, completely submerged. A monstrous metal tube lies across the top of it.

"This is our home from the outside," Hobbes explained. "It looks completely inactive and destroyed to anyone out there, no matter how close they might get. The government has been attempting to locate this place since before I was born, but thanks to my father, grandfather and his father, all efforts have failed. There was a time before Jack that this building was only used to safeguard knowledge and those that sought it out, the freely thinking people of our time. We would race to find smart children before the government or ONE could capture or dispose of them."

Hobbes stops to cough several times. His body shudders as each dry cough racks his insides. When the spurt of coughs end he is out of breath and a string of spit hangs off his chin. He regains his composure while he wipes off his face and adjusts his glasses back into their proper place. They had almost fallen off the tip of his nose.

"Are you alright?" I ask carefully.

"Yes I'm fine let me continue," he says. "They would raise the kids and then use their intelligence to make better products or find better ways to control the people of this sad city. Often the two went hand in hand, which is why the government and ONE are now only separate in name and it has really become quite confusing as to who is in charge. The two leaders now, are brothers and unfortunately they get along quite well. But enough of that, let me show you what we came up here for."

Hobbes strikes another button and several other screens switch on and fill the room with a dull blue light. A slew of numbers and maps scroll across some of the screens while several others produce moving images. All I can manage is a quiet "whoa." He swivels the chair to face me while extending a hand up toward the wall of monitors.

"I'm not from the camp that enjoys bragging, but all of this was constructed by me and my father quite a few years back, before the glasses and the grey hair," he says. "We used to believe we were hidden so well that this place would never be found. After a number of close calls we decided that hoping was not as good as knowing. Now from this chair I can monitor our power, which comes from that submarine that landed here some time before my great grandfather's father. And a number of motion sensors have been set out, along with cameras, within a quarter mile radius so we can see who's coming."

He cracks a smile while I stare at all the lights. It all seems too complicated for me as numbers flash and lights blink on and off. I begin to tell him this and it seems that he knew what was coming.

"Sam, listen," he grabs my hand. "I know the look. Bear gave me the same one. I don't need you to know how to rebuild anything like this. If the system were damaged that heavily, rebuilding would be the least of our concerns. Bear is my only help though. If Jack's desire for confrontation is realized, Bear may be taken away from me. I need more people to help me maintain what has already been built and watch these monitors when I can't. Even if Bear and you both survive this harsh world and the probable conflict that seems to be charging toward us you will both eventually grow too old to go out into the ocean."

With Hobbes blathering on like this thousands of questions arrive at the front of my mind. I have a feeling they won't be answered soon so I don't ask. "I'll do whatever you need me to," is all I say.

"Great!" Hobbes smile widens. "Every other week you will come up from the cave and work with either Bear or myself until your training with Wolf is done. The skills we teach you will be basic and all geared towards repairing equipment along with other simple tasks. And if there is time we will simply teach you. Now go find Bear we'll start next time."

He shoos me out of the room and down the ladder. He doesn't follow so I take myself to Bear. He's sitting cross-legged on a folded blanket reading a large book. He peers over the edge and continues to read until I make it across the room to him. He licks his thumb, folding over the top corner of a page and closes the book, causing a large cloud of dust to rise up towards the light above Bear. He sets the book back onto its stack against the wall and gives me a pleased look. He is much more like himself now.

"Hobbes hates that, but he still hasn't given me a bookmark," he says as he wipes off the dust that has collected on his shirt. "Give me a hand up, yeah?"

He reaches out an arm and I pull with both of mine. He stands so quickly I almost tumble to the ground. He catches me in response and lets out a small chuckle. For someone so powerful I find it incredible that he enjoys such insignificant moments.

"So did all go well with our friend?" he asks.

"Yeah. I guess I'll be helping you guys out," I say.

"Good, maybe soon I will finally have more time available for reading," Bear lets out a sigh and rubs his lower back as it cracks several times. "I could also use a break. But for now let us worry about taking you back down below. You've been away for some time and my brother

---

---

quite enjoys opportunities to yell."

"Oh I know," I say.

We quickly walk to the lift and say little on our way there. It seems that this training is going to be even more difficult and slightly complicated now. I step into the lift and Bear closes the gate behind me. He has a somber look on his face. I don't know if it is because I am leaving so soon or if he is worried for me. Either way, I don't bother asking because I know he won't answer. He flashes a measly pair of fingers and his thumb as a wave goodbye just as I fall from view. I nod back to him trying to appear confident. When the lift reaches the bottom Wolf is there to greet me. Arms folded and scowling, he seems ready to prove his brother right. In the distance behind him the targets are still smoldering. The smoke has created a haze throughout the entire training ground.

"Whatever it was that my brother wanted it had better of been important," he says in his usual abrasive manner. "But I know you didn't want to miss training for today so I saved you a target. After fifty successful hits you will run the course four times and we will rectify the issue of your piss poor hand-to-hand combat. Even without training you should have put up a better fight when you were being beaten. Let's hurry it up, I won't be sleeping much tonight either."

It continued this way for four more months. Most days were simply training and the conflict between trainees slowed and eventually stopped altogether, except when someone would make a mistake. The days I joined Hobbes and Bear were difficult. We would spend the whole day working with machines and electricity, something I rarely saw my whole life. After getting shocked, burned and pinched, a number of lessons were learned. The most difficult part was coming back to train with Wolf through the night. It would take me several days to catch up on sleep. It also made Wolf angrier and no less tired of yelling.

Eventually both trainings were coming to a halt and even Wolf started to show appreciation for my progress by letting me sleep from time to time. I wasn't the best at anything, but I could do everything. Wolf said he would have started calling me "Jack Of All Trades" if it wasn't a potential offense to Jack. And after I had learned everything Bear and Hobbes needed me to, we started to do the fun part of the work. We would spend a good amount of time in the water, triggering motion sensors and making faces in Hobbes's cameras. Whatever was malfunctioning got replaced. And fortunately for us, Jack never knew I'd left the building. Hobbes had a back door air lock, which was built by his paranoid grandfather. When the workload slowed down I started to spend the days above reading with Bear. I would pick a subject and he would help me find it so I could learn about whatever topic was currently stirring up my interest.

I discovered the past of the city. From what the last history books could tell me the city of New York hasn't been dry for more than four hundred years by our best guess. It used to be one of the greatest cities in a vast, interconnected world. As the water rose all over the planet the people of this city, like many others, fought the flooding. Until eventually no wall or machine could stop the ocean. Unfortunately no book can tell me what happened between now and then. However, Hobbes and Bear were able to tell me some of the stories that have been passed down through their families. They told me that in the beginning everyone just wanted to survive. So they worked together to gather food and supplies. Rooftops were made into gardens and people learned to rebuild their lives.

When people began to settle they decided to unify in an attempt to recreate something similar to the government they once had and they appointed leaders. Other people wanted to be free of having to make everything for themselves so the leaders were given the responsibility of handing out tasks. People worked well together for a time, but when the leaders died their families wanted to hold on to what they had. So sons and daughters were given what mothers and fathers once had. When the people asked for change the families withheld food and water. The people tried to fight, but they had no real means to. And now for over two hundred years Hobbes' family has taken refuge in the library and they've allowed all they can to join them. Only recently has there been a newfound resistance, slowly pushing back. Bear, Wolf and Jack started it and when they needed a place to hide Hobbes found them and saved them as Empire was closing in. Bear only recently told me that Hobbes lost his father just before he found them holed up on an abandoned level over ten years ago. He hasn't left the library since they returned that day. Bear thinks he doesn't trust anyone but his own blood to watch it, unfortunately he has no family left.

On the last day Bear said to me, "Enjoy these days, for as much as you hated training with Wolf and tiring your mind here, seeing battle will be much worse. Don't assume that the scuffle we had with the patrollers long ago is how it will be. Some of the people you have grown fond of down below will most likely die and you may die. Also, don't believe Wolf when he says not to care for your fellow man. I would rather more people survive and you lose a battle than you stand victoriously on a pile of corpses. Most people in this world are more scared and confused than you could ever understand. You're too smart and brave to really know how that could ever feel. Many of the people you fight are fighting you because they were made to believe they had no other option."

The advice hit me hard. Not only was I now fearful of my impending graduation, but for the first time in a while I took the time to think of my family. Not only those that I had left behind, but the ones I had lost as well. At least I knew, from what Azalea told Bear that the rest of them were subtly being taken care of by rebel aids in the field. Bear kept me updated on Azalea as much as he could. Without him telling me, I knew that she wanted to see me again and that I was lucky Jack had not yet figured out her feelings for me despite her obvious behavior.

"He would never allow it," Bear said to me during one of our library sessions. "He would have to die for it to happen and he may even be too stubborn for that."

The news was hard to take, but not as stressful as what Wolf told me on the day before graduation as I was packing up my things. "It's you," He said while walking with me to his shack. "Despite all of the added challenges you encountered you have persevered, you are the squad leader. You know the ins and outs of every task your group could ever be expected to accomplish. Those who are great at one or two things are good and even great soldiers, but someone like you can more easily lead and you have already been doing it without knowing. They all respect you now and even more to the point you proved me wrong. It doesn't happen often, now you just have to deal with Jack as your commander. Of course, after you and your squad graduate."

Like always Wolf had a lot to say, but he always answered my questions before I could ask them, pretty much the opposite of his brother on the average day. Even with my questions answered I was still distressed. Now if we failed it would be seen as my fault and it would be that way until I died or was replaced, both would be a failure. I knew there was no way around it.

CHAPTER SEVEN

The squad got through graduation without an issue. Wolf tells me it was the first time the ceremony didn't have an audience and was hosted on the training grounds. I'm sure that has something to do with me succeeding where Jack had hoped I would fail. I managed to come out of that pit with two people that are more than just fellow soldiers. Paul and Dylan, not surprisingly the most hesitant to lay a hand on me on the first day. We depended on each other heavily through most of our training. Now that we're done I want to relax in our new living quarters and stop moving for just one day, but from what I understand we won't get to. Jack already wants to send is back out into the world. Bear tells me he hopes we will be split up like most groups. He says that we are expected to be more like watchful guardians than soldiers. But there are rumors of Jack wanting to commit to a full attack on Empire Tower.

I'm walking to Bear's quarters to see if any of this is true, hoping that if it is, the squad and myself won't be involved. I arrive at his door and hesitate to knock. I walk past and down the hall as some other soldiers pass by. After they pass I gather more courage and knock on the door with authority.

"Open it yourself if you are so eager," came the familiar booming voice.

"Oh it's you," he says as I step in.

He is sitting cross-legged on a blanket with his eyes closed. I stand nervously not wanting to disturb his meditating and lean against a shelf, waiting for him to finish. He breathes deeply before opening his eyes and motions for me to help him up, a kind of ritual we have formed.

"Well I can't call you kid anymore, you're not so frail anymore and I have little left to teach you."

I smile and thank him for the compliment. We sit down on the edge of his cot and I ask him the question that had kept me up through the night. "Is Jack really hoping to attack Empire Tower?" I ask. "If so, is my squad going with?"

"So that's why you look as though some thief has taken your last few days of sleep," he sighs. "He is trying to convince all of us that have a say. As much as he would like to have authority over these decisions, it was decided long ago when we first set out that these issues would be solved with voting, even though he is our appointed leader. So far even his wife is against him, but I worry he may take a small group to the tower, even without consent. So the answer I have to give is that I have no idea."

"Why does he want this?" I ask. "Just because his mother has died. He can't risk everything here for that alone. It isn't even his in the first place. It's not fair to us, when we have all lost. Just because he has power he gets to choose when the time is right for revenge? This just isn't fair."

Bear opens his mouth, hesitating before he speaks, "It most definitely is not fair and I share your sentiment. Though, this is one thing I do not think I can speak further on, my young friend. Jack has been too close to me and I would not feel comfortable sharing his thoughts from a dark time. All I can say is that you must hope for the best."

He grabs both of my shoulders and looks at me sternly, "This is the last lesson I can teach you Sam. From here on out you will have to learn on your own and start making tough choices. There are many things in this world you can worry about, but it is important to only think on the ones you have power over. And if you do that you should do everything in your power to keep it from becoming what you fear. Now go back to your squad, I'm late to meet with Hobbes."

This is the first time Bear has scared me without his size being part of the reason. I thank him again for the compliment and the advice before leaving. I am afraid because he seems afraid. What will it mean if Jack leaves us and goes his own way? Bear might be asking himself the same question. Though it means significantly more to him. To me, Jack is just some prick, but he's been friends with Bear for more than ten years.

As I make my way up the stairs back to the cot room my squad is in, several small children run down past me. They almost topple me as I trudge up the last few steps. Madison slowly follows, holding her relatively newborn child. She is smiling but looks just as tired as me.

"Howzit?" I say quickly.

"Very well, I'm glad to see you made it through," she says with a wink. She tries to mask her obvious sadness with a smile. I don't mention how tired she looks or anything about Jack and quicken my pace to avoid further conversation, giving her a slight wave as I round the corner. Before making it the full way around Dylan comes running into me. He would have spilled onto the ground if I hadn't caught him. He tries to speak through his panting, but the words can't be made out.

"Just take your time," I tell him.

He shakes his head, "No time," he gasps. "Have to come back quickly. Looking everywhere for you. Hurry."

He points to our door. Following his finger I break out into a jog until my worry has me in a full run. "What's Dylan all excited about," I ask out loud to the whole room, bursting through the door. Several members of the squad belt out answers at once and they all begin to crowd around me. From what I can gather Jack came through and relieved me of the squad, then Paul refused an order and is now being held in solitary. The rest of the squad is to report to Jack before sun up and leave before breakfast.

"So I take it Paul and I won't be joining?" I ask over everyone else's panic.

"No," Dylan says, having just made it back to the room. "Jack told us that you technically don't qualify to have a squad because you never had basic training and Paul has another three more days before he is released. So I guess I'm in command of the squad now."

"Did he say what the mission was?" I ask.

"All he said is that we would know when it was appropriate to know," Dylan tells me.

I tell him I'm grateful for the heads up and his continued belief in my leadership and ask him and the rest of the squad to get ready for their mission and get some sleep. They all continue to respectfully listen to me despite my loss of any real authority. As I pass through the small crowd they part to pack bags and undress for the evening, I realize how right Wolf had been. I don't take the time to enjoy it and instead rush to my cot and pull out my jacket and cap. I have to go see Paul and nothing can be left for the guards to scrutinize.

I arrive at the back of the library and pass by the first set of guards to the holding area. All it takes is a nod and the insignia that has yet to be pulled off my uniform. I may not have a squad anymore, but my jacket still says I do and that's enough to get me in. Hopefully it's this easy the whole way, considering I don't have any kind of plan if I'm stopped. I come up to a desk and attempt to walk past without a word. Before I can an outreached arm blocks my way.

"Are you authorized to be in here during dark hours squad leader?" a helmeted guard asks me.

"No sir," I don't bother lying. "But it is important that I see someone being held back there." I can't tell what the guard is thinking behind the mask of his helmet.

"Who do you need to see and why, squad leader?" he asks.

"I need to see Paul." I tell him.

"I have orders for no one to see him as he has information on a highly secretive mission," he informs me.

This time I lie, "I'm aware of that. The commander asked me to confirm how much he may or may not know."

The guard eyeballs me from behind his helmet. The facemask adds to this feeling, a smiling monster is painted across it. The bright red stands out against the shadowy visor of the mask. He comes within an inch of my face and even through his mask the stink of his hot breath hits my nostrils.

"We will see," he hisses. The smile seems to change into a ferocious scowl as the painted creature's demeanor changes with the tone of the guard's voice.

Sweat rolls down my neck collecting on my lower back as he picks up a radio. I just hope Jack is too busy planning his mission to be bothered by a simple guard. He grabs his radio and it squawks as he turns it up for me to hear the conversation.

"Commander?" he says cautiously. He releases the talk button. A crackle of static follows for some time before he tries again. After no response he places the radio back in its holster. "Just a few minutes," he says pointing down the hall.

I hold back my relief and amble past the guard as though I don't even need that long. Once I pass through the door my pace quickens. The hallway is dimly lit and the names on the doors are barely visible. I look through the slot of each door until I find Paul huddled against the wall. The only light comes from the open slot. Half of his face is still hidden in the dark. He covers his eyes. Hiding from the light he crawls across the floor until I can only see his feet. They are filthy and bare. Small, fresh cuts leave splotches of blood on the floor.

"Go away I've had enough" he croaks. "I won't yell anymore."

"Paul its Sam," I whisper through the opening. "Come back into the light. Let me see you."

I can hear his hands scrape against the wall as he pulls himself up. He walks toward the door, doubled over and shivering. He is careful to keep his face out of view. His teeth chatter as he stumbles closer. It is surprisingly cold down here. When he reaches the door his breath escapes through the slot.

"What happened and why won't you let me see your face?" I ask.

"Jack made me the squad leader," he says as he slides to the floor. "I refused, stating that I wasn't qualified or willing. After that the commander brought me here. One of the guards knocked me around and said it was a warning not to speak of the commander's plans."

"What is he planning?" I ask without pause.

"Exactly what everyone has been saying," Paul says. "He wouldn't tell anyone the details. All I know is, he is planning on taking three squads to Empire Tower. They leave sometime tonight, he wouldn't even tell me the exact time. By the way you do realize how silly it was to ask me that right? You're lucky we're friends."

"Thanks Paul," I reach my hand through the slot and grasp his hand firmly. "I'm going to talk to Bear and the others. Hopefully I can stop this and get you out of here."

"Take your time," he says.

Just as he says this, the door to the hallway slams shut. My senses heighten at the sound of the latch closing and quiet footsteps making their way toward me.

"Yes Sam take your time," comes the angry, quivering voice of Jack. "In the cell right next to your friend."

He pulls the door open with an incredible force, stops it with surprising control and motions for me to walk through as though he was politely holding it open. I consider rushing him until two masked guards come out of the shadow. Without hesitation I step into the deep dark of the cell. Jack slams the door behind me almost catching my heel. I sit on the floor not wanting to walk into the walls.

"Don't beat on this one Chrysler," Jack's muffled voice comes through the door. "I'm trying to win a war for all of us. That doesn't happen by hurting our own people. If it happens again I'm throwing you in a cell next. That goes for you too, Orion"

Both guards stand to attention and let out a loud "Sir!" acknowledging his command. The hall door opens and closes without any more being said. I sprawl out on the floor and call for Paul. He doesn't respond. I assume he can't hear me through the wall or doors. With nothing else to do I crawl to the wall to get my bearing and try to get some rest. In the darkness by myself it becomes difficult to tell how much time passes. At least I finally have the time to catch up on all the sleep I've been missing. At least until being jarred awake by the sound of the slot of the door being opened. Light cuts into the room and blinds me. A small plate of food is being pushed through the slot. One of the masked guards is yelling at me as my eyes try to adjust.

"Grab the food before you're eating it off the floor," he growls.

I snag it from his hands, fearful that he would let go at the last second. To my delight the food is still better than what I've spent most of my life eating. I knew that they grew food down here but I never thought they would waste it on detained soldiers like myself. I get a better idea of how much time has passed with how quickly I eat. After finishing I force the metal plate through the slot and let it clatter to the floor.

The hall door bursts open and a guard jumps through.

"What the hell…," he mutters. "Next time just leave it until the next one comes."

"Sure thing boss," I sass, rolling over and going back to sleep. The darkness and lack of movement have left me feeling exhausted and I doze off. Flashes of dreams haunt me. Skulls shred through my body and pull at me as they fight over the scraps. I claw at the eyes and pull on tentacles each time, but it doesn't even irritate the monsters pulling me apart. They keep coming back, pulling me in, continually taking pieces of me. Sometimes everything goes dark as the tentacles wrap around my face, but it continues to scratch and bite. Just as the dreams and pain become unbearable a light shoots out of a beak and the squids all burst open in a cloud of bubbles and dark blood. The beam reaches through, cleansing the water and eventually evaporating all of it.

For a brief moment I'm standing on something soft and tan, mounds of it roll ahead of me and a strong breeze sends ripples through it. Small pieces of brown are lifted from the ground and harshly brush against my face. It builds up higher as the wind continues to push into itself. As they reach upward they start to look like slow moving, gentle waves lapping against the side of a tower. Except these waves don't seem to fall. Each time they build high enough, the wind begins to take each mound down by each individual piece.

"Why am I always finding you when you're in trouble," comes a soothing and familiar voice, it pulls me from my dream. "It's time to wake up, we could use your help."

I open my eyes to a face I can't quite make out. Several other people are standing in the doorway. The once dim light of the cell hallway is now painful. I cover my face and the figure nearest to me helps me to my feet. As a hand finds my waist I recognize Azalea's touch. She helps me to the guard station and the other's follow. Azalea and I take a seat, she hands me the sunglasses from before and tells me to put them on. My eyes finally open as they slide over my face.

"Sunglasses," she tells me.

I don't bother to give her any lip about knowing what they are. I look around the room and find myself in the company of Bear and Hobbes. Wolf comes out of the hallway helping Paul. They sit down on the other side of me. Paul is also wearing a pair of sunglasses. Bruises creep out from the edges of the tinted glass and lips are cracked, but otherwise he seems fine.

"Nice to see you again squad leader," he cracks a smile. A bit of blood is still caked onto the side of his face. I smile back and we both laugh. I'm not sure why we do. It's just a relief to be out and amongst friends.

"Good to see the cage didn't dampen your spirits," Wolf says. "Toughest kids I've ever had the pleasure of training. We're going to need that."

"What's happened?" I ask, looking around the room.

On the floor I notice the guard with the painted facemask, Chrysler, knocked out. Next to him is Orion with his hands and legs all tied together, arched over his back. The last one had taken off her helmet and was chatting with Bear. Her streamlined face and small eyes give her the look of a beautifully crafted weapon. Bear takes a pause from his conversation with her to answer my question.

"Well if you're referring to the mess that surrounds us, we knocked out this one," he says kicking painted mask in the head. "Then we tied up this asshole and Grace was kind enough to join us for the excitement." Grace nods at me from around Bear's wide shoulders giving me a nice wink. Everyone down here winks.

"I never liked these two," she says. "But they usually give this job to the creeps like Chrysler and Orion, they enjoy this shit."

The one with the painted mask moans, rolling to his side. Grace swiftly kicks him in the ribs. He clutches them but stays quiet. Bear and

Wolf take the both of them to the same cell. Two loud thumps come from the hall as they toss the guards in. They chuckle to each other and whisper excitedly like two young boys that haven't played together in a few days. Not wanting to interrupt I question Hobbes and Azalea. "So what are you all doing here?"

They look at each other, waiting for the other to speak first. Azalea finally responds. "Well, if all of this happened as it seems it did, my brother left for a mission shortly after locking the both of you up," she says. "He took at least half of our people that are trained specifically for fighting. Two of our people came back twelve hours after the mission was supposedly started. They were both seriously injured so I'm not sure how they avoided becoming lunch."

"Who?" Paul and I ask in unison.

This time Wolf answers the question, "Dylan made it back in one piece, just got nicked by a pulse gun, and he was carrying Penn in on his back when we found them at the airlock. Penn lost most of his left arm."

"Where is everyone else?" Paul asks.

Everyone becomes uncomfortably quiet at the question and shifts their attention to Bear and Hobbes. Bear talks first. "From what information we could get from Dylan it sounds like most everyone else died in the first few minutes of fighting. They were in back and made a run for it. As they were getting out Dylan says he saw Jack and at least eight others surrendering."

Hobbes speaks up to answer the next obvious question, "We have no idea if they are still alive, but Bear and I have decided that it is imperative that we send in a small team to confirm if they are. If so we need to recover or kill Jack along with whoever remains."

No one objects to it, including Azalea. It's hard to tell what she thinks about all this. It would be nice to believe that she cares more about everyone down here, especially myself, but I have to wonder if she wouldn't choose us over her brother. I don't know if I could choose anyone over even just one member of my family.

"I understand that there are feelings against this," Hobbes assures us. "On one hand you are wondering if it is worth lives to save lives and killing them just seems, well, like the most backwards way for us to do things. But we must understand and remember that they will torture Jack and anyone else to find the rest of us. We are obligated to attempt a rescue or destroy any information concerning this base and its location and most likely killing them means that the team has, for lack of a better description, miserably failed. So don't assume this comes from a place of selfishness."

"So we have to die, whether or not we like how we got into this situation," Paul states flatly.

"Not if our plan goes as we hope it will," Hobbes says. "We'll go get you some food while we catch you up."

CHAPTER EIGHT

In the mess hall there are just as many people as ever. Except a general hush makes it apparent that the bad news has spread through the whole library. Only the sound of utensils scraping and clanging on dishes can be heard through the room. One suicide mission followed by another has everyone nervous and in poor spirits.

"If we lost so many soldiers why is this place still so cramped," I ask Azalea as I squeeze into the seat next to her.

"Most of us do what I do," she says. "We take care of everyone we can, within our limits of course. We act more like caretakers, taking care of the sick and hungry and bringing those in danger down here. We usually never act in violence unless it comes to us first. You were just lucky enough to be brought down when Jack had a ban on any new people being brought in."

"So what else…" Hobbes cuts me off by talking over the few conversations that have started up at our table.

"It's time we went over our plan," he says. "I'm sure Sam and Paul have recovered enough strength to comprehend the details. Now Bear, if you would please," he waves his fork towards him.

"The plan we have is one that Hobbes and myself have decided has the least risk associated with it," he says with an already defeated look. "Sam and Paul are going to go in with the two patroller suits we obtained last month with Wolf and I as prisoners. The suits are baggy so we can sneak in some explosives and weapons. Grace will be waiting at the bottom of the tower with several zoom tubes. We don't have an idea of exactly where anyone will be and we are unsure of how we will get there. If it comes down to it we will shoot our way through."

"So where does us being walking bombs fit in?" Paul interrupts.

Bear smiles weakly, "That's the unknown variable. If need be we will use them on those who have been captured and ourselves. Otherwise, if we get the chance we can blow out enough support columns to potentially bring the building down. Maybe both outcomes, it's hard to say what will actually happen when we get inside. Jack's quite likely the only non-government person to step foot in there since the war, over three hundred years ago."

Hobbes cuts in before Bear can make the situation seem any bleaker. "We've already told you all that none of this is ideal," Hobbes adds. "Unfortunately this isn't a volunteer operation. Our other lethal forces are already spread through the towers. Jack took just about everyone with him."

"So how do we get in?" I ask.

Wolf grins so wide that his teeth actually show through his ever-growing beard. "I'm glad you asked," he says.

We find ourselves taking cover in a collapsed tower twenty levels below the surface directly across from Empire Tower. It lays horizontal, supported by two smaller towers that it landed on. Most of the insides have been gutted out and it is more of a steel box than a tower. For the mission Hobbes has given us one of his recent creations, or as he has modestly called it, part of his hobby. He gave all of us masks that create a pocket of air around our faces so we can use radios to talk. To me the gear says more about the mission than it does Hobbes' ability to create. Basically, we need every advantage to not die today and any mistake or miscommunication could throw the whole thing off.

Wolf calmly lays out the next step of our impossible plan. "All right, listen up," he commands. "This is going to be rough, fortunately it's too late to back out. We are going to jump the underwater rail that brings supplies from ONE directly to the tower."

"What! How?" Paul yells so loud his radio squawks.

Wolf grins, "Well that's why I tied these cables to our harpoons."

He hefts his up from around his backside showing off his handiwork. Paul gives me a look like he's about to fill his mask with the last meal we had. The feeling is mutual.

"Now when you fire your harpoon be sure it's still slung around you," Wolf explains. "If you just try to hold on you're going to rip your arms off. So when the tube comes by, keep in mind that it is plenty long enough to take your time with the shot. No mistakes, you miss, people will probably die. Get ready, no pressure, it should be here soon."

Paul and I move one window over from the brothers. The giant metal cargo doors of Empire Tower begin to slide open, letting us know to get ready for the shot. We already have our harpoons pointed at the rail. The broken down tower begins to rattle, disturbing rubble and dust.

Despite the vibrations I'm caught off guard as the tube starts to pass overhead without a sound. It is a sleek, chrome cylinder with a pointed tip, not quite attached to the rail, but held close to it by several large magnets. Small bolts of electricity bounce back and forth between the rail and the tube riding it. I begin to feel weighed down as displaced water pushes past me. I start to worry that we will miss our chance by the time Wolf and Bear finally shoot.

As their harpoons hit Wolf screams out in excitement over the radio. "Like a breath of fresh air brother!"

They are pulled up toward the rail and leave a trail of bubbles and dust. Paul and I fire next. The shots soar through the water leaving a trail of bubbles behind them. When they reach the tube mine silently deflects off the rail and floats down. "It's over," I say.

"Not yet," Paul says, wrapping his arms around me. "Hold on, Sam."

I hook my arms around him and wrap the strap of his gun around my wrist and we rush through the water so quickly that my mask is pushed into my face. I start sliding down Paul's torso as we swing up to meet the tube. The strap slides up to my hand before cinching and I feel pressure build up in my fingers. My shoulders make a popping noise and start to burn and I worry that they might actually tear off if this ride doesn't end soon. Ahead of us there's nothing except for a cloud of bubbles. We come to a sudden stop and they begin to dissipate. Wolf and Bear are already swimming towards the bottom of the rail support beams. As our momentum continues to slow we start to sink down towards them.

Paul and I roll over each other through the water as we try to untangle ourselves. Instead of talking we grunt as we continue to push and squirm harder until gently bumping into a post. The feeling of our momentum suddenly stopping causes me to lose control of my sense of direction. Bear comes to our aid righting us in the water and pulls me free of Paul's gun strap. He motions for us to sink deeper, towards the floor of the cargo hold as patrollers appear through top of the water. We huddle together at the base of a rail support column and hope we aren't seen. The tube slowly moves through the midsection of the tower, as each section is emptied out. By the time it's finished my mask has fogged over from my anxious breathing and I can barely make out Wolf's shape as he rises to the surface.

"Clear," Wolf states.

We all swim up to meet him. Paul and I strip our gear off quickly to make our transformation into patrollers. As we do Bear hands out the explosives and weapons for us to strap to our chests. He takes our gear and puts it in his bag. Fortunately Bear and Wolf can hold onto the non-lethal gear and we can pretend we found them this way if anyone asks.

The red cap of my uniform spills over my forehead. Wolf gives it a flick while sending a glare my way.

"Look the part, soldier," he says. "Remember, nothing can be amiss. You can pretend to be a dumb patroller, most of them are. But they all know how to dress."

I readjust the cap as he continues to scrutinize me with his eyes. Normally I would have gotten defensive with him but our lives depend on me looking the part. He tugs at the uniform a few times until he is seems satisfied that every crease is in its proper place.

"Sometimes I wish we had uniforms," Wolf says. "But for obvious reasons..." Wolf trails off and turns his back to me. With his hands reached out behind his back to have his restraints clicked into place around them and his ankles. Paul and Bear do the same. Even the most dedicated patroller won't be able to see that the locking mechanism has been adjusted to release when enough force is applied.

"We'll take the door straight ahead," Paul says, taking a look at the small map wrapped around his wrist. "Then we take a few turns until we hit the lift. After that it's as easy as walking past a few guards on the detention level."

Hobbes had managed to make a small touch screen device and had somehow been able to put the most updated map of the Empire Tower on it. Updated, of course, only meant best guess and what little information Dylan could give us. Though we had all agreed that the detention center would most likely be on one of the levels with blacked out windows. The bottom most one was our first guess, if we got it wrong we would just keep going up and hope no one noticed.

"Let's get moving," Bear's voice waivers.

Bear is sweating and his face has gone pale while his brother smiles, twitching with energy. It was strange to see these brothers so extremely different from each other. Leading the way, I take us through the first door with Wolf shuffling in behind me. As we reach the first intersection of hallways Paul whispers from the back for us to turn left. I turn the corner to an empty hallway. Some of my anxiousness recedes. If we can make it to the lift without running into anyone we won't have to explain why we're bringing prisoners in from the wrong direction.

We turn down two more hallways before we make it to the lift. Still, there is no one in sight. At this point my relief is turning back into worry. Why isn't there anyone in this building? If they cleared it out it means they know we're here. I want to tell Wolf we should go another way, but decide not to, this is our only option. Taking forty flights of stairs would take too long with shackles and could be even more of a risk. Instead, we wait for the lift to arrive.

A small bell dings and a light flicks on above the large metal doors. Paul grabs his holster in response. I hold my breath as the doors slide open. They reveal an empty, bright enclosure. I hesitate to step in until Wolf gives me a nudge with his shoulder.

"Don't worry it's just fancy," he says.

We all pile into the lift. Bear starts to remove his restraints until he realizes Wolf still has his on. Paul hits the button marked sixty-two. The bell sounds again as the doors quietly slide into each other, closing with a gentle thud. The lift starts up with a surprising ease. I can barely tell that we've started to move. No one speaks and I focus on the hum coming from the walls of the lift as it continues to rise. As the number fifty lights up the lift slows down.

"Don't panic," Wolf says. "But we are slowing down too soon."

I panic and reach for my gun and begin to pull it from its holster as the doors open.

"You won't need that yet," Wolf whispers in my ear.

I listen to him, holstering my weapon as a small man is revealed to us. He is shorter than myself and wearing thick, round glasses. Dressed in all white with his magnified eyes, he gives off the appearance of a human size rat. He waves to Paul and myself. We return it but don't speak. He faces the doors as he presses a button for a level above the one we're headed to. The lift starts back up and the tension rises to a stifling new high and I worry that the new passenger will feel it.

He ignores us until we start to slow down for our stop. "Excellent job catching these two sad excuses for rebels, it smells like they can't even clean themselves properly, much less fight," he tells us. "I'm sure they will enjoy their stay with the rest of those troublemakers. We were worried for but a moment, as the all clear came only seconds after the alarms had been set off, such a sad excuse for a resistance movement. I'm certain Astor will have a day's worth to say about it and maybe you'll even be on his show when they drop these two off a tower like that last one."

He reaches out to shake my hand as the doors start to crack open.

As they inch open a barrage of pulse fire bursts through. Several shots rip into the small man, pushing him to the floor. The rest of us dive to either sides of the lift. I forget that I'm still holding the man's hand. I look down his arm and see that most of his right side has been burnt black, the frame of his glasses have melted into his cheekbone. These weapons were obviously powerful, but training never prepared me for this. I throw his hand away and pull out my gun. Paul has already returned several shots down the hall before my safety is turned off. A hole has already melted into the back of the lift from all the plasma flying above our heads and beads of metal dribble down. The lift has started to rattle from the continuing force of every shot. As I start to fire back Wolf's hand reaches over my shoulder and rummages through the front of my uniform. He produces two more guns and tosses one across the lift to Bear. Instead of firing out the doorway they shoot up at the middle of the ceiling. At first it burns and pieces of melted chrome start to glob up and fall to the floor.

"What the hell are you doing?" I yell.

The lift falls and answers my question. The suddenness of it gives me the sensation of all my blood running to my head. My stomach feels suspended. Just as quickly, the fall stops with the sound of grinding metal. My face slams into the ground crunching my nose and several of my teeth poke through my cheek. All the blood that had flowed to my head was now a small puddle on the floor.

"If I hadn't gone before we left I think I would have shit myself," Wolf laughs.

I doubt I'll ever understand how Wolf finds these moments humorous or exciting. I sit up to look at him and try to glare at him, but only manage a grimace.

"Let me fix that for you," he says pointing at my face.

Confused I lean towards him. He takes both of his hands placing them on either side of my nose. With a sickening snap air rushes back into my nostrils as even more blood spills out down my face. My vision blurs from the tears that well up, but the blood slows and only trickles along my chin and neck. Still, it's enough to turn the blue jumpsuit purple. My sleeve does a poor job of wiping the blood off my face and instead it smears across my cheek.

As I continue to furiously wipe, Bear approaches the doors of the lift and begins to pry them apart. Something inside the carriage groans along with Bear as the muscles on his arms ripple. The doors snap and fling open without any more resistance. Bear almost falls into the opening, but he steadies himself by grabbing the wall next to the control panel. A small opening is revealed between the top of the lift and the floor. Through it is just blank, white hallway.

"We need to move now," Bear commands. "Get out, you first Paul."

Paul climbs up and scrambles through the opening with the help of Bear. I go through next and my hips barely squeeze through as I frantically wiggle my body from side to side. My legs clear it as the sound of footsteps clomping down a hall echo from somewhere nearby.

"Hurry," I scream back into the lift as I rip my plasma gun clear of the holster.

Wolf slides through next. His mane of hair pops out and his slender figure scuttles through the hole with ease. As he clears the opening he turns to help pull Bear through. He makes it one shoulder at a time and Wolf starts to pull on his arms. Bear comes to a sudden stop with a soft thunk from inside the metal doors. Something else clangs to the floor below Bear as he gives his brother a panicked look.

"We're going to need some time," Wolf calls out. "Cover me

while I pull on tubby. The one day you forget your honey Pooh Bear," he grunts out while tugging on Bear's arms.

Both brothers breathing turns ragged and panicked as they continue to struggle with Bears oversized waist. The sound of stomping boots draws closer. A stampede of patrollers must be on its way to take us down. Before anyone comes around the corner of the long hall Paul releases the first blue projectiles. He hits the first patroller to take the corner twice in the chest and once in the neck. The man screeches, clasping at his throat as he stumbles backwards to the floor. The next two patrollers step over him without a glance. Their guns are already drawn, shots fly past my head as I dive forward and chunks of burning wall fall on my back and legs. The temperature in the room rises rapidly as the fire spreads. I ignore it and fire back.

I clip one of the patrollers in the arm and he drops his weapon. As he lunges for it Paul expertly hits him in the back of the head, instantly caving it in. Adrenaline shoots through my veins and sweat rolls down my face and back. My vision closes in around the end of the hall as the other man fires two shots. They whiz past, completely missing both of us. Wolf lets out a cry as he finally pulls Bear's hips loose. He falls over on his side. One of his legs has been grazed. It smolders and smoke rises from between Bear's fingers as he places pressure on it. Bear fishes around in his pack with his other hand, producing a small chrome ball. He twists it and it extends into a more ovular shape, revealing a ring of small holes.

He tosses it to me yelling over the sound of plasma melting into the walls, "Chuck it."

I send it soaring over the heads of the now three patrollers charging toward us. A trail of mist is left in its path and the haze goes unnoticed by the men in red caps.

"Well that did fuck all," I mutter to myself.

A cloud of blue flame roars to life just as the words leave my mouth. It rides the cloud of mist, engulfing at least five patrollers as they continue to rush in unaware. And as quickly as the fire came to life it sucks back into nothingness, leaving a trail of scorched corpses. The hall fills with the putrid smell of burning flesh and parts of the ceiling and walls still burn and fall to the floor. One remaining patroller comes into the hall with his hands raised and no gun in sight.

"I surrender," his voice wavers and cracks. "Please."

A single shot lashes out and takes half his face. He falls back into a sitting position. What remains of his face contorts into a confused and frightened look. His arms go limp and fall to his sides as he crashes down onto one of his comrades. Wolf's outreached arm holds a still crackling plasma gun next to my face. He grunts as he pulls himself to his feet, using one of the fresh holes in the wall to support himself.

"Those are my conditions of your surrender, coward," Wolf spits.

The charred heap of men lay in front of us. No one speaks as we walk through them. The nausea is overwhelming, but I fight it, not wanting to soil the men we had just killed. They may have been our enemies, but until today, they could have just been trying to get by however they could. Every hungry person thought about what it would be like to join the patrollers. Who's to say these men hadn't been hungry too? As we reach the end of the hallway Paul gives in to his stomach. He pukes and falls over. I help him back to his feet as he wipes his mouth with his sleeve and steadies himself.

"Thanks Sam, I just couldn't hold it," he says.

"We should be quick about finding some stairs," Bear says absently. Yet for a moment no one moves. The level has gone quiet again. It still feels like we are cornered. The silence is anything but comforting.

"Won't they be waiting for us in there?" I ask.

Bear hesitates to respond, Wolf answers for him, "He's right, if we take the stairs we could easily end up cornered again. Everything seems like an attempt to corner us. Stairs would be perfect for that. We aren't lucky enough to make it through two straight on encounters, especially since we'll have to cover our front and back."

As he explains this, the sun comes over the horizon, blinding me as it peers through a window down the hall. An idea takes shape in my head. Bear and Wolf are grumbling to each other and I have to nearly shout to grab their attention.

"What if we climb the outside of the building?" I offer. "While they're all in the stairs waiting for us we can sneak past and the sun will hopefully be blinding to anyone still on the detention level."

"Great idea, except if we don't keep them in the stairs we're still screwed," Wolf says. He pauses, thinking, before his eyes light up, "I suppose a good distraction would solve our problems. Sam, you and Bear are taking the cables. Paul and myself will make the patrollers believe we're taking the stairs. Give me the explosives. If we can step in fire a few shots, drop a bomb and run like hell, everything should work just fine. And blowing them up along with the stairs will probably put a damper on their plans to stop us."

Paul and I unstrap the bombs from around our chests without question and pull all of them from the inside of our stolen uniforms. Wolf takes them and instantly goes to work shortening the time on one of the charges.

"Paul it's a good thing you just finished training, I know you can still run fast," he says.

Just as Wolf starts to head towards the stairwell Bear embraces him and whispers something in his ear. "Yeah, you too, you big bastard," Wolf says, pushing him away. "Now get off me, you're squeezing the bomb."

Paul hands me the two remaining cables and I give him my extra plasma gun. We shake hands. Our parting is much less dramatic, though I have a feeling we want to tell each other more. At least I know that I want to, but I don't know how to put it into words. Our friendship is new and we're still unsure of each other in that regard. At least I am. If we're lucky we'll get the chance to see each other when the mission is over.

As we part, Bear's face turns from worry to determination. We don't talk, but he gives me one of his reassuring claps on the back as we set up next to the window. I tie my cable to a harpoon before loading it. After I strap my plasma gun to my thigh Bear hands me one of the small chrome balls.

"We each have one," he explains. "Be careful with it. We don't want to burn the people we're attempting to rescue. I'm sure there are worse ways to die, but I would not wish it on a friend."

He finishes his warning and crashes the butt of his harpoon gun into the window. It shatters and the pieces of glass reflect the blazing orange light of the sun as they tumble downward. We stand at the edge of the frame and lean out the new opening. Below, water gently laps against the side of the tower and a calming breeze washes away the stench of the dead and cools me. The air feels clean and full, it opens up my lungs and my heart slows. It's calming until a gust of wind comes surging upward almost pulling me out into the air. I lean hard against the wall to keep my feet below me and give Bear a haggard smile. He returns a cool smirk.

"This is going to be tricky," he says. "Don't shoot the glass, for all the obvious reasons."

He takes a step forward grasping the frame and leans out. With one arm he aims the harpoon gun, turned grappling hook and shoots. Over the sound of the ocean and wind there is still a solid thunk. He throws the gun to the floor and tugs on the cable. It doesn't come loose so I lean out the window to do the same. The gun is heavy in just one hand and my arm shakes slightly. I try to time my aim in between the spasms. With the squeeze of the trigger I'm rewarded with the same solid noise of metal piercing cement.

" Beautifully done," Bear says. "Now uncoil the rest of the cable and throw it over the edge, it might be our only way out in a few moments."

As he says this the crackle of pulse guns starts up deeper in the tower. Bear stops to listen for a moment before attaching himself to the cable and pulling himself out of the window to start his ascent. I follow as quickly as my arms allow. Despite Bear's red face and heavy breathing he makes it to the window before I'm half way up. When I catch him he has already produced his pulse gun. I pull mine out and start it up. As it spins, Bear motions with his gun for us to shoot the window and dive in.

He mouths out a countdown. His lips exaggerate, three, two, one, before he flings himself through the window. He's through before I've managed to budge. He shoots as he dives and is inside and moving while I'm still struggling through the window. Flying shards of glass strike my face, sending me into motion. I shoot out my half of the window and scrambled in after him. He has already taken out the two guards that were left behind.

As I approach him, he's already digging through their pockets. He's frenzied, even tearing pockets off the uniforms to search them more thoroughly. He finally finds a set of keys on the body of the second guard. They take flight when Bear rips open the pocket they were in. I snag them off the ground as they slid toward me.

"Great job," he says.

Not sure of how much of a job I had done I hand the keys over without accepting the compliment. He takes them graciously and seems to be calmed by the metal being placed in his hands. With the keys dangling from one hand and a gun in the other, he approaches one of the two doors in the room and flattens it with an effortless kick. At the same time the other door blows off the hinges followed by a ball of fire and a smoldering body.

The force of the explosion sends a wave of energy through the floor and I feel myself lifted by it, sending me to all fours. The ground is unusually hot. I share a disoriented look with Bear as he pulls himself off of the door he just kicked in. Our moment of confusion is interrupted by Jack's familiar and angry voice.

"Before you knock the whole building down maybe you could get us out of it," he belts out.

"You can rescue yourself next time," I yell back. "Or maybe not get captured in the first place."

"You brought the kid?" Jack questions Bear. "How much has he already messed up?"

Bear says little in response, "Less than you. He is still free and fighting."

The obvious tone of disappointment is enough to finally subdue Jack's temper. "Just get us out," he says.

Bear tosses the keys into the cell. He walks away and joins me in the other room. The heat from the level below begins to subside and a cool air seeps in from the stairwell. A thick white cloud follows into the room. I stand transfixed on the doorway. Out of the fog, a patroller club flies at me. It strikes my thigh and the pain paralyzes my leg. A woman encased in dull metal emerges through the door. Each step produces a clang and hollow thud. The grey, scratched metal is layered across her body like the scales of a fish and it moves with her flawlessly. The head of the armor resembles the head of a roach, with giant bubbled out eyes and two large pincers hanging from the jaw. She runs a set of claws along the chest of her armor. The harshness of it pierces my ears.

I start crawling away faster, willing my leg to work, but the overgrown cockroach quickly reaches me. She raises her foot up over me and I instantly remember every bug I've killed. Before the armored figure can replace my teeth with her toes a tattered man flies over me, sweeping the legs out from under her. They wrestle as the rest of the former prisoners race to the window behind me. Jack doesn't take a second look at the man who risked his life to distract the metal pest. I'm helped to my feet by one of the members of my former squad, Evan. He brushes me off before giving me a brief salute.

"Good to see you sir," he says with a grin. "You don't look too terrible."

"You either," I say. "We should get out of here now."

We rush towards the window as Bear comes back towards us. He starts to speed up until he is in a full sprint. As he brushes past I realize he's running towards the doorway. Another metal plated body has entered the room. This one has two large spikes growing out of his head and a bizarre snout. Without hesitating he charges towards Bear with a lowered head. At the last second Bear manages a side step and grab his stand off partner by the spikes. His muscles tense as he pulls and whips the metal man over his shoulder.

He tumbles through the doorway and slams into something else metal deep in the fog filled stairwell. Bear starts into the stairway only to turn his attention to the giant bug that has regained her feet. She mercilessly slams her attackers face into the floor until Bear grabs her by the neck with both hands and throws her to the ground. The roach struggles as Bear replaces his hand with a foot.

"Take him and get out, Sam," he commands, pointing at the man with the bashed in face.

Evan and I grab the nearly unconscious man and rush him to the window. I send him down with Evan. He barely manages to hold on the cable as he fights to stay awake. As soon as he starts to shinny down I turn my attention back to Bear. Though he is still stepping on the bug's throat she is gripping him tightly and he can't seem to get off her. Her companion returns from the stairwell, the face and chest of his armor is bent and cracked. Several of the scales have fallen completely off. A small amount of blood trickles out from under his eye and I can see a patch of vulnerable flesh under the plates on his chest. Bear struggles violently to take back his leg, but the metal fingers gripping him dig in and thin ribbons of blood start to trickle down.

Before the armored man can get a grip on Bear I fire several shots at him, trying to hit the exposed skin. Each shot fizzles out, dissipating upon impact with the armor and my shots are far from accurate enough to directly hit the bare spot. He marches toward me at a casual pace and I try to back away while still firing. I trip over a crack in the floor created by the explosion and he is on me. He lifts me up above his head with both hands. His cold grip slowly squeezes around my throat. Black spots with white rings around them fill my vision while I fail in an attempt to draw another breath. My feet kick wildly and hit nothing.

My vision goes completely dark and there is muffled chuckle as my struggling slows and the strength fades from my limbs. The sound is drowned out by an incredible boom that tears through the air. Within a second several things happen. There is a loud clang quickly followed by a low grunt and I fall to my knees coughing and grasping at my throat.

As my vision slowly returns another crash comes through the air followed again by the sound of metal impacting metal. There's no clue as to where it's coming from, but I'm grateful to be breathing again.

Bear limps over toward me. While I lie there as he yells for me to get up. He slaps me and screams in my face for me to move. The two metal behemoths lay on the ground clutching at themselves and blood spills between the plates of armor.

"What did you do?" I struggle to ask Bear.

"Nothing," he says. "Let's just be grateful for whoever did do something because without them we would be dead. Now go out the window."

Both of us hobble together toward the window, helping each other move as efficiently as we can. We each take the same rope down so we can descend together. We catch up with the recently freed prisoners only to find that they've stopped climbing down.

"Why is it that we've stopped?" Bear calls down.

Jack answers, "It looks like the other part of your rescue party destroyed too much tower. We can't reach any lower levels unless we try to swing in and I don't think we're in any shape for that."

"Jump to the water then," is all Bear says.

No one argues. One by one they all start letting go and those of us at the top climb down further to make the fall shorter. By the time we reach the end of the cable the fall is only ten levels down. Soon it's time for Bear and I to take the plunge. My stomach rolls and my grip tightens around the cable. Bear can sense my hesitation and simply decides to grab me as he lets go. Instinctively I clutch onto the cable with both hands. Our collective falling force pulls the cable loose from the side of the tower and brings down several large hunks of cement with it.

When we hit the water a million bubbles come to life around me. They tickle my skin as they float up past me and through my clothes. It's the last thing I really remember before a large slab pierced through the top of the water and smashed into my face. There was the sensation of sinking but everything else went blank. It was a dark and empty feeling, like being sucked deeper and deeper into a pit with no end.

CHAPTER NINE

"Here we go, I got 'em."

I wake up to the sound of grunting and my sternum cracking as a strong set of hands lays a rhythmic pressure down on my chest. I try to brush the hands away while at the same time violently vomiting up water that had collected in my lungs and stomach. Hands and a light rush into my face. I try again to shove them away, but a large set of hands restrain me. The collective pain of my broken sternum and my arms being yanked high above my head sends a tearing sensation through my torso.

"Take it easy kid" the indistinct voice from before shouts at me "You took a nasty bump to the head right before we sucked you in."

I have no idea what that means. Sucked in? From what? The last thing I remember was falling into the water. What tower can suck in anything?

"How is he looking?" comes a second voice from further above.

The first voice responds, "Well we burped him and now we're trying to give him his bottle but he's putting up quite the fuss."

"Jokes aside give me an honest assessment of his current state Ed," the voice from above sounds irritated.

"The kid was in the middle of drowning when we sucked him in and he received what appears to be a grade five concussion at some point before that. The swelling is extreme and I don't know if his head can take it. Also, he drowned a little bit and we ended up cracking his sternum while trying to pump the water out. At this point it's still taking four of us to hold him down and give him an examination," the voice belonging to Ed says matter o'factly. "If anyone can make it through these injuries I would put my money on this kid right here."

My mind slips away from the conversation as it continues in a distant part of my pain filled world. I forget about my body and wrap myself up inside my head. Everything goes white and all there is, is me on my own, lying on a slab surrounded by light. Even though I'm filled a surreal comfort, worry overtakes the pain as I begin to wonder where everyone else ended up. Am I the only one sucked in or is everyone else here and just unconscious like myself? Then I hear Bear speak up and the world around me comes crashing back into place.

"I told you he was a tough kid, Jack." Bear says.

I quickly realize he was the one who had taken hold of my hands so I couldn't interfere with Ed's torch of a light burning through my eyes. And though they had lifted my lids I still hadn't gathered enough of myself to really see what was going on. My world is filled with black and purple spots and the occasional white out caused by the menacingly bright light that the Ed guy is wielding. When I finally get over the flashlight I realize that Bear said Jack's name, which reminds of what had brought us here.

"Hey Jack," I whisper through gritted teeth. "Give me one good reason for you to be here."

Before Jack could come up with a reply I pass out. That's one way to get the last word in. When I wake up again my head is on a pillow and my body is on something soft up above the floor. I can't move much or complain either. Whatever I was laying on was the most comfortable surface I've ever experienced. Before getting lost in the softness, some movement at my feet makes me aware that someone is watching over me.

"Bear? Jack?" I mumble trying to sit up.

"Nope kid, it's Ed again you might not want to try that," he calmly states as a shooting pain travels from my neck all the way down my chest and back. I gingerly lay back down panting from the rush of sudden pain.

"I would have been better off dead from the way my body feels, but thanks for the assist anyways. I guess I owe you one," I say this through strained breaths and open my eyes for the first time while also taking in the view of my scraggly savior of the day.

Ed's face he looks worn and leathery but his stout body looks like it's used to a hard days work. His clothes, though dull, like most of the people in Empire, appeared much sturdier. They are thick and brown instead of grey and filled with patches. The way he sounded I had expected someone younger than 30.

"I know that look you're sneaking at me right now kid," Ed says in his calm yet constantly sarcastic tone "Some of us have it a little harder down here than you folks in your towers and it shows. Sure we eat more than you, but we work for it every day."

After that comment a lot was suddenly coming together and I

was finally recognizing that this wasn't a tower. The ceiling is higher than usual and bright lights hang from cords every few feet. The walls and arched ceilings are lined with glossy white tiles. It was once most likely a beautiful place, but now the tiles were chipped and missing in some places and crumbling cement showed through. Beyond the half open curtain there is really only one floor and not a window in sight. It goes on as far as I can see. Though the floor drops off a few feet away. People quickly walk back and forth, occasionally climbing up or down between the two levels of ground. The taller of the two is only half the height of most people walking past, it seems odd to me to have a half level.

"Bit of a shock I imagine," Ed chuckles "I gave your towers the same look the first time I came up to the surface, two worlds filled with opposites, one stacked on top of the other. When you decide to get your ass out of bed make sure you stick with me, most of us down here don't like you folks from above. It's why you never hear from us. By the way most people call me Unfound Ed but you should call me Ed, that will go over better."

Stick with me? When I get out of bed? If anything Ed would have to stay with me for some time. There is nothing that could make me want to sit up again. When the curtain to the room rips open and I realize that there may not be a choice in getting up or lying down. Jack charges into the space with a very displeased looking woman on his trail.

"Help me get him up Ed. It's time for him and me to get ready to go," Jack says in a surprisingly calm voice.

The petite woman pushes forward and fills the room with her voice, "Do not touch that boy! Just because he's been in a coma for two months doesn't mean he's well rested enough to go fight your war or even walk for that matter. You've recruited plenty of people while he slept. What's one more? Haven't you taken enough of my people that you can leave one half healed boy?"

For what she lacked in size she made up for in the way she commanded her authority. And for the second time in my life Jack hesitates and before he can object to her Ed speaks up.

"This kid is tough as nails, he'll be fine," he says. "Besides he's one of theirs."

"Then you can go with them and you will make sure that he stays that way until you're dead or they have finished their task. Now take Jack, find the rest of those fools and gear up. We'll be sending you up within the hour," She states.

Both Jack and Ed suddenly burst into protest, Ed citing reasons why his help would not be necessary for my survival and Jack claiming that he needs at least a day, but she waves them off without a word. As they leave it's obvious that neither of them really have any confidence in my current ability to fend for myself. After they do she turns her attention to me and I wish that Ed's watch over me had already started. Her eyes shoot into me, cold and grey. Her sleek face and steel colored hair give off the impression of an intelligent predator. I'm being read and it seems like there is nothing she doesn't know about me. Despite her size the presence of someone else in the room would be a comfort.

"Sam, I know you but you don't know me. My name is Zora and I am the elected leader of these tunnels. My title would have me called the City Station Mayor, but I think Zora is good enough. I wanted to spend some time with you before you left, but it appears my anger may have shortened that opportunity. When this conversation ends I normally would say I hope to see you many times again, but it seems that you may not live long enough for that to be possible," she sighs and moves closer to me. "Your supposed commanding officer is determined to waste all of your lives, including a fair number of my citizens. I suppose it's best that he leave now so he doesn't convince any more of my people to take up arms with your resistance," she sighs again and the authority drains out of her face. "Eventually you people will realize that you can't fight the tower. Even if you tear it down, ONE will still be too big for you. And if you do somehow win, do you really believe your leaders will be any better?"

"What do you mean?" I ask, finding it hard to give an answer to everything she said and asked.

She smiles at me the way my mom used to when I would ask her silly questions as a child. It makes me feel as though none of my experiences carry any merit compared to hers. "Your so called leader desires to be the new leader of the city. That is, if he manages to tear down the current leaders. If the desire for power is what's driving him, he will ultimately end up like the fallen predecessors and I believe that it is exactly what he is after despite what he says." She stops speaking as a new idea strikes her as though it had been patiently waiting for its turn, "I know a lot about you from what Bear has told me, one of the most underprivileged people of our time and still you quite possible have a better heart than us all. A time when almost all of us are deprived of what should be freely given and you've seen the worst of it. Still, here you are trying to do what is right, for you and others. To add to it, you're quite

the resourceful young man. Literate by your own doing, in such

conditions that is a true achievement. That is why if you rebels are

successful and you live, it is imperative that you make voices like yours

known. For once let there truly be a voice for the people if you can. This

way they may actually get to choose how their new world will form. Do

all you can to keep Jack from taking power or he will keep them quiet.

You know what kind of man he really is."

"He isn't a bad man," I don't know why I defend him.

"He is a product of the current world, a necessary evil," Zora

says. "When the fighting is over he will have no qualities to offer for the

betterment of your people or mine. Even worse he knows about mine

now. He breaks things, he does not build and he will bring those towers

crashing down on these tunnels. I am sorry to involve you in such

conversations. In an ideal world you would still be a boy, more

concerned about whether or not some girl's smile meant something or

getting into trouble late into the night with your friends. Instead you are

having conversations about how our world should be shaped in the days

to come after gruesome conflict and others your age have already starved

to death, some of which have left children of their own behind. Someone so young should not have to be bothered with the great task of shaping the fate of their people. I sometimes find it amazing how older folks like me can have such a lack of respect for young people, but still expect so much."

"I don't know if I can do any of the things you're asking of me," I say. "Who am I to stop Jack or empower the people of Empire? Like you said, no one listens to people as young as me. And this is all supposing we do somehow win, which you just said we won't."

"Selfishly, I would prefer you did not, my people would remain safe. However, I've seen what determined minds can do. It is almost as powerful as hope, but much more dangerous. Hope is often for people who desire good, whereas determination can be a tool for anyone trying to accomplish anything. Either way there will be conflict and opportunity for a hope to blossom. When and if the time comes I think you will find more help than you expect," she replies and tenderly brushes the hair from my brow. "I can't tell the future though, so for now why don't we go for a walk and see if we can't convince some people to leave you here. Also, Bear has been eagerly waiting for you to finally wake up."

She pulls the blankets off me and I see that I have been clothed in something similar to the man in the Empire lift. They feel like expensive sheets. They are weightless and cleaner than anything I've ever worn. With her help my feet find their way off the bed and onto the floor despite the pain that screams for me to lie still and I walk for the first time in weeks.

"Moving is going to smart a bit, at first," Zora explains. "You haven't moved your muscles in a long time and they aren't too happy about it. That and you had quite the list of injuries."

She's right. Every joint feels caked in rust and my body refuses to cooperate, but by the time we've reached the doorway it is already easier to move. It is incredibly tiring and my body begs to lay back down as we walk into a thin stretch of space. More closed off beds line the station and a set of stairs up to somewhere that I can't see. At the edge of the platform the floor drops about four feet. Most people simply climb up and down the small drop off, but Zora leads me to a small set of steps made out of crates. She takes my hand and guides me down each wobbly step. Zora leads me into a less well-lit, arched hallway. People stroll past in either direction, avoiding the two thick metal rails that cut through the middle. And a number of people line the walls, either sitting together or taking a snooze on cots. Everyone down here seems smaller than most people in Empire, but they look incredibly tough and well fed. Ed wasn't kidding.

"Believe it or not this used to be a tunnel for transportation throughout all of Empire during the dry times," Zora breaks through my moment of wonder. "A long time ago during the first great flood the people who came down here managed to seal large portions of it off. Fighting the pressure of the ever-rising water was difficult and still is, but we've been expanding ever since. Oh, you may find amusement in this, take a look."

She points to the wall on our right as we come to another open section filled with small metal columns and stairs. A faded map of many colored routes is on the wall, along with strange signs. One of the large painted rectangles has a golden M. The faded words "I'm loving it," are quoted across the bottom.

"Unlike you tower dwellers we've kept a slightly successful oral history of our ancestors," she tells me. "You see at one point there used to be so much food here that people would compete to get others to eat at their kitchens."

I stare in awe at the painting, wondering how a picture without any food on it could get someone to eat anything. Zora tugs on my arm to pull my attention back to her and leads me up another set of crates. There are more rooms like the one I woke up in and before I see him, Bear's complaining reaches all the way to me. I shuffle in a rush to see him getting one of his arms stitched up.

"Careful," he cries out.

"Such a big guy shouldn't cry so much," the man stitching his arm says. "You said it didn't hurt when you were cut, so how am I hurting you now."

"If you knew how to use a needle…Sam!" he exclaims upon seeing me. He leans forward in excitement before wincing as the needle pricks his arm again.

I painfully chuckle at the sight of his insignificant discomfort in comparison to constant ache and gingerly take a seat next to him on the cot. He has several new scars all down his arms and he looks tougher than ever.

"What have you been up to?" I ask.

Zora answers for him, "Bear has been kind enough to help us clear more space in return for our hospitality. We recently found what was formerly a large station and without him I wonder if we would have ever managed to clear it out."

Bear nods in humble agreement as he lets out one last yelp when the other man finishes the last stitch. He swats at the man as he scurries out of the room.

"One would think you would be more careful if you disliked stitches so much Bear," Zora says. "Also, if you're going to be so mean to my nurses maybe you can learn to do it yourself. You might find it isn't so easy and just maybe you would stop getting injured."

Bear blushes, "I'm sorry we can't all be sleeping angels like Sam over here."

He nudges me and now it's my turn for to flush red. "I was told you wanted to talk to me Bear," I say, trying to brush past my embarrassment.

"Yes, I did indeed. Ever since you've been unconscious I've wanted to tell you how sorry I was for pulling you down from the cable. It was decidedly a foolish act. I know you would have jumped eventually. Such a mistake is too naïve for someone with my years of wear."

"How could you have known all that would have happened?" I ask. "I don't blame you at all. All I want to know is what happened after you dropped those rocks on my head."

Bear's relief is as instant as my forgiveness, but something still seems to bother him as he starts to explain. "Well the mission was an overall success. We retrieved all of our people. Even the one that had the piss beat out of him by that metal bitch. We are currently unaware of what occurred on Wolf and Paul's side and we couldn't find Grace after we fell. We also haven't been able to contact any of our other people. We didn't have enough gear to get back to the library and we were running out of 02 when their doors opened up and we were sucked in. I believe the everyone above assumes that we died in that tower. At least *The Voice* said we all did."

"So is that part of why Jack wants to get out of here so quickly?" I ask him and Zora.

"No, he couldn't care less about the library now and he prefers to be thought of as dead at the moment," Bear says. "There aren't any soldiers left who will join him there, except for those two guards and maybe a handful of others that have been riding the line. I've already told him that I intend to stay here a while longer to help these people and then return to the library when things have settled. Our bond is very much broken. Fortunately there is enough of his soul intact that he has decided to take his army somewhere other than our home."

"What do you mean settled?" I ask.

Zora speaks up this time, "All of Empire is in an uproar. The government and ONE have sent hundreds in search of you and your base. They have almost discovered us several times since your arrival. A few submarines have been hurried through production. Every time they pass, our foundations rattle. We fear that if Jack leaves with his small army we will certainly be found."

"You aren't leaving with him?" a suddenly frantic Bear asks.

"No, given the choice I would never follow him, especially if it meant leaving you behind," I say. "I just had no idea that was an option until now."

"Good, I'm glad," is all he says on the subject.

"Bear has actually been doing a lot more than clearing space by the way," Zora says to me. "Out of what some have called paranoia I have diverted most of our resources to getting an underground rail going again. It will be completed in just a few hours and we will be loading it with supplies and those who cannot walk. I've decided it is time to move to our new home in order to guarantee our safety. It was a controversial choice and part of why so many have signed up with Jack. But I do not regret my decision. These people voted me into my position. I am a servant to their well being and I see this as my only option to guarantee the lives of those who are staying."

At the same time Ed pops his head into the room. "What're ya'll doing in here? Am I still leaving with Jack and the kid?" he asks.

"Why don't you ask him yourself," Zora says. "He's standing right in front of you."

"Well bucko what's the word?" he addresses me.

"We're staying, or at least going where Jack isn't," I say.

"Well I can't say I'm upset," Ed says.

"Then why do you sound slightly disappointed?" Zora asks.

"I can't really say, that Jack man ignites a fire in you," Ed says. "He really makes you want to get up and do something. I don't agree with his anger or desire for guns and cheering, but when he starts talking to you it's hard to see it any other way than his own. He made me believe for half a second. After I came looking for you and Sam I became less angry and more myself the further I got from him."

"Well it's history and Jack will soon be a memory as well," Bear speaks up. "And unless we hurry we may find ourselves in the past with him. Why don't you help me finish checking over the station?" he asks Ed.

Ed's face brightens at the request. He follows Bear out and down the stairs. It was surprising to hear Bear speak about his former leader this way. They were close friends for a number of years. Shortly before my arrival things had even been going well.

Zora slides an arm around my shoulders and leads me from the room so that we can observe Bear and Ed working together. From the top of the stairs we watch them load their tools into a small rail cart that has appeared in the tunnel. Ed starts the engine as Bear loads the last heavy items and steps aboard himself. Bear waves for us to join.

"You go ahead," Zora says. "I have some things to do here. I haven't seen my new home yet, but I've heard it is grand and most definitely worth the effort. Your only job is to observe and confirm this for me, don't let those two rascals make you lift a finger."

I tell her that I will do what I can and shuffle toward the cart as quickly as my aching legs will shuffle. As I reach up to the side of it Bear easily picks me up from under my shoulders and sets me down next to him.

"You weigh even less than when we first met," he tells me. "We need to fatten you up, starting now," He throws me a compressed rectangle of grains. "They call it a grain bar. Full of energy and fat."

"A very long time ago they called it granola," Ed interjects. "At least I've been told by some of the stranger old ones down here, but this barely resembles it according to them, but they don't even know for sure."

"How do you grow food down here?" I yell over the sound of the cart as it picks up speed.

"Well, much like you rebellious people we steal from ONE every now and then," Ed explains. "I imagine they blame it on you guys. It's a good thing we make sure to avoid all contact with the outside world, at least until you guys showed up. Some of you might be quick to throw some of that blame our way. Anyway, we stole a number of sun lamps a long time ago, we've only had one go out so far and we've had them for twenty years or so."

I give a look of approval to Ed as he takes a seat across from us. He puts a bag of supplies behind his head, before leaning back he tosses one to me. I take a hint and lay back on it. The hum of the cart drowns

out all other noises. The sound is comforting and as I gaze at each

passing light on the ceiling it sets me into a trance. The tiles have now

been traded for what appears to be a complete lack of ceiling. All that is

above me is a trail of lights that brighten the tunnel every couple

seconds. The hypnotizing flashes swiftly send me to sleep.

Sometime later I am woken up by a loud screech and a jolt as we

start to slow. Ed is back at the controls and sparks are flying on either

side of us. Bear is still soundly dozing next to me. Ed is pulling on a

lever and as we come up to an opening he puts it down all the way. We

bounce back and forth as we jerk to a halt and Bear finally wakes up.

"You sleep sounder than a baby," Ed says to Bear as he rubs his

eyes.

"You would too if you ever did any of the heavy lifting around

here," Bear counters.

"Maybe if you could drive," Ed says with a smile.

Completely ignoring me in the middle of their banter they gather

their gear and start walking into the opening and up some stairs. I finish

what's left of my bar before following. They almost lose me down a hallway. Fortunately with they're heavy tools weighing them down it isn't too difficult to catch them. Ed groans softly as he shifts his pack on his shoulders, but Bear seems to have no trouble. He still stays a few steps behind Ed, waiting for me to reach them. I get to them just as they walk out into a clearing. Bear points an empty hand, sweeping it across the ceiling and I stop. It is at least forty or fifty feet high. Large metal plates are interlaced and riveted near the top where there were once windows, much like the library. And some are placed randomly along cracks that cut along the green ceiling. The longer sections of wall to either side of me have large portions of them covered, more than I've ever seen done. Each section is held close by a series or rods placed between the exterior wall and large columns that hold up the high ceilings. Water dribbles down the sides of the thick stone and scattered puddles litter the floor.

"She's a beaut' ain't she?" Ed yells back. His voice carries through the space and bounces off the walls. "She's still a bit wet but we're almost done drying her out."

They are walking towards some men and women on the far side of the building. When we finally cross the empty stretch of floor the sound of rushing water starts to drown out the sound of our steps. Four workers are struggling to push a metal plate back into place. I kick a rivet and find a number of them lying broken on the floor around.

"A little help here big man," one of the women yells.

Ed tells Bear, "Get to it."

Bear shouts to the woman, "How did this happen?"

"We had just pumped out the last of the water and as we were taking off our O2 gear the thing just ripped open," She says. "We started the pump back up so we're fine if this is the only one that pops, but we can't get it to shut again."

Bear drops his gear except for the large hammer he has been carrying. He takes the few steps up to the other workers and they scatter as he lifts it high over his shoulders. He puts all of his force into the swing and it crashes down on the plate with a loud bang that rings through the air. The metal bends in response and closes half way. Water splashes across the wall and everyone else, but the flow has already slowed significantly. He hits it again and only a small amount of water trickles through.

"Get another sheet of metal over this and let's check the rest," Bear says.

The crew hurries about, hefting a large piece of metal up the stairs and they get to work, sealing off the flow of water completely.

Ed chuckles, "That man is some kind of miracle. And only he would call that hunk of metal a sheet. You have the best guardian angel I've ever seen. Thanks for passing out for two months so we could borrow him. That man is the real hardware down here. That hammer does nothing without him swinging it."

Instead of thanking him I have to ask, "What's an angel?"

He laughs again, "A real savior, not that crap the government spews to you tower folk, but a hero. Some of us even say they have wings, but I say it's just a good person who will sacrifice her or himself for the lesser folk like us, without discrimination."

I let the image soak in and watch everyone as they go to work, climbing the sides of their new home checking every crack and seam for the slightest drop of water. After a while I lay on the floor and watch until falling asleep again. I wake up in Bear's arms, as he carries me back to the rail cart. When he feels me stirring he sets me down and takes some gear from one of the work crew.

"It's all done?" I ask.

"Yes siree," Ed hollers. "And you get to tell Zora the good news. We'll all be living here by tomorrow if we want."

The trip back feels almost too brief as everyone in the crew laughs and jokes with each other. Their conversation isn't about the work they've done, but they are all relieved and excited for it to be over. When we arrive we are given a real welcome. The much smaller home is now packed with hundreds of people. Many more than I thought were down here. Zora is at the front of the group and she helps me down. Once both feet reach the ground she embraces me and the cheering continues. The rest of the crew is greeted similarly, except for Bear. From the moment he stands up on the cart to the moment Zora plants a kiss on his cheek the people roar with delight and the air shakes with their applause. My head vibrates as I start to walk through the crowd. Dozens of hands reach out to touch the crew and myself. They grab at my back and shoulders, pat my head and try to shake my hand. I don't even attempt to explain that I did nothing.

A hush falls over the crowd and I turn to see Zora standing on the cart with her arms raised out towards her people. She points at the crew and motions for us to join her. The crowd pushes us back toward her and we take our place next to Bear who is still standing below her.

As everyone quiets again she shouts out in her deep commanding voice.

"People of our hidden city!" she cries. "For those of you who have decided to stay with me through this controversial and confusing time I thank you." The crowd collectively shouts out in delight and applause. "Though it has taken much of our resources and time we have achieved something great and we have proven to ourselves that we will always be capable, not only of survival, but of governing ourselves. We have avoided the corrupt men and women who have enslaved the tower dwellers for many years. And with this achievement it would seem that we have bought ourselves many more. Though I will not lie to you." As she says this, a murmur glides through the crowd.

"We must be careful in the days to come," she continues. "War is coming, and though it may not be directed towards us we must not forget that we occupy the same city. Violence may come without warning at any time. We cannot forget this. Conflict will cause pain to many, worst of all, those who do not desire to be a part of it. It is worse than Hell and we should pray for the men, women and children that are taken by it. We will hope that none of our own brothers and sisters will be taken by the inevitable violence to come. Even those who now leave with Jack are in my thoughts. I hope that someday they will return to us, but enough of this sad talk. It is time that we move on to our new home. I have been told its sight is beyond words. Those of you who can walk please start as soon as possible. The rail will follow shortly with our supplies and those who cannot walk the long distance. Leave nothing you desire to come back for. We do not plan to return, nor will we be able to."

The crowd, much more somber than before slowly falls apart as Zora finishes her speech. Those who had already prepared, start their journey down the tunnel. Others take Zora's advice and collect their valuables. The old and sick wait there for the tube to arrive so they can be helped aboard. Zora jumps down and joins the work crew.

"If you desire, you have all earned a seat on the train or one of the rail carts," she says.

The crew graciously declines the opportunity, sighting several reasons why they can or should walk. Everyone but Ed, Bear and myself runs off to join their families and gather their things. We all quietly watch groups of people mill about. Most people don't seem to be in a hurry to leave.

"Have we ever moved like this before?" Ed asks Zora.

"As far as I know we've only ever expanded," she says. "But it's time we all start moving. Ed and Bear grab your gear, you know what to do," she waves them off. "Sam, come with me."

We walk down the tunnel towards where I first woke up and a cart slowly pulls in a much older and square tube than the one I hopped into Empire tower. And this one is made up of eight separate sections. The exterior is severely dented and there are numerous patches of rust. Many of the windows are cracked or gone altogether. It screeches past as the driver of the cart pulls on his brake. Looking through the windows, I can see that the first four sections are completely filled with supplies. The remaining four are empty and set up with beds and cushioned seats. As it comes to a halt, I notice that a portion of the last section has had its walls removed.

"That's where we'll be sitting on the train," Zora says pointing at the open section. "I hear you're a decent shot with a plasma gun. We'll be a part of the team that covers our ass end, just in case."

She winks as she walks past me and hops onto the train. The people are loaded from the back and Zora personally helps most of them aboard. Several more capable men and women who were already aboard help them find a seat or place to lie down. After attempting to help one elderly woman I find myself strained and take my seat. As the last few passengers board Ed and Bear reappear. They are each carrying a much larger version of the plasma gun. Bear is almost bouncing with excitement.

"I don't care if I'm not even going to use it," he responds to something Ed said. "If you're not pulling one over on me and I'm truly holding this before they have been issued to ONE security I'm a happy man. Wolf would be jealous."

"Just remember," Ed says. "The shot has less oomph but it shoots significantly faster now. Also, be careful of it overheating on you," then he imitates the sound of an explosion.

Bear adjusts the rifle in his hands and his face takes on a more serious look. They climb aboard the tube and take seats across from Zora and myself. Ed drops his rifle to the floor and Bear jumps.

"Relax tough guy," Ed says. "They don't just blow up for any reason. Want me to give yours to the kid?"

Bear grips the gun more tightly and glares at Ed. Zora and I laugh at this and after a moment Ed and Bear join in. It feels good to be laughing again. It hasn't happened much since leaving with Bear months ago. As our laughter dies down the tube starts moving again. Metal groans and squeals under the pressure of the fully loaded train and I fall into Zora for a moment when it starts to pick up speed. It starts to click and clack as it chugs along.

"I safely assume that the two of you finished that last bit of work?" Zora addresses Bear and Ed.

"Yeah," they both say. Bear continues, "When we detonate, enough of the ceiling should collapse to close off the tunnel, we just have to hope water won't come rushing in after us."

"Hope?" Zora asks.

"What he means is we'll be fine," Ed says.

As the rail makes its way completely out of the opening, the lights of their old home begin to flicker. Dust and stones start to spill from the ceiling as vibrations echo down through the tunnel. The buzzing becomes overwhelming.

"Is that us?" I ask through chattering teeth.

"No," Bear says just loud enough to be heard as he jumps off the rail and onto the ground.

Ed follows him and they both start up their pulse rifles. They spark between one another as their large batteries spin up next to each other. They walk backwards, slowly distancing themselves from us. Zora starts up her own gun and I do the same. The lights go completely dark. The sound of stones crumbling and falling overcomes the sound of the hum.

"Zora what's happening?" a woman from the inside attempts to quietly ask through the window nearest us.

"Get down," is all Zora says. Our guns give off enough light that I can see her face. If anything she looks fiercer than the first time I met her. Hopefully she is as ready as she seems because I'm in no real shape for a fight.

The figures of Bear and Ed have gradually gotten smaller as we've chugged along. A beam of light appears in front of them and it is quickly extinguished as they both fire upon it dozens of times. The shots are followed by sounds of shouting and returning fire. The tunnel lights up with plasma that seems to come from everywhere. Suddenly the lights from Bear and Ed rush back toward us and blue flames fill the tunnel. Their shadows sprint along the walls with them. Several men emerge from the flames as they die and fall to the ground.

"Hit it!" Ed yells over the continued gunfire.

"We're too close," Bear shouts back.

"They're too close!" Ed's voice becomes shrill.

Neither says anything for a moment as they continue to run and I'm knocked out of my seat as an impressive wave of energy surges through the tunnel, causing it to collapse around us. Zora grabs me and rolls both of us under the seats. The rail stops and debris continues to pile up around us until neither of us can move.

CHAPTER TEN

Rubble shifts around Zora and myself as we try to dig our way out. Every time something moves we pause in fear of being crushed by the wreckage lying on top of us. Dust fills my lungs as I take in deep anxiety filled breaths. The debris starts to move more violently, Zora grips my hand tightly and I expect a rock to cave in my head any second until a faint blue light of a plasma rifle leaks through the cracks in the rocks. Bear groans as he lifts another boulder off of us. After he sets it aside he pulls me out from under the seats by my shirt. He sets me down on a rock next to him before he does the same for Zora. We are all covered in a mix of grime and blood. Instead of sitting Zora scrambles over the rocks to find her way inside the tube so she can check on her people.

"Where's Ed?" I ask Bear.

He quickly turns away without reply and goes after Zora. I pause for a moment and look for him before going in myself. There's nothing but a wall of rock. Most of the people inside appear to be in good shape despite the ash that has caked onto their skin and clothes. Most of them just seem afraid. In the second section a large piece of tunnel has fallen through the roof of the compartment. A bed is underneath it along with its occupant. It is too large for even Bear to move and no one really wants to see what is underneath anyway. I move around it being careful not to step in the blood. Bear and Zora are further ahead.

A bony hand snatches my arm as I try to pass into the next section. The icy grip stings my skin and my first thought is to pull away, but I realize the woman who has grabbed me simply needs help. A patch of blood is soaking through the ash on the side of her head and mattes down her pale hair. With her other skeletal hand she shakily points at the giant rock.

"Help my husband," she pleads. "Why won't anyone get him out from under there."

I look at the rock and back to her stammering. She has me at a complete loss. There is nothing comforting to be said to her. As much as I wish for someone else to answer, no one comes to my rescue. I wipe the soot out of my eyes as sweat smears it down my face. The woman starts to wail for help as I search for an answer. Eventually I lie to her. "Your husband is up ahead," I say. "I'll find him and bring him to you. Don't worry, I'll be back shortly."

She calms herself almost instantly, soaking up her fresh tears with a dirty sleeve. She smiles as she patiently places her hands over the bag that rests in her lap. "Thank you so much, young man," she tells me "I don't know what I was thinking." I move away from her quickly, collapsing at the next section of the rail. I sit on the floor sobbing as the commotion of the injured and those seeking to help swirl around me. After some time a hand gently grabs onto my shoulder. One of the women who helped move people onto the train is crouched down before me.

"Hey I'm here to help," she says with a smile. "Is anything broken or injured?"

I shake my head and point towards the woman looking for her husband. She gives me an understanding smile and moves on. After she leaves I manage to collect myself, getting to my feet. I run my sleeve across my face and start moving. Most of the people in the remaining two sections seem fine, they cough and shift around in their beds or seats. Most everyone seems to be in decent condition. A few scratches and bumps, but that's it. I finally catch up with Zora in the first supply cart. She is asking some of her people to take another round checking on everyone and find as much water as they can. When she notices me approaching she points me ahead to the front of the train. At the front the first half of the section has been completely caved in. Bear and several others are already working to open up a hole.

"You can't help here right now Sam," Bear says as he pushes a slab out one of the windows. "Go back to the other end and tell me if anyone is trying to dig through to us. Take the rifle."

I grab the rifle and make my way back through the rail as quickly as my body can take me. Rods of pain shoot through my stiff muscles. I push through it, even though it seems unlikely that anyone could be left to try digging to us. If someone is still coming after us there isn't much we can do to stop anyone at this point. I can't fight, much less a whole squad of ONE's security force. People begin to call out for water or continually hack as I squirm through the mess. I come to the realization that I could use some water myself. My nostrils fill with dust as the quality of the air continues to decline.

At the other end of the train it is much quieter. I sit and listen for even the slightest noise. The only sound comes from the few people coughing behind me. I start up the rifle anyway. Time goes by slowly as I pass it by trying to wet my mouth. Some time later I jerk awake, not sure when I had fallen asleep. In a panic I check my surroundings, peering at the wall in front of me to make sure it hasn't changed since I last looked at it. Everything seems fine and I lay my head back as the pebbles start to shift and fall down the pile.

I fall away from the wall and roll to the floor as I reach for the rifle, it's battery still humming. More rocks fall until a hand is revealed. I raise up on it, ready to shoot until I realize it can't be the cause of the moving rock. It twitches, but doesn't move enough to push the rock. I scramble up the debris to reach it. As the rocks continue to shift about Ed's face is revealed. He is unconscious, but breathing. Dust blows into the air away from his mouth, which means he's at least breathing. I pull on his arm until his body is halfway out of the rubble. He goes into a coughing fit, but does not wake up. The vibrations help to loosen the rest of the rocks that still hold onto his legs. One is badly broken and his shin is poking out through his pants as evidence. Ed moans as he slides onto the tube and his legs slam to the floor. Several others quickly come to my aid when they see me dragging him inside. I hand him over and run to tell Bear about the vibrating wall.

When I reach him they haven't gotten much further. Almost everyone but Bear is taking a break, sipping on the little water they have. Bear wheezes as he claws at the rock. It takes me a few minutes to catch my breath before I can talk.

"Bear, the wall," I say through my own ragged panting. "It's vibrating."

Bear drops a large rock at his feet and turns away from the wall. His face is ashen and sweat is pouring down his front, mixing with a thick layer of dust. "Back to work!" he yells. Everyone jumps to their feet and starts hacking at the wall with whatever tools they managed to collect. Bear doesn't wait to hear anything else, he pushes past me and starts swimming through the supplies and passengers. It's easier to keep up after he has knocked every thing and person up against the wall and out of his way.

As he reaches Zora he takes her gun out of its holster without a word. As I reach her, her confused look turns to fear. She leaves a bandage half wrapped around an old man's arm and chases after us. When we all arrive at the wall, we just stare at it. The vibrations have turned into a low rumbling.

"What do we do?" I finally ask.

"It's a race," Bear says. "We have to finish digging before they do."

"We'll never make it," Zora says. "It sounds like they have heavy machinery and we only have a slew of tools and our bare hands. With only three of us left to fight we're done. There's nowhere to go."

As we stand there staring in despair a commotion starts up behind us. Ed is trying to get up despite his obviously broken leg and is actually fighting a woman who is trying to keep him down. "Get off me dammit!" He yells inches from her face. He pushes her away and swings his legs to the floor. Using his arms to grab at the ceiling and his good leg, he manages to hobble toward us.

"You know, it's not good bedside manner to talk about all of us dying where people can hear," he says leaning out the broken back window. "I also happen to have a way for us to get out."

He pulls out a small block of explosives and grins despite the pain he must be in. "I know it's risky to use more explosives, but it's the only way you're getting your happy asses out of here."

"Well if we don't, we'll die. If we do, we might die," Zora says. "I'll take a maybe over certainty today. But if we blow our way out they could still catch us."

As if he knew she would say this Ed produces a second block of explosives. He tosses one to Bear and puts the other back in his shirt. Bear palms his and hands Zora back her gun before he sets off back to the front. As he leaves Ed's smile breaks into a frown and the pain he carries becomes real.

"I'm staying to blow the second one," he says. "It can't be detonated too soon, then it might only help them. Too late and they could already be past it. Once they get through I'll hit it." Zora starts to protest, but Ed cuts her off. "I can't walk. And I don't mean like how some of these old fogeys shuffle about, I mean I can't move. Even though Bear can carry me, who stays behind? I won't let someone else do it, even if they are some old fossil."

"Let's get you set up then," Zora says through a tear.

Zora and I help Ed hobble out to the wall, I set his charge while she gives him one last swig of water. He thanks her and they share a brief embrace. She whispers something in his ear and he nods his head. She leaves without looking at me. I hand Ed the charge and the rifle. As I go to leave he says one last thing to me. "Take care of the big guy, I think he's the one who needs you," he says with a smile.

"Thanks Ed, I will" is all I can utter before walking away. Another friend and loved one is leaving me. I have always wanted to have a chance to say goodbye before a moment like this, but now I can't manage it. For Ed, I can't ask him to try to come with and I know I would cry if I said anything more to him.

An explosion comes from the far side of the tube as I start to make my way there and it rattles the metal walls. I fall into the lap of the older woman from before. She smiles at me as I brush us both off and apologize. More dust and rocks clatter as they hit the roof of the rail. A hush falls through the section as we wait to see if the tunnel will fall in on us. It holds, I find Zora and we start to usher the passengers to the front. Thankfully the woman has forgotten about her husband. As we get there, Bear is waiting to help people down. One able bodied person is sent with every group of ten and they start their long march. After they have all filed out we jump down to Bear.

"So he is staying," Bear says. "He has to I suppose. Sam, we should wait here to be sure the job gets done. Zora, go with your people. I sent a runner to get rail carts. Hopefully your walk won't be too far. We'll catch up shortly."

"You have to," she says. "It's your job to look after Sam again."

She tilts her head up and kisses him on the cheek. "Be careful," she says to us both.

She takes off at a jog to catch up with caravan of sick and elderly. When she is out of sight Bear hands me a large hammer and starts up his gun. Looking down at the tool it becomes apparent how desperate this moment really is. If we don't kill every single person coming after us, thousands of people may die.

"At least they have to come through the rail," Bear says. "Hopefully it doesn't come down to that." He looks at the hammer.

The vibration from the digging has now reached us at the far end. My teeth chatter as I lean against the outside of the tube. Eventually it turns into a rhythmic pounding and the rocks really start to move. When it stops, an incredible light shines through the tunnel and Ed yells, firing dozens of rounds.

"Get some!" He belts out in one last sarcastic roar.

Several shots are returned and Ed cries out. He lets out a defiant cry and the lights dim and flicker as an explosion rips through the back of the tube. The ceiling falls and a storm of dust billows through the tunnel towards us. The whole tunnel goes dark and the lights remain extinguished. We silently wait in the darkness for everything to settle. The aftermath is slowly revealed to us as my eyes adjust to the dark and tears clear out the soot. There is almost nothing left of the far end of the compartments. Still, we wait for any noise to reveal a threat. Nothing happens for a long time. We only leave when a rail cart comes to retrieve us.

On our way out we don't say anything. Bear doesn't slap my back with his palm, no one tells any jokes. Now I more fully understand Zora's contempt for conflict. If it weren't for people like Bear, Jack and myself this hardship may have never brought itself down to these people. And one of them sacrificed themself instead of us taking the hit. Even though ONE or the government may have been the attackers, I feel responsible for Ed's life. It certainly seems like we had a hand in this. A debate has started to rise in me. Is it worth all this loss to have a little more? If we stop now would it dishonor those that have already died? I just have to keep thinking of what Bear told me. Don't worry about what I can't change and do my best with what I can.

CHAPTER ELEVEN

After two weeks we still haven't seen any sign of ONE security or government forces. We have felt the rumblings of passing submarines several times, but so far it seems that we successfully escaped and somehow we have remained hidden. The tunnel was blown several more times. Digging all the way here would be too great of an undertaking for anyone now. Just yesterday a quiet ceremony was put on for Ed, someone I had hoped would be a new friend for a long time. The ceremony was small, but worthy of the man. It wasn't decorations or the number of people who took time away from their daily tasks, but the words said about him. It seemed like he alone had been the cause for the happiness of many in this damp world. It was the first time I've ever seen Bear cry. I cried too, it had been so easy to feel like his friend in such a short time.

After everyone was done speaking Bear and I started to pack our things. My last night was spent guarding the tunnel and Bear spent his last night with Zora. For his sake I hope we return and that these people will be safe without us. But, it is time for our own people to get some good news. The thoughts of the library, Azalea and my family have been on my mind for a long time. I'm glad we're finally going back. My last few things are packed in the morning while Bear says his final goodbyes to Zora. I walk over to them with both of our packs as they finish a long embrace. Bear looks gruffer than ever and Zora's eyes shine with held back tears. They have already said goodbye. I give Zora a quick hug and say nothing to avoid prolonging the pain of their parting.

An airlock has been finished a short distance away in another tunnel. Bear tested it out the day before. It leads into the bottom of an abandoned tower so that we can exit without being seen. We now float at the edge of the interior, waiting and watching. The world above ground has changed significantly since we left. There are mines scattered throughout the water at several depths. Bright orange flashes that go off in unison give each one away. For every three scavengers there is a ONE security squad. Cold, white lights cut through the dark water, sweeping the ocean floor. Even from inside the tower the beams blind me momentarily as they pass just a few feet away. After they leave my eyes struggle to see in darkness that resumes. They shoot down from the submarines that are now more plentiful than ever. There are at least five sources of light gliding over and between towers. Prior to the war Hobbes had told me there were only two in all of Empire.

Bear starts to rhythmically tap his hand on a wall as he readies his harpoon gun with the other. The subs have a pattern and Bear is trying to get the timing of it down, so I get ready to move. Without a word he stops tapping and propels himself out into the open, swimming as close to the ground as he can. I follow without hesitation as we half swim half crawl through the wreckage of the ocean floor. The remains left by the old dry world shield us from anyone that might still be looking. We swim in and around the metal skeletons of machines that were once used to get around on the concrete, which is now cracked and covered in seaweed. As we near a scavenger we slip into a large patch of weeds and watch for anyone that might be looking.

The field of dead machines has thinned out here. Though a few pieces of the machines that have been deemed useless for their fragile nature lay scattered and all of the growth has been cut away. An enormous amount of space lies bare between the next building and us on our route. Signs larger than a cube litter the ground and buildings around us. Some of them have been rebuilt or repaired by ONE to display images of propaganda. We wait for the scavenger to turn his back after a squad swims past as Astor's face appears on the screens. He slams a fist on his desk. A vein breaks through his red face, as he shouts into the ocean. The scavenger momentarily takes notice of the giant man across the way as the screens flash blue and white light onto him. He nods his head in agreement before returning to his work. Once sparks start to fly we scramble across the ground as quietly as we can, boosting ourselves towards a large sign marked Star Cof. We launch ourselves through the remains of a glass door and gently land behind a counter. The sucking sound of my regulator fills my skull as I start to inhale too quickly and my pulse pounds out through my ears. I put a hand to my chest to help get it back under control.

When we peer out into the opening, except for a swirl of sediment, it looks like we never passed through. The scavenger, still with his back to us, continues to cut away with his torch and the squads lazily kick past. We made it just in time. A submarine now lowers to the ocean floor where we had just passed and the squads change out. As they do we head to the back of the building, swimming through several hallways to make it to the back door. It is like a small maze and we have to double back several times before we are out in the open again.

Behind several small towers we watch another sub gently lower itself down, eventually disappearing from sight. The guards are changing out so they can refill their oxygen. We take the opportunity to attempt an all out sprint to the opening of the library. Before the subs have lifted up again we're rounding the last corner to the entrance. As Bear lifts the cover, one of the subs explodes behind us just as it climbs above the shortest towers. The remains scatter and crash into the side of one of the surrounding buildings and wedge themselves into the guts of the tower. The tower slowly sways before settling and a giant cloud slowly rises up from the foundations. We watch as several zoom tubes shoot out from cover several towers away. One of the other submarines tries to give chase, but it is not nimble enough to follow into the tight spaces and it quickly gives up. Instead, each of the remaining vessels dumps every squad out into the water and they begin to sweep the entire area. Not wanting to press our luck we push ourselves into the hole and Bear closes and seals it without wasting a second. When the water drains and the airlock opens only Hobbes is there to greet us. The rest of the hallway is deserted.

"So I'm sure you two have just heard, the war has started," Hobbes says as another explosion reverberates through the hall. "Jack came by about a week ago and commandeered some supplies. He also convinced a few more people to leave with him. But at the very least you have returned, a shred of light to brighten these dark days," his face changes over to a more pleasant look. "I was beginning to worry about you two, but I never completely lost faith," he says with a forced grin.

"We have much to do in little time don't we old man?" Bear responds.

"Yes," Hobbes says. "And without the both of you I doubt we would ever be able to accomplish it. Also, I've told you I don't like the word old."

"Did I just miss part of the conversation?" I ask. "Because it seems like the two of you already have some kind of plan underway."

Hobbes and Bear manage to utter some kind of confirmation, but instead of telling me they move on. So I follow them through the library and I find myself sitting in a room I've never seen before. It is plastered with maps, pictures of faces and towers. Names of people and towers are scribbled across the walls. Across from me is a large table with one last map laid across it. Bear and Hobbes stand on either side and pore over it. Quiet yeses and grunts of agreement come from them as I patiently wait to hear what they have planned. Eventually I obnoxiously clear my throat to remind them I'm still there.

"Yes, yes, yes," Hobbes starts. "I suppose now would be an appropriate time to fill you in. A few years ago a group of us got together and came up with a plan to take out several key members of Empire and ONE. We concluded that if we could destroy their propaganda, chain of command and supply lines, the resulting confusion would allow for us to strike a heavy blow to their infrastructure and manage to cause an uprising of the people. The result would be both ONE and the government crippled while the people fight for us. Which if they all did there wouldn't be much fighting at all. The people outnumber patrollers and ONE security about thirteen to one according to our last census."

"But I don't see how killing a few men and destroying a few buildings will make any of this happen," I say. "What gets the people fighting and why should they do it for us?"

"Two things will happen if we succeed," Bear says. "The propaganda will stop, patrollers won't know where to go or what to do. The fear will stop. When food and water becomes even scarcer people will not only lose their fear, they will get angry. And when we arrive as the only help, they will join us. All we have to deal with after that are the patrollers that are true followers and the ONE-security forces. And if the people fight it will ensure that they are the ones who take power."

"That's a great plan," I say. "Except it needs to be changed."
Bear and Hobbes look at me confused. "What happens with Jack in the
mix? And if the people fight each other instead of together" They both
pause and neither seems to know what I'm getting at or don't want to.
"We'll have to fight him too, at some point anyway," I say. "But why
don't we let them fight for now and when both sides have exhausted their
resources we step in and hopefully no one else has to do any fighting.
We would still have to take out some of these people you were talking
about, but maybe Jack can do most of it for us and if he doesn't die in the
process we can kill him when the war is over."

"We can't kill Jack," they say together.

"But what happens when it's all over and he still has an army?" I
ask. I continue before they can respond. "Do you doubt that he would
assume ownership of what he has taken? He would destroy every bit of
the city before giving it up." Zora's ideas and words spill out of my
mouth.

Bear continues to protest before Hobbes cuts him off, "No Sam
is right, did we not just months ago talk about stripping Jack of his rank
and his privilege to vote? When he found out he went into a rage and
took full operational command. He wants power and he doesn't deal with

opposition well. If he doesn't die and tries to assume control we are obligated to stop him. We let him become the war hungry monster when we hesitated."

"He has been my friend for years," Bear says.

"When was the last time he was really your friend?" Hobbes asks.

All Bear can say is, "Let's get ready," before he leaves.

"I suppose that means I should fill you in more deeply while he goes to hit something," Hobbes says. "Once Paul and Wolf are cleared by myself. Yes, by the way did I mention that they are alive and mostly well? Paul lost part of his hand and needed surgery and Wolf has an impressive set of scars on his back, for having been blown up they are in impressively good shape. You should take Bear to see them in a moment. That should lighten his mood. Anyway, enough of that tangent, as this war grows there will be some confusion on both sides, which is perfect cover for the team to roam somewhat undetected."

"Just tell me what we're doing Hobbes," my patience finally gives out. "If you keep going on about a plan without sharing the details it won't ever get done."

"Right, well you're going to begin this mission with a rather rotund man who you know as the voice." Hobbes pulls down a picture of a bald man whose face is covered in scars. "You may have seen his cleaned up, pudgy face on those screens they installed in the towers some time ago or quite possibly when we've had the chance to get the broadcast down here. Before his new illustrious career, he was in charge of information gathering along with a terribly wicked man named Caldwell. When Astor grew tired of the blood he dug up some old equipment to entertain the people. Now, not only does he claim to be the voice of the people, but he also runs the entire propaganda machine for both ONE and Empire. Luckily for us he is an overconfident prick and sleeps where he works, in the America Tower. So if we get to him there we can destroy his work along with him."

"How are we getting in?" I ask.

"Fortunately for the sake of so called transparency it's also been the least guarded building," Hobbes says. "Astor likes to claim anyone can visit him any time. No one ever has though."

"So we're just going to walk in, kill the guy and burn his stuff." I say. "I guess that sounds less complicated than the last mission."

"Simple right?" he says. "That's all for now. I'll tell you the rest when everyone is gathered. I would prefer to tell the plan in its entirety just the one time. So grab Bear and take him with you to collect Paul and Wolf. Also, don't forget to tell Bear who our first target is, he always hated that man. In the meantime I'll prepare your gear."

"Just make sure it works better than that hot stick," I tell him as I leave.

As I walk down to Bear's room my footsteps echo through the hall. The library is eerily empty and I only see two people between the lab and Bear's door. The muffled sound of him hitting something comes through the thick door. I wait to knock until there is a pause. When I finally build up the courage to knock I am greeted by a bloody handed Bear and a gaping hole in the wall behind him.

"What is it?" he asks between heavy breaths.

"We're going to go see your brother," I say confidently.

He grunts and grabs a jacket from his closet. We walk together in an awkward silence, leaving a trail of blood behind us. I've never seen Bear this way before. I feel like he might punch a hole through me at any moment if I say the wrong thing. He hasn't bothered to wrap his knuckles and I haven't bothered to bring up my concern about infection.

When we arrive at the rec room his mood barely lifts. We walk in to see both Paul and Wolf doing a strange sequence of stretches as a third man leads them through the process.

As we watch I whisper to Bear, "We're going after Astor first."

He nods and stares at his brother. Wolf has his shirt off and scars overlap each other all the way down to his pant waist. Next to him, Paul struggles to balance as they go down to all fours. His right hand is missing a couple fingers and does little to help him balance. Paul looks between his legs and sees us. His eyes light up and he tumbles to ground, bounces back up and trots over to us with a smile.

"Enjoying the view," he says with a wink. "Wolf and I hear from Hobbes that some big cloak and dagger, multi-stage mission is going to take place now that you two slackers finally made it back."

Bear keeps his sulking face on, but I embrace Paul with a firm hug. I hold him at a distance and tell him I'm happy to see him again. He tells me the feeling is mutual. As Wolf finishes the last stretch he comes to join us. Bear reaches out a hand, Wolf swats it away and wraps his arms around the much higher shoulders of his brother, swaying him side to side until Bear finally cracks a smile.

"What have you been feeding this guy?" Wolf asks me. "He must have put on twenty pounds of muscle since I last saw him." He slaps Bear stomach with both hands. "Stiff as a rod and you're not even flexing. I have some catching up to do."

Bear lets out a laugh despite his best efforts to look stern again, Wolf joins in as he boxes at his brother's chest. By the time they've settled down I've begun to explain the little that I do know about our mission to Paul. Bear and Wolf listen intently once the name Astor is brought up again.

"You mean we finally get to kill roly poly?" Wolf asks. "I can't wait to get my hands on that fat bastard."

"You'll have to beat me to him," Bear says.

"Did he do something to you two specifically?" I ask.

"When we first started our high paying careers as rebels with a cause we were seen one too many times and the grease ball mocked up some fairly scathing wanted posters," Wolf explains. "It's also why we have all the facial hair, so patrollers don't recognize us. When we venture outside of these walls. We also got our nifty code names from it too."

"What did you two do to earn that?" Paul asks.

"Well between Bear punching holes in people's faces and me blowing up a supply tube twice in a week we managed to piss off a few people," Wolf says. "The good old days, before we realized covert was a better route and got less people hurt. So much more enjoyable though."

By now Bear's mood had changed significantly. "Let's go get suited up then," he says. "I'm sure Hobbes has plenty to show us."

We walk quickly and talk in an excited manner about everything that had happened since we had last seen one another. After we told them of our time in the tunnels they explained what had happened to them from the explosion in Empire Tower up until now. They took turns describing the short fight in the stairs and how they had been much too close to the explosion when the bombs went off. Wolf covered Paul, despite his previous advice to me and took the brunt of the blast. They never would have made it if Grace hadn't decided to come looking for us. Incredibly she had managed to carry Wolf and help Paul walk as they painfully took every step to the bottom. Paul had still been strong enough to use a zoom tube and between the two of them they dragged Wolf along as they made it back to the library. Since then the two of them have been rehabilitating to get ready for our return.

When we get to Hobbes' lab Dylan and Grace are already there being fitted for the new gear that Hobbes has been working on. They greet us with a mixture of waving and hellos from across the room, much to the annoyance of Hobbes who is trying to stuff a vest over Dylan's shoulders. The workbench is littered with several more vests along with a number of rifles and other weapons that Hobbes has modified or made himself.

"Everyone put on one of those vests and get it fitted," Hobbes says. "Obviously the very large one is for Bear. When you get it on it should begin to conform to your body. If you want you can make slight manual adjustments for comfort by pulling on these straps."

He demonstrates by pulling tightly on Dylan's vest. He winces in response and lets out a sigh when Hobbes shows us how to loosen them. We all throw a vest over our heads. It is incredibly light and it gives off the sensation of deflation as it wraps around my chest and lower back. I make adjustments to it until I have a full range of comfortable motion.

"What exactly are these for?" I ask.

"The vest has two main purposes," Hobbes begins to explain. "Firstly it protects you from all types of projectiles and pointy things, more so knives than plasma. You're not invincible though. There is also a device that Wolf has aptly named 'round two'. It reads your heartbeat. If it stops an electric charge will go off several times in an attempt to restart it. This of course only works if the vest is on snugly. And in theory it should have a success rate of sixty percent. That's about it. Any questions?" No one asks any questions, but we all tighten our straps. As we do Hobbes moves back to the workbench and begins to explain the weapons.

"Each of you will have one of the new pulse rifles along with three fireball grenades," he says. "I have added modifications to three of the rifles. For Grace and Paul, I have slowed the firing rate of these and developed a telescope that can sit on top of them for better long distance shooting. You can also take it off and switch over to a three shot burst. Wolf yours has a launcher on the bottom that fires an explosive, which is set off by impact after twenty feet of travel. Otherwise it's just an obnoxiously large projectile. For Bear and Sam I did nothing because you can't put dumb luck or care for other humans on a gun. However, since I know you lost your last one Bear, here is a new knife. It's a harder metal than before so don't lose this one."

"Great when do we leave?" Grace asks looking through her scope.

"We'll leave tomorrow," Bear says. "The war has already started, but let's let it brew for a bit longer before we go out there."

"Before you all leave to prepare in your own ways let me share the basic idea," Hobbes says. "Entering from some point below the water, I have left that part up to Wolf, you will make your way to the first equipment floor. Paul will have a map of the building…"

"We got it," Wolf interrupts. "Well, I've got it down already. All you need to know is get in, burn everything and kill the fat man. Then we leave. Work for you Hobbes?"

"Well I'd say you might be missing some details," Hobbes says. "But you will most likely end up winging it whether or not I share the minor details."

"Alright," Grace yawns. "I'm going go sleep with my gun then."

She walks out and no one else makes a clever comment. We all slowly leave, not sure what to do with ourselves. Paul, Dylan and I walk together towards our squad's quarters. Sadly, we are already the only three still alive from our squad, which we know of. As we get closer they start to give each other a strange look.

"We're going back to the exercise room," Paul says. "Have fun."

I don't know what he means until I open the door to the quarters. Inside is Azalea and my family. Before I can let out a hello Lily is already wrapped around my leg smiling up at me.

"You're here!" she exclaims.

Everyone else greets and hugs me as I wade my way through them. When I reach Azalea she plants a kiss on my cheek. My younger siblings let out an excited *ooooooh* that gradually gets louder. Despite my embarrassment I still smile and I make the noise back at them. It makes them all giggle and they go running out the door and into the hall. As they exit my mother approaches me and grabs my face.

"You look so much older," she says. "At least it looks like someone's been feeding you better than I ever could." She pulls her hands away from my face. "Oh!" she yelps. "I didn't even see that you have stubble now!" I could tell she was holding back tears as her eyes glisten. "I have to go watch your brother and sisters." She hurries out the door in an attempt to hide her tears. Alison punches me on the shoulder. "We all missed you," she says. "We've been waiting in there for an hour now. Hobbes picked you and Bear up on the cameras so we decided to hide as a surprise for you."

"How long have you all been down here for?" I ask.

"Azalea and a couple other rebels came and pulled us out of the towers a week after you left here," she tells me. "We though you had died on us, mom almost couldn't take it. Lily wouldn't shut up about you though. We didn't tell her you were dead, she's been asking when you would be back almost every day. That's one question I'm happy to not have to hear anymore." She rolls her eyes.

"Seems like you've been doing just fine without me," I laugh. Just then Lily comes running back and latches herself onto my leg again. She smiles up at me and sways back and forth, taking my leg with her.

"Lily!" my mom shouts. "Give your brother his leg back." And Lily comes running back to her, giggling. She whispers something in Lily's ear and she runs off to join Dakota and June. "They are nothing but trouble down here," my mom says. "We certainly missed you."

"I missed you too mom," I say. "Have you been holding up OK?"

"Yes, we've been good and we're doing better now that you're back," she pauses. "Alison can you watch them before they disappear and Hobbes finds them somewhere they shouldn't be?"

"Yeah sure thing," Alison says and trots off.

"I'm sure you're tired," my mom continues. "Get some rest. I know that they're sending you out again. But before I go I just want to tell you that even though I'm scared for you out there I'm incredibly proud. Your father would be too. Just, please do your best to make it back here. We still need you too and we all love you very much."

"I love you too."

She leaves and closes the door behind her, leaving Azalea and myself alone. She quietly scans the room and the silence is unbearable. I've never been alone with her and suddenly I have nothing to say. Azalea dives into my arms and I realize I don't need to say anything. When she kisses me it feels better than the time before. We are left alone for the night. In the later hours of the night we're still awake.

"Why is it that there are only six people with the ability to fight who are willing to do it for all those that can't?" Azalea asks out into the darkness. "I just don't get why it has to be for control or power."

"I don't think most people want to risk their lives just to give something away," I offer. "Maybe all some people will fight for is gain, at least when it comes to leaders. What other reason could there be?"

"Well," Azalea says. "To give people opportunity to rise or fall as they choose their own path, instead of forcing them into cramped

boxes and giving them just enough food to work the next day."

"I don't see how fighting is going to do that" I say.

"Fighting on it's own won't and it will certainly make things

worse. People up there are dying either way though. It's just a big knot of

questions with ambiguous answers. When do you fight back? Why?

How? I don't see a clear answer, but now that the war has started we

have to see it through. All I know is that all the wrong people will have

to give too much for it to end. Your siblings might be grown up before

you can find your way back and if you don't you'll only be a memory or

a distance thought."

"We're all going to come back," I whisper. Before she can say

something more I turn over.

I only find a couple hours of sleep before there is a banging on

the door.

"Get dressed, we're leaving soon," Bear shouts through the door.

"I guess when this place empties out you actually can get some

privacy," Azalea says as I walk across the floor to my clothes.

I smile in response, trying not to think of last night's

conversation and start to dress myself. I take my time not wanting to leave the room. I feel happy and sad about this moment. A great moment, but it's only a moment. I know when I walk out the door all that waits for me is cold water and spilled blood. Azalea's eyes watching me with curiosity as I pull my shirt over my head. As it slides past my eyes Azalea appears next to me with a blanket loosely wrapped around her. She leans in and kisses me one more time. Before pulling away she whispers in my ear. "You have to come back," is all she says before she returns to the cot and I leave without a word. I feel less confident with each step.

When I open the door Bear is there to greet me with a smile beneath his beard. When he sees the serious look on my face his smile fades. For once it is my turn to be moody. We don't talk the whole way to the airlock. Hobbes has already assembled our gear there. I start to put on my vest when Bear finally speaks to me.

"How about breakfast?" he asks me.

"Nope," I say.

"Take this, eat it now or later," he tosses me a grain bar. "Last one. And you will be needing the energy for today."

I eat it despite the feeling of my stomach being filled with rocks and saltwater. I adjust my vest in an attempt to reduce the feeling, but it doesn't help. Grace and Wolf arrive as I finish. They mumble tired *hellos* and begin to go through their things. Paul and Dylan arrive a short while later. Dylan stretches and cracks his body several times.

"You're welcome, Sam," he says with a grimace.

"Thanks," I say.

"So that's a yes," Dylan says, jabbing Paul in the side. They both laugh.

"Hush up you two," Grace says. "Keep it together. Today will be tough enough without two kids making dick jokes all day. You need to be men until the job is done."

After that no one speaks while we finish preparing ourselves. I'm grateful that no one is pretending to be in good spirits. Last nights conversation continues to run through my head and I find myself mouthing the words as they pass through my thoughts. It makes it difficult to gather myself as I float between the past and the task at hand.

I had already slung on my harpoon gun and plasma rifle and was struggling to find a spot to put my fireballs. My hands search for any kind of pocket to put them in until the vest rips one out of my hands and it holds just above my hip. I grab at it and it pulls off with ease. I put it back and add the other two. Paul has figured it out as well and has started jumping up and down to test out whether or not they would stay on their own. They don't wobble in the slightest. Paul lets out an approving *Sweet.* By now everyone else had also figured it out. We were all getting our O2 masks and cylinders on when Hobbes comes running down the hall.

"Wait," he tries to yell while running. "There is something you all need to see. Come with me now."

We dropped the O2 equipment, but bring everything else with us to the lab. Fortunately he had installed a large screen that can get a live feed from his equipment so we didn't have to cram into the monitor room. But instead of an outside shot of the library Astor is on the screen.

"Men, Women and children of Empire," he starts. "This message has been recorded and is set to repeat for the next twenty four hours. Currently, outside my very door men sent by our government and ONE are trying to come and stop me before I can deliver this message." Sweat pours down his face, as he goes to wipe it away the sound of a door being slammed on causes him to whimper. "I don't know how long I have so I will be brief with you all. Over the past years I have been held as a captive, forced to lie to all of you poor souls. Do not trust them, they only need you for the labor that this city survives on so they can continue to live in luxury. While you squabble for slop they eat food you've never seen or heard of. Their lies of us all being one and coming together to make it through tough times is a lie. Each and every day has only been made worse for all of you. I have desired to be the real voice of the people and it seems when I finally have found the courage the moment will be short lived. You must come to realize that you are all individuals, we are one and many all at once. I urge you beautiful people of Empire to take what you deserve, rise, rise!"

His face flushes red and he wipes his face again, then starting again more quietly he says, "rise to join the man who will lead you to a better future, a better order and a better world. He is the true savior. Join Jack, the leader of the rebel forces!" As he finishes the sound of a door caving in comes from somewhere in the room. "No, please!" he cries out.

He raises his hands to protect his face. It doesn't do much to slow the plasma fire that cuts him down until all that remains of him resembles nothing more than a human sized piece of coal. After a moment the screen goes to black and Astor's sweaty face returns and he starts again. Hobbes turns off the screen and throws the control to the table and slams his hands down on the table.

"He beat us to it," he says. "He's following the plan, but he's changing it to suit his needs. Now they will think any help we give has come from him."

"Bitch," Wolf states.

"Indeed," Hobbes remarks.

"So what do we do now?" I ask the room.

"Jack won't burn Astor's propaganda machine like we would have," Hobbes says. "He'll need to keep sending out recordings like this. We have to get in there so we can send out our own message, take the equipment and destroy whatever we can't carry. We have much more to worry about now. Now it's time for you all to go."

Hobbes walks with us to the airlock rattling off a list of items and their descriptions, the equipment we would need to start our own machine if need be. At least if we had one ours would share the truth.

Before I get a hold of my O2 Hobbes pulls me aside and we walk to the other end of the hall. "If you run into Jack out there I want you to kill him before anyone else has the chance to," He says. "I know this request makes me quite the hypocrite. I always asked Jack to use less violent methods and now I'm asking for his head."

"You're asking for me to take a life now?" I ask. "I thought that you were still against that idea. What happens to Madison and their kid after Jack is dead?"

"I know," Hobbes stammers. "Did I not just say that? I know what I've said in the past. I just want you specifically, to take this life before Bear has to and before Jack has caused too much harm. And in regard to the other matter, Madison has locked herself away with her child. She doesn't know what we plan to do, but I doubt she would protest, considering she refused to leave with Jack. They will be taken care of though."

"All right," is all I can say to Hobbes. The idea of being the one to kill Jack is a shock. I never thought I would have to be responsible for the words I spoke earlier.

CHAPTER TWELVE

As I walk back everyone else is already in the airlock, buzzing with impatience. Dylan actually bounces on his heels in rhythm with my steps. I quickly throw my O2 mask on and heave the tank over my shoulders and take my place between Paul and Dylan as the door begins to shut. Before the water fills all the way Wolf already has his hands on the latch. As soon as we are submerged he is out into the open. He hovers over the hole with a harpoon at the ready as we pop out one by one.

"Hurry," he says through his mask. "There are plenty of people floating around that I would prefer not to see."

As I come through the hole it becomes obvious that Empire has seen a lot in only two short days of war. The water is thick with oil and blood. Shadows of dead bodies float in the distance. Clouds of red mist follow them, making the water murkier. Several sharks and skulls can be seen cleaning up the mess. Large black scars pepper the ground below us and nearby towers. Two more submarines lay dormant and have landed on some of the lower towers. Their sides are blown outward instead of in.

"Maybe he's using suicide bombers now" Grace coldly states.

Wolf looks at her and then Bear, shakes his head and moves out. It seems like we might have missed the entire war. There is no one else to be seen as we make our way through the silent carnage. Even the scavengers have disappeared. The sun no longer cuts through the water to light up the ocean floor. The metallic smells of the fight leak into my mask. I can't find a single thing that has gone untouched.

As we cross the vacant space between the library and the America Tower a floating body emerges from a cloud of grease and into our path. It bumps into Paul and he panics, becoming tangled in its O2 tubes. I manage to cut him loose after calming him down. I push the body and as it floats away, the mutilated face that once belonged to a man stares back at me. I would have reacted exactly as Paul did if that face were only inches from mine. The body seems to wave goodbye as one arm wheels above its head. As it nears a pile of rubble, a pair of long white tentacles snake out, grabbing it by the same arm and slowly pull it into the shadow.

Despite all the predators in the water, none of them seem to think we are worth their time, during our short trip to the base of the tower. During war it seems that they can afford to be lazy. The longer this continues the fatter they will grow. A shiver of sharks swims past us without notice. Pieces of tube and flesh hang from their jaws. The more I see of the floating dead the more I wonder how long this can continue. How many people could even be left? For all I know the fighting could be over, or this could just be a fraction of the damage, but I doubt either side would give up so easily. When we near the tower we have yet to see a single living person. Wolf brings us to a halt with an upraised hand and we conceal ourselves behind a large part of hull that fell from a submarine.

"That was all very delightful," Wolf says as we settle in. "My thought is we swim up through from the very bottom of the tower instead of scaling the outside."

"I don't want you to be in charge anymore," Grace says. "Sure we won't be seen that way, but seriously?"

"It'll wash off," Wolf says.

"Excuse me," Dylan says. "What is going to wash off?"

"Shit," Grace grumbles. "Shit is going to wash off. We're going to the lower, unused levels of the tower. Back in the day when you flushed it went down into the unused floors. When the windows all broke that wasn't possible anymore, but the stairs and shafts for the lifts are still filled."

"How many levels do we have to go through like that?" I ask.

"Most of the them until we near the deadline," Grace says.

"Delightful," Paul mimics Wolf's harsh voice.

We enter the building with Wolf at the front. The bottom level starts out wide, but narrows quickly and bottlenecks us. Everyone else tries to push to the back of the pack. When we arrive at the stairwell I find myself on Wolf's heels. For now the water seems fine and I try to tell myself it can't be that bad, but as we get to the ninth or tenth level the water starts to take on a brown hue. Wolf stops us as the water becomes murkier. He hands me a thin rope.

"Tie it around you and pass it on," he says.

As I hand it back to Grace she grumbles loudly. Paul and Dylan make a similar noise in agreement. Bear just takes the last bit of rope and remains silent. As we continue our ascent Wolf becomes a shadow and then disappears altogether. Eventually, only his kicking feet can be seen.. The water gets thicker and each pull with my arm becomes more strained.

"Why can't they just flush this into the open water?" Dylan gags.

" I suppose they do now that all the towers are filled like this," Grace tells him. "And now that most of the windows are blown out they can't store it anyway. It's just that no one ever bothered to clean out the stairs."

"Well it is a crappy job," Wolf says from somewhere in front of me.

He chuckles to himself for a bit. No one else laughs as the water continues to feel more like slop. At some point I close my eyes and simply feel my way up the stairs. It's easy until the water becomes so thick that we have to walk. I'd still rather look at the blackness of my closed eyelids instead of the brown cloud I'm forcing my way through. Just as the smell starts to leak through my mask there's a tug on the rope from in front of me. I look up from my feet and see that the water has cleared and the deadline is just above us. Wolf is already out of the water and he is pulling me out. I begin to untie myself as I set my feet on the stairs.

When Grace gets out after me she rips off her wetsuit and all of her gear and jumps back into the clear water before everyone else has had a chance to get out. She scrubs herself violently. "Disgusting!" she yells out as she stomps up and out of the water. Everyone else follows her lead. I still don't feel clean enough to touch my own face by the time I get out.

"What's wrong Sam?" Wolf says. "You basically bathed in water like that your whole life."

"Yeah I know," I say. "That's why I stopped bathing."

"Tough stuff," Wolf says. "I say we stay in the stairs, we'll be less likely to run into someone that way."

"Agreed," Bear says as he emerges from the water.

We leave the O2 tanks and masks along with the harpoon guns and start our climb. By the time we've already gone up twenty levels my thighs ache. With each grueling step my rifle strap pulls harder on my shoulder. I start to switch it from side to side every few flights.

"How close are we?" I eventually ask.

Paul pulls out his wrist map and we all take a seat while we wait to hear. As he scans the specifications for the building everyone's heavy breathing sounds off erratically. It's comforting to know I'm not the only one that needs a break. Finally, Paul looks up from his wrist with a smile.

"Just up to the next door," he says.

"Let's sit here a moment longer so we can be ready to move when we go in," Bear suggests.

No one argues and Paul takes a seat on the stairs next to me. We rest our heads against the cool wall. I even close my eyes for a while until Wolf nudges me. He hands me a container of water and I take a generous gulp before passing it down. When it comes back up I take another swig before handing it back. By now everyone's breathing has calmed and Bear is already standing. We seem ready.

We all get up and take the remaining steps in stride. My legs still resist, but the burning sensation has left them. Wolf gets to the next-door first and is already peering through it as I take the last step. He reaches back a hand signaling for me to duck. When I do everyone behind me crouches down wherever they are on the stairs. Then Wolf raises three fingers, closes his fist and raises five.

"Three by five," Grace whispers. "So we have fifteen guys on just this level."

"Now there's thirty," comes a familiar hollow voice from above.

Boots stomp down the stairs towards us and before we can start our guns there is one so far in my nose that the plasma wouldn't have to travel far to fry my brain. We all give up our weapons and our hands are bound behind us. They start to march us up the stairs. Chrysler stands above us on the next flight with his ever-growling mask on. His arms are folded across his chest and in one hand he has a coiled rubber cable with some wires poking out of the end.

"Get them moving," he shouts.

The soldier behind me shoves me in the back and I fall at Chrysler's feet. I try to get up, but can't with my arms behind my back. As I roll to my back and try to sit up Chrysler steps on my chest and lashes me across the legs with the cable.

"Don't fall again," he says pulling me up by the vest.

I start up the next set of stairs while the soldier continues to prod my back with his muzzle. We take the corner of the next platform. Grace is taking up the rear. She stops in front of Chrysler and spits on his mask.

"Nice to see you again, pretty boy," she laughs.

"I missed you too," he says before whipping her in the face.

She cries out and falls down with her knees and forehead supporting her. Blood pours from the gash just below her eyes. Chrysler kicks her in the stomach and she slams into the railing. Wolf struggles with his handler in response. He kicks out the soldier's knee, the snap echoes up the steps. The other two subdue him quickly. One takes the butt of their gun to his face and he stops his struggle. They pick him up by the arms and start to drag him up the stairs by his armpits.

Bear looks back at Wolf and one of the three soldiers watching him jabs him harder. His face tenses and he glares over his shoulder at the man that poked him. "I hope you don't care much for your face," he says. And the man let's him turn for a moment to check on his brother.

"Smart move," Chrysler says from below as he pulls Grace to her feet.

We are herded up one more flight of stairs before being shoved through a door and into a level filled with electrical equipment. Men and women run about, busily moving large pieces of electronics and massive tangles of cord. They are all wearing the same white uniforms. Most of them scurry out of our way as we are forced through the chaos. One man trips on a rogue cable and falls into our path, causing us to stop. The soldier leading me along pushes him out of the way with his foot. The man cries out an apology and hurries to go about his business.

As we make our way through the heart of the propaganda machine I realize that we are headed towards a large room with glass walls. Inside is a large table with several beat up chairs. Jack is standing at the end of it. He is going over a map with several other men. They nod in approval as he continues to talk and sweep his hand wide in a grand gesture. Jack sees us as we draw closer and with the wave of his hand the men with him leave.

Chrysler is the first one in. "Found these assholes in the stairs playing with their shit," he says.

"Thank you Chrysler," Jack says. "Now wait outside."

"But," he protests.

"And close the door, thank you," Jack tells him. Chrysler slams the door as he leaves and the whole wall shudders. Jack waits for it to stop before he addresses us. "My friends," he says with distaste. "I see you saw my message. At least I assume that's why you came here. But more specifically why are you here so heavily armed? You know the broadcast was my doing."

No one speaks and Jack's calculating eyes scan over us. He takes a seat in the chair behind him and crosses his legs. I start to sweat and a bead trails down my spine. Outside Chrysler impatiently paces along the glass wall nearest us. After a few minutes Jack waves Chrysler in. He goes straight to Grace, kicking her in the back of the knee. She drops to the floor and he punches her in the back of the head. She crumples, going completely limp.

"You know why we're here," Bear shouts.

"Yes, I do," Jack says. "It's just nice to hear it from a pal. I honestly thought you would have waited longer. This war has only just begun. Why not let the ranks thin a bit longer?"

"Well, we have obviously come here because of your broadcast," Bear says. "We couldn't let you continue this path."

"And what then?" Jack leans forward in the chair, slamming his arms on the table. "My army just disbands and you take out Carnegie all on your own and then his patrollers and ONE just give up? No you need me for now. However, I don't need any of you. In fact, it's becoming apparent that I would have gotten along fine without you all along. I might have even done this a year or two earlier. You fools would have had me wait until my hair thinned and greyed," he motions at Chrysler again. "They're yours."

Chrysler starts by dragging Grace out of the room by her bound hands. He drops her limp body just outside the door. As he does the soldiers from before come to take us away. Both Grace and Wolf are carried in front of us as we are led back to the stairs. This time we go down one flight. The level is riddled with plasma burns and dead patrollers lie everywhere. Equipment still smolders here and there. There are also a few people dressed in their formerly all white uniforms. They lay face down with their hands restrained and burn marks in the back of their heads. We are careful not to step on any of the bodies as we shuffle past them. At the center of the level there is a wide, charred body tied to a column. *Silence is Golden* is written beneath it. I safely assume the body is Astor's.

"You should have heard him cry before we set him up for that last broadcast," one of the soldiers says.

"Oh good for you killing a defenseless, fat man," Dylan says.

The same soldier claps him over the head, "We're about to kill you too, Sally."

Dylan goes white without a counter and we keep walking. They stop us at the edge of the building where most of the windows have already been broken out. The floor near the edge is soaked red. They tell us to get on our knees and look out the window. The ground is still wet. Everyone else fades from my mind. Paul whimpers as he's forced to the ground. I look out at the few closest towers and try to remember their names. The too familiar sound of plasma guns buzzes behind me and I close my eyes to ready myself for the scorching impact in the back of my head.

"Can't say I'll miss you guys too much," Chrysler says.

Dylan cries out first and the smell of burning flesh enters my nostrils. Before he hits the floor the lift lets out a soft ding in the background. Chrysler and the soldiers stop and wait to see who is coming. I open my eyes and see Dylan writhing in pain on the ground. They only shot him in the back.

"This wasn't part of the deal," comes a raspy voice. "I get first crack at the prisoners."

"Haven't we given you enough Caldwell," Chryslers says to the voice. "Besides these ones are different, they're for me."

"Oh, well I like the sound of different," Caldwell says. "Give them to me for a few days and then you can have your fun. You don't even know how to play with your food properly. You eat to live whereas I live to eat. You can still get your meal if I leave them breathing."

I shuffle around on my knees to see Caldwell. Bear kicks my foot and mouths *no* at me. It grabs the attention of Caldwell and he slides up behind me, breathing down my neck.

"I don't think you'll find yourself so curious after a few hours with me," he whispers in my ear. He's so close his breath wets my skin. "In fact, you'll wish I'd let this fool burn your hide right now. And who's this?" he says slinking over to Bear. "Hey fuzzy buddy, you still mad about your pop pop? I hope you won't cry again"

Bear stares out the window with his jaw locked. A single tear rolls down his face and he starts to tremble. Caldwell starts to massage Bear's shoulders and Bear starts to shake wildly. Caldwell grips him even harder and throws a knee into his back. Bear lets out a low grunt but doesn't fall down.

"We'll break you yet," Caldwell hisses. "And what have you

done here," he turns his attention to a still squirming Dylan. "You shot one of my play things. Ooooh he's all crispy now. He won't be nearly as much fun. I'm going to have to tell daddy about this one."

"Just take them out of here, freak," Chrysler says.

"Says the man with the silly mask," Caldwell tsks. "All right boys pick them up and bring them to my place."

Caldwell returns to the elevator. Chrysler and the soldiers pull us to our feet and take us back to the stairs. We walk down a number of flights before we stop and at this point I'm exhausted. My feet start to drag and I almost trip once or twice on the way down. Paul's head nods in front of me. At one point he falls into the soldier in front of him. They slap him and he barely reacts. We had just all accepted our death and I can tell no one wants to do it again. So now we are defeated, even Bear's head hangs low.

When we finally stop at a door I slouch down against the wall. No one stops me and everyone else still conscious does the same. Fortunately for Wolf and Grace they are still knocked out, so they've been carried all this way. They also won't have to remember having a gun to their head.

The soldier in front slams a fist on the door several times with no response. We wait so long even Chrysler takes a seat on the stairs. "That prick has to make everyone miserable," he says. "I wish Jack had just killed the guy. *No he can be valuable*," he says in a mocking tone.

Bear looks at him, "I'll kill you, if I'm ever given the chance."

"Oh yeah," Chrysler says standing up. "I'm going to gut you with your own knife if Caldwell leaves anything left."

"Wretched little thing you are," Bear says and spits at Chrysler's feet.

Just as Chrysler reaches up to hit Bear the door slams open and Caldwell steps out with a cigar lit in his mouth. He's well dressed and his dark hair is slicked over, revealing a handsome face. Still, I can tell that he is old by the wrinkles near his eyes and the sag under his chin. Chrysler lowers his hand and heaves Bear up to his feet. They stare each other down before the descending the last few steps.

"What took you so long my friends?" Caldwell says with a smile.

"Screw off," Chrysler says. "Just take them, I'm out of here."

"Bye bye, you base creature," Caldwell's voice goes from sweet tone to a rumble. "I'll try to keep them somewhat fresh for you."

As Chrysler and his men leave the rest of us either lay or sit on the floor. Caldwell walks across the pristine, white room and takes a seat in a bright and heavily cushioned chair. Next to him is a glossy, wooden table with a half-filled glass of brown liquid resting on it. After a puff of his cigar he picks it up and takes a loud slurping sip. He loudly yawns with his mouth wide open as he sets the glass back down.

"You know before this silly conflict started just two days ago I was one of five people in all of Empire that could afford liquor," Caldwell says. "Have any of you even heard of what this is?" he swishes the liquid around. After no one responds he continues. "Well my new friends maybe if you play nice I will give you some. But you'll have to be on your very best behavior because I have very little left and there may never be any again and soon there will be very little left of you. No," he pauses and swishes it around. "I won't be sharing then."

He finishes what is left in the glass and lets out another obnoxious sigh and slouches down in the chair spreading his legs wide. His shoes squeak as they slide across the floor. Once he is comfortable he closes his eyes. I decide to do the same and before long I fall asleep on the cold floor.

CHAPTER THIRTEEN

I wake up to the sensation of my leg being tugged on and the sound of Caldwell's raspy voice. He is saying something about me being heavy as he hoists me into the air by one leg, the other dangles uselessly. I try to move as my head scrapes across the ground but my body doesn't react and my vision is blurred. When the jostling stops, my vision focuses on an upside down Caldwell.

He has changed clothes since I fell asleep. Most of what he's wearing is shiny and black. His hair is still slicked back and he is smoking another cigar. He blows smoke in my face as he spins me around, slapping my thighs and stomach. Everyone but Bear is hanging sporadically throughout the room. My eyes finally find Bear on the floor, tied to a chair.

"Early to bed, early to rise," Caldwell says while licking my ear.

He spins me again, causing me to hurl. Caldwell shushes me while he wipes off my face and gives me a swig of water. I swish it around in my mouth and spit it out at him. It misses completely but still gets his attention.

"What bad manners," he says. "Do it again and I'll pull out your teeth and tongue."

By now the others are starting to stir. Wolf and Grace both let out shouts of surprise as they finally become aware of our situation. Caldwell takes delight in spinning all of us around as he prances through the room. He cackles as Paul and Grace also puke. Caldwell cleans them up but doesn't give them any water.

"I've woken up in stranger situations," Wolf says.

Caldwell approaches Wolf. "You and your brother both know we're far from strange," he says. "You know I like to take things slow my dearest fuzzy wuzzy."

Caldwell grabs Wolf's face and shakes it furiously. Both of their faces flush red. Caldwell hits Wolf in the stomach several times until he is gasping for air. As this happens Bear starts to frantically shake in his chair. It wobbles and scrapes against the ground leaving dark marks on the otherwise clean floor.

"Are you both so eager for my attention?" Caldwell says. "You must stay patient there will be plenty of time for me to get to everyone. But if you insist I can start with you, Bear."

Caldwell walks over to the small table next to his chair. The glass has been replaced with a small metal tray. On it there are six syringes and a pair of gloves. He starts by pulling each glove over his hands, loudly snapping them as he does. Afterward he takes both hands and interlaces his fingers. The gloves squeak as he wiggles them together, pushing out small pockets of air. Then, picking out a single syringe he strolls over to Bear. Caldwell straddles him as he continues to struggle and shout, but the restraints are too much for Bear to push him off.

"My, what beautiful veins you have for me," Caldwell says as he plunges the needle into Bear's arm.

Bear's struggling slows and eventually he goes limp and his eyes glaze over and roll back. Caldwell, still on top of him, says something to him that can't be made out. As he gets up, Bear starts to sweat and moan. His hands squeeze the arms of his chair so tightly that it starts to creak.

Caldwell backhands Bear and the squeezing stops. The moaning gets louder until Bear is screaming.

"No, don't touch him," he yells. "Let my dad go, he isn't a rebel!"

Caldwell starts to whistle and smile as he retrieves the remainder of the syringes. He comes to me first, I try to lift my arms up away from him, but he calmly grabs my face and stabs the needle into my neck. The liquid burns through my muscles, but chills me at the same time. Beads of sweat form almost instantly, rolling off my forehead and falling to the floor.

"I'm coming for them all," Caldwell tells me. "I'd love for you to see it."

His voice resounds in my head until it's all that is there. The sensation of hanging and the pounding in my head leaves me. The sound of Paul screaming brings a flicker of my senses back before everything goes dark.

The first thing I hear is Lily's voice. She's crying and trying to wake me up. I sit up and my blood rushes from my head. I lay back down to keep from passing out, but Lily won't stop crying so I force myself up.

She still won't calm down. She points and continues to sob heavily. Words try to escape between each wail. Nothing makes sense as she wails and snot starts to run down her face. I use a blanket to wipe off her face and pick her up. We leave our cube and she continues to point the way. As we continue to follow her directions the floor becomes whiter and the level gets brighter. The cubes start to spread out and eventually fall away. Even though I'm going where Lily wants to, the tears keep falling.

Eventually we leave the cubes behind and there is nothing but open white space. Somehow the far side of the level is still out of view. The light becomes blinding as I continue to follow my sister's finger, until I can barely see where I'm putting my feet. I raise a hand to my forehead. Several figures come into view in the distance. Quickening my pace I slip, almost dropping Lily to the floor. She clings tightly around my neck as I lean over to see what has made a mess on the spotless tiles. A small dot takes shape next to my foot and I run my hand through it. The spot smears and feels warm on my. I turn it over and see that my hand has turned red.

Panicking, I try to wipe it off on my pants, but it only smudges and spreads. I forget about my hand and keep moving only to slip again and find several more spots. Eventually the spots become puddles and as I reach the figures my feet splash on the ground with every step. There are six people ahead. Five of them are sitting and one is standing in the middle as though he might be talking to them like members of an audience. I join the circle and I'm delighted to see Azalea, my mother and all my siblings. Even Lily has taken a seat. The man in the middle has his back to me. He's dressed in white and muttering to himself. I ignore him and run to my mom to talk to her.

She acts as if I'm not even there and stares blankly at the man. Everyone else reacts similarly to my presence. As I circle around the chairs the man continues to keep his back to me. When I move towards him he drops his hands to his sides and stops muttering. Blood drips from his fingertips onto the floor and I remember the puddle. I hesitate and look back to Azalea and see that she is covered in blood. Her clothes are soaked and cling to her. They feel sticky when I pull on them to look for signs of cuts. It doesn't make any sense. Why are they covered in blood? I try to pull them out of the chairs, but they won't even look at me as I yank on their arms and shout in their faces.

Adrenaline and panic take over and I start to shout at Alison and shake her. The only response is the loll of her head. It eventually falls forward and rests there. I give up on them and charge towards the man in the center of it all. Just as I reach for his shoulder to turn him around he spins on his heels to face me. Caldwell stands before with blood spattered down his front. In his hands is Lily's stuffed toy. It is soaked red and ripped along the neck and arms. Grinning Caldwell hands it to me and lets out a high pitch chuckle.

"I really wish you could have seen it," he says. "But teddy did and he can tell you everything you missed."

When I look up from the toy he is walking away and the chairs are empty. I shout for him to wait and run after him. At the edge of the circle my foot thuds instead of slapping in the puddle and it sticks. I pull as hard as I can to release myself and catch Caldwell. After each tug my foot sinks further into the floor. When the blood reaches my waist hands start tugging at my legs. Six pairs tug until my pants rip and they start to slide down the skin of my leg. They pull harder until they use nails to get more purchase on my flesh. When it is up to my shoulders Lily's head floats to the top of the blood, completely dry.

"I really wish you could have seen it," she says. Then she grabs me by the hair and pulls me under.

A splash of salt water to my face pulls me out of the dream. It startles and chokes me momentarily. It takes a few seconds to remember where I am. Caldwell is staring at me upside down again. He looks like he is taking notes in his head as he tilts it to the side with a look of intrigue.

"Was it really so bad?" he asks me.

The only response he gets is panicked breathing. My dry mouth barely opens enough for air to pass through my lips. The rest of me hangs loosely without answering any thoughts to move. The images from the injection are still leaving their mark on my brain. Caldwell loses interest and goes through the rest of the room, splashing water on everyone. Eventually the cries of anguish come to a halt. Bear is the only one that doesn't get splashed. He is already awake, looking drained and breathing heavily. His shirt is ripped in several spots and his face is swollen. Blood trickles out of every orifice and his eyes are bruised and puffy. I continue to coax my limbs to move in an attempt to grab his attention, but I'm unable to take command and barely twitch.

When he sees me looking at him he tries to smile, but only manages to widen his lips before cringing in pain. In the mean time Caldwell continues to inspect every one of us that hangs from his ceiling. He grabs faces, spins us and hums to himself the entire time. After awhile he comes back to me.

"I suppose you've all been hanging long enough," he tells me. "It wouldn't hurt if I were to let you down before you pop and spill all over my nice floor. We haven't finished our play date yet and they won't be sending someone to clean up just yet and I do sincerely hate a mess."

He pulls out a knife and cuts the rope around my ankle. I try again to move in order to catch myself as my head and shoulder crashes into the floor. The fall sends me sprawling out on my back and the pressure that has built up behind my eyes slowly recedes. Four thuds follow and Wolf tries to get up. He stumbles and lunges for Caldwell, but he easily side steps Wolf and kicks him to the floor. While his back is turned Grace tries the same thing. She grabs his legs only to be struck in the face with his knee. Both of them were merely able to flail wildly, far from in complete control. Then both Grace and Wolf lay there exhausted.

"I was going to allow a short reprieve, but it would seem some of you don't quite realize the rules of this game," Caldwell says. "Let me remind you that it is I who decides who gets hurt."

With a menacing grin he stomps down on Grace's arm. She wails as the bones in her arm crunch and splinter out of her skin. Blood splatters across Caldwell. He wipes off his forehead into his hair, slicking it down further. He inhales deeply through his nose, a look of delight slides across his face. He leaves Grace to writhe on the floor in pain and grabs Wolf by the neck, dragging him across the tiles. He throws him down next to Dylan whose back is still splotched with burns from his botched execution.

Caldwell quietly walks to the far end of the room and taps the wall as he approaches it. A solid white rectangle lights up and a drawer slides out. Metal gently clatters as he thumbs through the contents. Every few seconds he places a chrome object in one of his pockets and he starts to whistle again. When he finishes he taps the wall to the side of the drawer and it shoots back into the wall and the light slowly fades, leaving no evidence that it was ever there.

He returns to us, still whistling and attends to Dylan first, tying him back up to the ceiling. Dylan lets out a low moan as he is jostled and hoisted into the air. He moves on to Grace who is now rolling on her back clutching her arm. He drags her closer to Wolf, stopping a few feet away. As he does Wolf props himself up and manages to sit upright on the floor. At this point all I can manage is to turn my head to see what's happening. Caldwell digs deep into his pockets. His hand knocks around the tools, creating a muffled sound of metal on metal until he finally pulls out two objects. He tosses one to Wolf. Caldwell has just given him a particularly sharp set of scissors. Wolf grabs it off the floor as it skitters towards him. His eyes light up and clear, but before he can stand up Caldwell has the scissors to Grace's ear.

"We're going to play a nice quiet game now Wolf," he says. "I like to call it mirror, because you will do exactly as I do. For example I will cut," he waves the scissors around Grace's face. "Her hair," he finally says as he snips off a lock of hair. "Now you will cut some of your hanging friend's hair.

Wolf drops the scissors to the floor in defiance. Caldwell says nothing but slowly slices off a sliver of Grace's ear. As he does she feebly claws at him, with both her broken and unbroken arm. As he goes to cut again Wolf quickly picks up his own pair. He uses Dylan's hanging body to pull himself up before he cuts off some hair.

"What next?" Wolf asks.

Caldwell simply taps Grace's still bleeding ear. Wolf's tired body sags further as he grabs Dylan's head and cuts off part of his ear lobe. Dylan's eyes crack open and he starts to thrash wildly as he momentarily comes back to a full state of consciousness. He grabs Wolf's vest and starts screaming with a savage look on his face.

"Why, why, why, why did you, did you do that?" Dylan stammers.

Wolf's eyes fill with tears, but he doesn't respond. Eventually Dylan let's go and fades back into his unaware self. Wolf faces Caldwell, the chromed scissors now smeared with blood. Caldwell smiles and takes another turn at twirling the scissors around Grace's head.

"How about here?" he asks Wolf as he taps Grace's pointer finger from her broken arm.

Wolf says nothing as tears now roll down his face. The scissors hang loosely in his fingers as his unresponsive body slumps back to the floor. He grips them more tightly as Grace's finger is quickly sheared off. This time she doesn't fight, she collapses at Caldwell's feet staring up at him with a wide-eyed lifeless look. Wolf's fingers turn white as he clenches his hand around the grip. He snags Dylan's hand and quickly chops off a finger. Dylan screams again for a moment but his reaction is less than before. Blood is now spattered across the floor. It continues to drip from Dylan's hand and the scissors in Wolf's.

"I just realized," Caldwell says as he taps his own bloody scissors on his cheek. "His arm isn't broken like hers is. Lower him and stomp on his arm until it looks like this one."

He lifts Grace's arm up and then lets it flop back down to the floor. It creates a sickening smack as the shattered mess lands on the ground. A small puddle of blood is starting to take shape around her arm. Her face has gone completely white and her chest slowly rises and falls as she lies on her back.

Wolf hesitates until Caldwell hunches over and puts another finger between his blades. Then Wolf carefully attempts to cut the rope holding Dylan, but cannot reach. Caldwell does it for him with a considerate demeanor and Dylan's limp body falls to the floor in a tangle of limbs. Dylan is completely unresponsive as his arm is laid out. Wolf looks over at him with a broken sadness as a hammer is tossed into his lap. He looks at me instead of Caldwell as he drops it on my friend's arm. A small grunt comes out of Dylan that is barely audible over the sound of his arm breaking. Blood pools underneath it too quickly. Wolf reaches down to compress the wound.

"Have I helped her with her fractured arm?" Caldwell asks. "Remember, only as I do."

The color in Dylan completely drains. The pooling from his arm reaches his face and his breath create ripples in the blood. Each inhale is slower and seems to take more effort. After a few moments it stops altogether. Caldwell walks over to him, his shoes slapping right through the bloody puddle. He reaches down and touches Dylan's neck. A few seconds go by before he stands back up.

"It looks like the game has to end sooner than I had hoped," Caldwell says.

"It's already over," Wolf screeches. "He's dead, there's no point in me doing anymore to his body."

The vest starts to work as Hobbes said it would, sending shocks through Dylan's chest. His arms fan out, smearing blood across the floor and his back arches in a rigid convulsion. He flattens back onto his back with a splat. Only to be shocked twice more until the vest finally runs out of juice.

"Quite right," Caldwell smiles. "Two points for observation go to my fuzzy friend. However, you have failed to realize that whatever happened to one was supposed to happen to the other. Grace now has to bleed out."

"Stop, Please!" Wolf yells to Caldwell as he crawls after him.

But Caldwell reaches Grace before Wolf can attempt to grab his feet. Caldwell pulls out a small blade from his pocket and puts it to

Grace's neck. Instead of slicing he just rests it on her neck and watches Wolf. He studies the look of anguish on Wolf's face and then smirks. His arm starts to jerk across Grace's face as a window blows out behind me.

Caldwell's arm flies from his shoulder and lands several feet past him. He drops Grace and rolls on the ground next to her. His legs kick and his remaining arm grasps at his shoulder. He doesn't make a noise as his mouth continues to open and close in shock. Something crashes through the window and I roll over to look. A man dressed in all black with goggles on strolls towards me. A knife in one hand and a strange looking gun in the other. There is also a long thin barrel strung across his back.

He walks past me as though I'm not even there. His hair is just as dark as his clothes. He seems empty or like he's barely there. Everyone but Caldwell quietly watches as he walks by in silence. His footsteps make no sound as he crosses the room. Caldwell finally takes notice of him and starts clawing at the floor with his one arm.

"Damn you!" he shouts. "That was my favorite arm," he tries to chuckle and coughs violently. "I knew you would be coming for me eventually, but you could have at least let me finish this one last game."

The man in black continues on through the white room, toward

Caldwell without a word. Just as he reaches him, Caldwell flings a blade toward the man. He expertly catches it and tosses it aside before slamming a knee down into Caldwell's remaining arm. Caldwell curls up and screams into the man's face, his disheveled appearance now fits his crazed mind. His black hair has lost its slick look and patches of grey stick out wildly and his eyes bulge out of his blood spattered face as he continues to grin obnoxiously. The other man's face is like a statue in comparison. His jaw is shut tightly and his eyes hold steady as he plunges his knife deep into the middle of Caldwell's chest. Caldwell grabs the hilt and hisses into the man's face.

"Why don't you smile just once when you kill someone," he croaks. "If for anyone, why not me, Emmett? Let me see those pretty... white... pearls...boy"

"How about some lead for yours?" Emmett finally speaks.

He stands up and slides back the top of his dark grey gun. It snaps back into place with a click. Each time he pulls the trigger the top slides back and forth, ejecting a small cylinder of metal. The gun cracks like thunder with each squeeze and the sound is deafening. Each shot goes directly into Caldwell's mouth, causing his head to bounce up and down with each hit. Blood starts to spatter across the room as the face of a dead man becomes more mutilated. Then there is nothing but a click as Emmett's finger twitches on the trigger one last time. He calmly presses on the side of the gun and a thin metal brick falls out and clacks to the floor. A new one quickly replaces it before Emmett jams his gun back into its holster.

From one of his vest pockets he then produces a small white bandage, which he softly presses onto Grace's arm as he kneels next to her. Blood quickly saturates it and he stacks another on top of it. Then with his free hand he tapes it down before firmly tying a cloth around it. She doesn't react, but her chest still rises and falls in a steady rhythm. As he continues to treat the wounds on her Wolf comes from behind him.

"Thank you," he says with an outreached hand.

Wolf stumbles and the hand brushes the shoulder of Emmett. Without hesitation Emmett grabs the hand and twists Wolf's arm. Emmett's eyes give a hint of the savage instinct that lies behind them. And just as quickly he lets Wolf go. Wolf falls to his knees clutching his wrist. His puzzled look catches Emmett's attention.

"I'm sorry," he tells Wolf. "I don't react well to being touched. Also, you should know that I'm not here, specifically for your sake. You're just lucky I wanted Caldwell dead more than anyone in this city.

And once I've splinted your friends arm I will be leaving you here."

"If you're looking for Astor he's pretty well done already," Bear's voice comes out gravely and weak.

"Ah that belly of a man," Emmett says as he cinches down another cloth over Grace's splint. "Don't worry I get the news. No, I'm here for some of my belongings and of course, this chucklehead." He kicks Caldwell's leg as he gets off his haunches. He pulls out his still bloodied knife and walks over to Bear to cut his restraints. Bear leans out of the chair and controls a fall to the floor as he sprawls out. He mouths *thank you* as his bones crack while his back is allowed some relief from the pressure of being tightly tied to a chair. At the same time Wolf has managed to cut Paul down from the ceiling. Just like me, he seems unable to move much. I roll my head back over to Emmett and he gives me a curt nod as he makes to leave. Before he can take more than a couple steps I call out to him.

"That was you before, right?" I say as a mixture of a statement and question. "You saved us in Empire Tower a couple months ago. Why?

"When you can all walk you will want to go down two flights and find the sky bridge to the Condé Nast Tower," he says.

303

Without another word he noiselessly heads to the door. He opens it with a creak and slides into the stairwell. As it swings back to close Bear starts to get up. He approaches the wall and begins to swipe his large hands across it until the panel gives off its glow and opens to reveal Caldwell's collection of blades. He grabs several large knives and leaves the drawer. He hands a serrated knife to Wolf. He grasps it firmly and quickly tosses the shears across the room. At this point I find myself at least able to sit up. I manage to scoot along the ground to the chair Bear was in and pull myself into it. My vision blurs from the strain and the room seems to tilt. For a moment darkness closes in around my eyes and everything is muffled. I drop my head to my knees when it becomes too much. When it is over I'm left with the sensation of the back of my head floating up and away from my face. Before I get lost in the euphoric feeling Bear kicks my foot and hands me the third knife.

"It's time for you to start walking," he says. "I promise you there is no other way out of here."

I push myself up and out of the chair before taking the knife. My legs wobble like a child just learning to walk. Still they somewhat listen and allow me to stagger forward. The light feeling in the back of my head passes and is replaced with more of an ache down the center of my skull. I'm glad for the pain to be there, it helps me stay centered. Paul doesn't seem as lucky, still lying on the floor with a drooping face. Bear simply points at him as he walks past towards the door. I take my cue to pick him up as Wolf slaps Grace awake and pulls her to her feet. She slouches into his shoulder and hip, struggling to drive each foot forward. I try to do the same with Paul, but he can't even throw an arm over my shoulder. I crouch down and heave his torso over my shoulders. His body flops wildly before I can get a firm grasp on him and he almost spills over me. With each step towards the door he bounces and moans. A line of spittle falls down my vest.

"Just don't puke on me Paul," I say. "I really don't need that right now."

He groans louder and I tell myself it means he won't. Bear holds the door open for all of us as we shuffle through. We start down the stairs. It takes all my concentration to keep myself from falling forward. Sweat fills the inside of my vest as I struggle with Paul's limp body. Before I've made it one level down and Bear is already prying open a door below. Shouting and plasma fire starts up and I pause, but I don't bother to stop completely. Even if Bear is dead there's no point going back. Without him we're not getting out of here. Neither Wolf nor I can carry someone and fight at the same time, especially without a gun.

At the top of the last flight is a bloody Bear leaning against the door. Inside two men lay dead. One still has Bear's knife in his chest. Wolf steps over and lifts Grace with him. Bear slides one of them out of the way for me as we come through the door. His vest smolders from one of the few shots they got off.

"My knife is stuck," Bear says as he reaches out his hand.

I fill it with mine and take a better grip on Paul. As I do his hands grasp the straps on my vest. It sparks a hope that he'll be able to walk soon. Other than us and the bodies the level appears to be empty. The door to every room is wide open and the inside of each has been thoroughly ransacked. Either Jack's soldiers did this or Astor destroyed as much as he could before being taken.

Ahead, Wolf turns left, following a sign that reads **Condé** with an arrow through it. Bear runs ahead to lead the way. I try to speed up so that I don't get lost. When I turn the corner the bridge is right there with Bear already at the mouth of it. The beginning of it looks like a whirlpool, but with a wider, open bottom, large enough to walk through. The glass almost seems stretched as the bridge closes in more tightly at the middle. Bear sends Wolf ahead of him with a wave of his hand and beckons for me to move more quickly.

"Not much further Sam," Bear says. "But you need to move more quickly, who knows when they will notice we're gone."

I let out an exasperated grunt as I shift Paul's weight and march forward. Each step threatens to buckle my knees as my legs become stiffer. My muscles feel like stones, pumping melted steel. And a thunder roars through my head from the drugs still finding their way through my system. I crash at the edge of the bridge, still without a rebel in sight.

"All right Sam," Bear says. "I'll take him across, but you have to get up now."

He heaves Paul over one shoulder like a sack and starts off at a trot. I claw at the glass for support and regain my feet and run to catch up with him almost catching flight with my lightened load. When we reach Wolf we both slow down. Paul is still drooling down Bear's back. We take up a casual pace, each of us exhausted. Then the rattling of metal on glass overtakes the sound of our collective exhaustion and a shadow spills over me. Through the glass and several levels up, a burning window and pieces of camera equipment fall down toward us and the bridge. Two bodies fall from the window, one riding on top of the other. They hit the bridge with a vibrating bong and the head of the body on bottom pops. The blood creates a red tint over the glass, dampening the sun. Both bodies begin to slide like a roach when you crush it against a window. The man on top starts to scramble and slide at the top of the bridge. It's just possible to make out Emmett's face through smeared blood. He manages to straddle the bridge and pull out his gun.

"If that bastard shoots the glass we're all dead," Wolf says.

Instead Emmett brings down the butt of the gun between his legs. It lets out a hollow bang that resonates through the inside of the glass. He tries several more times while we watch on with intrigue. Eventually he throws up his arms in frustration. As he does, two more men appear at the window he fell from. When they start shooting we start to run. Each shot cuts through the glass and it starts to peel away from the heat.

"Well if Jack didn't know we'd gotten away yet he does now," Wolf barks as he starts into a jog, dragging Grace's feet behind him.

As we reach the end, Emmett's shadow flashes past us as he jumps from the bridge and into the window next to it. He covers his face just before he crashes through. Behind me the center of the bridge droops and the mid section melts away. A single figure, backlit by the flames, now stands at the edge of the window. I can't say for certain, but something tells me it's Jack and he's watching me. We can't go back now. At least they'll have to get creative to follow us, much less catch up.

CHAPTER FOURTEEN

When we get into the Condé Emmett is already in the hall lying on a broken down door, picking glass out of his forearm. With each piece he lets out a slight hiss. He seems altogether less indestructible with every speck of blood. Our ragtag group hobbles toward him as he gets up and shakes off what remains of the glass and ash that has collected in his hair and clothes. Other than the few scrapes on his face there is almost no sign that it took him any effort to accomplish what six others failed to do.

"I honestly never thought we would crossing paths again," Emmett remarks, kicking at pieces of broken door. "Lucky for your bunch though I guess. So what's the plan? Hobble along until you get caught, maybe poke out an eye with your cutlery."

"I think with an army now more interested in you it may be you who is lucky to have found us," Bear suggests. "I even wonder if you chose your escape with more purpose than you suggest by calling this situation happenstance."

"I'll go with that one myself," Wolf says while wagging his knife at Emmett. "And I think if anything, this hit man won't do much other than get us killed or do it himself. In fact we wouldn't have a few hundred pissed off soldiers after us right now if it wasn't for you."

Emmett still in the midst of brushing himself off and looking smug suddenly stops. He seems like a charismatic man, but he's now realizing whom he was trying to pull one over on with just wit and a smile. His attitude takes a serious change at the sound of an accusation.

"I remember saving your life mere minutes ago," Emmett fires back. "Not only that, I bandaged her up." He points at Grace. "And I have a strong feeling that I did you lot of sore asses a bigger favor than you can repay. I blew out half of Astor's equipment before I took a ride out the window. Something I would want very much if I were you, I imagine." Now he stands nose to nose with Wolf. The eyes of two trained killers sit inches from each other, begging the other to unleash the fury that waits behind.

"You still haven't answered my question," I speak up to break the stalemate. "Why have you saved me twice now? I know it was you before."

Emmett starts to answer the question still staring into Wolf's eyes. "I owe you a life debt," he says and Wolf backs down. "A long time ago your father saved my life. Before I killed for Empire I killed for anyone that still had something to pay with. One day I found myself running from a dozen or more patrollers and he hid me. I got away, but they eventually figured it out and came back for him. They used him as shark bait that same day, while I watched from two towers away. We had talked briefly and I knew he had family and where you lived. The only reason I found you is because you look so much like him." He pauses to pick out a piece of glass stuck above his eyebrow. "Months ago when I shot the twins at Empire Tower was just coincidence. I happened to be there for something else, but that explosion you idiots set off caught my attention. Today, I came looking for you. I knew you and this motley band would be coming here and the way I see it I owe your father's flesh and blood my blood until I have nothing left. It also doesn't hurt if I get what I want too."

"What do you want?" I ask.

He takes a moment to think it through, tapping his lower lip with his gloved pointer finger. "Well killing Caldwell was a nice start," he says. "Otherwise I haven't given it too much thought. I've been made to do the bidding of the government for the past three years or so. Free will has seemed like an untouchable luxury until now."

"Made to?" Wolf says in disbelief. "You seem too capable to be made to do anything. And what's this crap of not knowing what you're doing. Is this supposed to be your crusade of 'Eh, I guess I'll shoot some guys'?"

"What a bunch of overly sensitive and critical punks you all are," Emmett exclaims. "What is a life saved to you ungracious lot? For me it's my whole life for the life saved. I could have just saved Sam here and kept a clear conscience. I owe the rest of you piss." He barely breathes between words and his flush face begins to glisten with sweat. "I decide to go out on my own, save lives, help people and what do I get? Nothing, I get shit."

"Welcome to the life, prick, where the enjoyment is the job itself," Wolf says as he steps over the fallen door and starts down the hall with Grace in tow. Glass crunches under his feet and as he passes the next door, it opens and a head pokes out swiveling from Wolf then to us. The woman that belongs to the head lets out a frightened, high pitch squeak and slams the door. No one moves and Wolf looks back at us.

"Screw her," he says.

"Where are you going to get to anyway?" Emmett asks.

Wolf pauses for a second and shifts Grace's weight against his before kicking in the door to his right. "Up," he says and walks through. I push past Emmett and hurry down the hall to catch up to Wolf, whose footsteps I can already hear echoing up the stairwell.

Behind me I hear Emmett say, "there's a lift just around the corner."

"We had an incident once," is all Bear tells him.

By the time I reach Wolf he's sliding along the wall to take some of the weight off his legs. I slide my head under Grace's other arm and take over, careful not to grab her broken forearm. She is barely conscious and each step takes all of her focus. The bandage is drenched in red and a steady drip falls from her fingers. Wolf sits down at the next landing, only to start again when Emmett catches up. Bear is on his tail with Paul now leaning on Bear for support. The color has returned to his face and from below he gives me a frail smile.

After several flights of stairs our group is stretched by our respective loads and stamina. Emmett is charging ahead, taking two steps at a time with Bear a flight behind. I've taken over Paul's care and haven't seen them or Wolf, who is carrying Grace again, for a few minutes. Paul urges me to take a brief rest as we get to yet another landing. I don't argue with him or the ache in my knees. I slump down against the wall and Paul more or less collapses. We're soaked in sweat and smeared with blood. I know I can't carry Paul much further, much less myself. My body begs for sleep and my eyes want nothing more than to close. The cool, stone wall makes it easy to relax. Until the sound of Bear's voice thundering down the stairs brings me back to my feet.

"We're at the top," He shouts. "Hurry it up."

Paul resists being pulled back up to to his feet, he almost drops as his sweaty palms slide through mine. Wolf passes us, now cradling Grace in his arms. His mane of hair is soaked and flipped back over his head and face. She whispers incoherently with every struggled step Wolf takes. His eyes look vacant, yet determined. We wait a moment before following. When we reach the top we are greeted by Bear holding open a large door with Wolf sprawled out on the floor just beyond it. Grace has been laid down on a cushy sofa and Emmett is somewhere in the interior.

He calls out, "hulloo!" loudly and in an obnoxious manner, followed by a second and even louder call for anyone that might have

315

been occupying the room when we arrived. Paul and I take a seat across from Grace as Emmett comes in from another room and plops down next to me. Bear has closed the door and is wedging a large table up against it.

"So this is it?" Emmett whispers with his head lying on the back of the sofa.

'Well, we needed a place to rest and heal," Wolf says from his spot on the floor. "Jack will assume that we're still following our protocols and we've always said that going up is just about the dumbest thing you could do when on the run. So here we are, where Jack supposedly knows we're too smart to be."

"Who lives here anyway?" I ask, scanning the lavishly built level, from the clean, white walls to the sparkling ornaments that hang from the ceilings. Art similar to some of what lies in storage at the library lines the room.

"This is Astor's playroom as he called it," Emmett says. He chuckles at my gaping. "Ceilings two levels high, three bedrooms with their own baths, a kitchen and this room. A real penthouse."

"So what kind of play does Astor do here?" Bear asks.

"He would take his women here," Emmett says. "He also hosted parties, consumed just about every available mind altering substance still available to the city and hosted a number of executions.

"So you mean he had a place like this just so he could have fun?" Paul inquires. "And by fun you mean I shouldn't want to touch anything in here."

Emmett smirks at Paul, "There's a lot more space than you may ever realize. A large part of the city actually remains vacant most of the time. All the big players hold at least half of all available space. And our dear late Astor would never actually sleep in a place he deems filthy like this. He can get quite messy with his victims and his women. Sometimes they're the same thing. So he has a whole other place like this that he keeps to himself. That's were he really gets weird. I've watched him some nights."

Paul face takes on a disgusted look, but he still doesn't move from his spot on the sofa. I don't either. It's too comfortable to care what's happened to it. I would even consider living here and still not throw a single piece of furniture away. Besides my cot in the library, the only furnishings I've ever owned have been blankets. While I ponder the worth of the soiled palace Emmett relieves himself of his seat and struts off to the kitchen, quickly returning with several red orbs. He hands one to Bear before tossing one to both Paul and myself. He gently places two next to Wolf who is running his fingers through Grace's matted hair.

"For later," he tells Wolf before biting into his own. The sound it makes is a mix of a pop and a bit of suction. Liquid spills down the sides of his mouth. "Eat, they're delicious and you may never get another chance to have one the way today is going." Emmett explains.

The smooth ball of food rolls around my palm as I inspect it. Paul bites into his and I hear that same crisp crunch again. As he continues to chew his eyes bulge with delight. When Bear gives the same reaction I decide to finally take a taste. The first layer of red is harder to break through, but when I do my teeth slide right through until they meet and I pull away my first bite. Juice unexpectedly fills my mouth. It starts out sweet and as I swallow, it leaves a sour taste.

"What is this?" I ask Emmett, waving it towards him.

"This is a delicious piece of fruit." Emmett says, holding it up to his face as though he were admiring it. "This particular type just happens to be my favorite, an apple. Many of the rooftops have gardens where food is grown naturally and of course, reserved for people of status. I have had the good fortune of convincing several members of government to pay me in fruit instead of currency."

"How much would it cost to get one?" Paul asks as he continues to scarf his down, even eating the hard middle section.

"They have no price, because they are not for sale," Emmett says. "This kind of food makes it's own vitamins. Nothing is added or taken out. Quite unlike the concoction of white something or other that many tower dwellers are forced to eat. Carnegie never wanted anyone to know that this was something they could strive to have."

"How much stuff like this is there?" I ask.

"Go up to the roof and look for yourselves." Emmett tells us.

Paul shoots up and points towards a door on the far side of the room. "That way?" he asks. Emmett gives a slight nod and a smile. Paul hops over the small table in front of us and starts off at a jog. I walk around and catch up to him while he waits at the open door. On the other side, a set of metal stairs leads straight up to another doorway. Wind howls through it and a sliver of light pokes out through the bottom of the door. Excitement takes over our tired legs as we take the stairs two by two. When we reach the door Paul moves to the side and offers me the honor of opening it.

We burst through it and out into the open air. Both of us are instantly calmed by our awe. The sun is setting over the city, throwing a wave of orange and pink through the sky. Clouds block the light and colors here and there. And a row of trees casts their shadows down on us. Most of the ground around us is covered in soft, spongy ground. Sweet smells of the plants around us mix with a fresh, almost metallic smell.

"All of this for one man," I say. "I wonder if he even uses it all."

Paul doesn't hear me as he wanders through the soil and the plants that have been placed perfectly apart for someone to walk through. I run my fingers through vines and leaves. Things I only read about and never thought I'd be able to see or touch. When I reach the center there isn't much to see besides leaves and a variety of plump, low hanging fruit. Paul meets me there, with an apple already half eaten. We find an old wooden bench behind a bush and take a seat.

"I wish Dylan could have been here with us," he says as he chucks the core of the fruit. It rustles some leaves before settling.

"I wish we could go back for him," I say with a tone of agreement. "I feel like his body will just lay there forgotten or get dumped out a window like something easily disposed of."

"Hopefully it gets burned up in the fire Emmett started," Paul fights back a tear. "It would just be nice if he had something close to a proper send off. I couldn't stand to find him like we did Astor."

"Maybe the America Tower is still burning," I offer. "If so the least we could do is watch and hope the level he's on burns up."

It feels strange to talk about him like he's still alive and hope that his body is burning at the same time. We silently make our way through the garden on the roof and find the edge of the tower. The sun is almost completely past the horizon and the clouds from before have formed together and roll over each other as they charge towards us. Instead of beautiful it looks much more menacing in the fading light as the sky has turned red and the clouds flash and crash with the threat of a coming storm.

Below us a cloud of smoke still spills out of the broken windows. I almost expected Jack to still be staring out the same window. Fortunately that part of the level has been completely taken over. It would be such a gift if those flames had captured and burned him. If only it were that easy.

Paul sits on the edge and swings his legs over the side. I join him and use the railing there for support. We watch the fire dance in and out of windows as it travels through the building. Metal starts to groan, out into the open. The thunder from the storm answers back as the clouds

begin to fill the spaces between the towers. Both Paul and myself lean

our heads over the bars of the rail to try and keep an eye on the fire. The

smoke billows out and the smell is almost too much. For a friend we stay

and watch.

Soon we can only see an orange glow through fog and smoke

that mixes with it. When it starts to rain the light begins to waver and

when the wind starts the smell dissipates. All we can do now is wait and

hope. It's not like we could go back anymore. If the fire goes out the

tower will still be in Jack's control, if not we can only assume Dylan at

least got some kind of send off. We salute him from our spot above and I

tell myself we did everything we could.

"Do you think it was enough?" Paul's worried voice shouts over

the sound of the storm.

"I hope so," I yell back. Rain has started to hit us as well as the

fire below. A cloud even passes along the top of the Condè Tower. It

leaves us blinded. Paul becomes a shadow next to me. He grabs onto my

shoulder as I get up. Even with railings, neither of us wants to get

separated and end up spilling off the side.

"We should probably head in," I try to tell Paul. He nods his head and stays where he is, looking over the edge. I can't tell if he heard me so I tug on his arm. He pulls back and I hear the first explosion. A bright yellow flash goes down below us. Followed by several more. They continue to go off one after the other. Larger orange blossoms of light respond close by. Glass shatters and beams groan and snap. Gunfire starts up in the America Tower. Sparks of light go on and off like a beacon in the higher levels. I struggle to keep an eye on everything as the storm lets more water loose and the thunder goes on without pause. With the mixture of noises it becomes hard to tell what exactly is going on.

"Any idea who might be winning?" Paul screams into my ear.

I shake my head, unable to take my eyes away from the continued show of lights. One sound starts to overcome the rest. The foundation and supports of the tower have taken too much and it sounds like the Tower is falling. Any lights that were coming from inside have now stopped, but the bombing from below intensifies. Suddenly, the clouds in front of us grow darker. Breaking out of the mist come the words America. It confirms my thoughts. The tower sways into view. Rebels and soldiers still shoot at each other as it tilts and a few shots go astray and hit the roof near us. The groaning of metal twisting and breaking becomes overwhelming and people start to spill out of the windows. The America Tower is falling into the Condè.

CHAPTER FIFTEEN

We turn to run and at the same time Bear begins shouting above the last cries of the dying tower. "What's happening out here? Where are you?" he yells. I try to yell back as we run towards the sound of his voice, hand in hand with Paul. Then the Condè shudders and throws us into the dirt. My mouth fills with and I find myself spitting out pebbles as I get back up. Paul is slower to move and has to be pulled to his feet. Closer to him now, I can see that his eyes have glazed over. A quick slap and a push get him moving. When we reach the door and Bear we realize that the Condè isn't falling.

We pour through the door and Bear slams it shut against the howling wind. The light goes out as one more round of bombs go off. We lean against the wall as the stairs shake. In the dark Bear asks his question again.

"What went on out there?" his voice shakes. "Did you see who was winning?"

"No," Paul tells him. "All we saw were lights and all we heard was the storm and the explosions. I can't believe that just happened. A whole tower just fell and almost crushed us. Do you think Jack is dead?"

"If we could only be so lucky," Bear says. "I doubt that he was still there. Most likely he went back to wherever he's been hiding or he's out looking for us. Those left in the tower were most likely just trying to gather whatever hadn't been destroyed by the fire."

"So they took down a whole tower just to kill a few of Jack's men?" I ask. "That's insane."

"No, I'm sure they had hoped for Jack to be there just as much as us," Bear murmurs distantly. "But I wouldn't be surprised by any continued extreme actions. I never expected them to float away quietly with the current just because someone finally took a shot at them. It's much more likely that they would burn the whole city down rather than lose it. This is part of why we need to get back to the library and tell Hobbes what's happened so we can decide what to do next. To start, let's get off these stairs and hope the penthouse still has power."

We grope our way down the steps with Bear leading the way. He finds the door handle and we are satisfied with the little amount of light that we do find. Nothing more than a green glow from several light sticks on the floor. At the edge of the light Emmett is strapping his gear on as Wolf adds another bandage to Grace's arm. She is standing and alert, but even in the low light she looks spent.

"So we're all leaving then?" I ask.

"Yeah I thought this place was safe for awhile. Can't Grace and Wolf stay for now?" Paul adds.

"Well, considering a tower was almost dropped on us, and the fact that every single patroller and ONE security enforcer is going to be scouring this area shortly, we might want to get moving," Emmett says. "Also, Wolf wants to get Grace to your base for more extensive medical attention."

Before we can get another word in, Bear adds on. "We found some gear in a safe room so we can get home. Paul, you're going with them right now." Wolf has already started walking Grace towards the door. Paul goes off at a trot to catch up. Before Bear continues, I hear O2 gear start clanging together.

"The three of us are going to look through what remains of the tower," Bear continues. "If we can I want to recover Dylan and I want to be sure Jack wasn't in it when it fell. I have a feeling he'll be hiding, if he doesn't show his face for awhile Carnegie may feel confident enough to call the bombing a success. However, I won't feel easy about it until I know he's gone for sure."

"But if this place is going to be full of people we don't want to see how are we going to do that?" I ask.

Emmett's face breaks into a grin, "We get to wear the big boy wetsuits. The top shelf stuff that personal guards get for watching people like Astor. His safe room had a few extra pairs. It should make sense to them that some heavy hitters will be down there now that Astor and Caldwell are gone. Either way no one will question us if it looks like we outrank them."

"OK let's get ready then," I respond.

By the time we get suited up and ready to head down Paul calls us over the radio to tell us that patrollers have already started pouring in from a submarine that has anchored next to the tower. Grace had managed to hold herself together for a few minutes until they all passed, which means the suits work. Some of the men had even stopped to salute them.

We leave the pent house with confidence and even decide to take the elevator down. When Emmett presses the button the lift dings and five patrollers spill out. They move right past us and sweep the room. They only use hand signals until they find one of Grace's blood stained bandages.

"Sirs, whose blood is this?" the one holding it asks us.

When Emmett shrugs they all reach for their guns. Before any clear the holster, Emmett has already shot everyone, except for the one holding the used gauze. He still hasn't moved and a dark spot starts to grow on his pants.

"You don't pull a weapon on a superior," Emmett lectures the remaining patroller. "Anyone else coming up here?"

"Who are you?" he replies.

"So that would be a no," Emmett says. He shoots the man in the face once.

The lift dings again and the doors start to close. Bear jams his arm between them and they bounce back open and ding again. We file in and Emmett hits the bottom button.

"You could have at least made an attempt to create some kind of story," Bear tells Emmett. "Those men obviously weren't a threat to us if you could dispatch them so easily."

"Sometimes it's just quicker to shoot before someone can ask more questions," he says with a shrug. "Besides I've always found it so tedious to try and sneak around. Now that the war has finally started there's no need. Everyone is shooting everyone."

"Has it really become so easy for you to kill?" Bear asks.

"Only when I make jokes about it or they would have killed me instead," Emmett says.

The lift comes to a sudden stop and we stroll out onto the bottom floor. On the other side of the glass the sub is anchored to the tower outside and two patrollers have stayed behind to guard it. The hull is marked with dents and streaks from the earlier fighting, but the two men appear to be free of any injuries. As we walk towards it they draw their weapons and tell us not to move. Emmett reaches for his own gun until Bear stands in his way with raised arms. The seams of his wetsuit scream at the seams in response to his movements.

"What the fuck," Emmett hisses from behind his back.

"We're fine," Bear mutters back.

"Ranks and names," one of them shouts as we continue to walk towards them. "We weren't told about any personal guards being stationed here. They've all been killed along with 'The Voice.' The rest have been brought in to guard Chancellor Carnegie."

"We were on a break," Bear argues. "We have no idea what's been going on since we lost contact with our squad."

"Stop moving and spread out," the patroller commands. "No one takes a break in Astor's pent house. Get down on the floor before I fry you."

Emmett glares at Bear as we slowly spread out and lie down on the floor. He doesn't say it, but his eyes scream blame. I can't see past my goggles with my face on the ground, but I hear wet boots hit the tile floor as they jump down from the sub. Their clean boots squeak with every step until they're right above our heads. Shackles jingle as they pull them from their belts. Emmett and Bear tense up as the patrollers hover over us. Before they attempt to fight an explosion rips through the air.

It's quickly followed by a large wave that rams the submarine into the tower. It rolls into the building and wedges itself between the floor and ceiling. The water pours over and around it and crashes into us. I roll

into the wall and try to use it to get to my feet. Bear does the same, while

Emmett has already taken a knife to one of the patrollers. Bear fires on

the other patroller before he can regain his feet. The patroller falls back

into the rush of water and gently floats away.

"I hope you're beginning to see this whole killing thing from a new

perspective," Emmett says to Bear as he drops the now limp body in his

hands. "Not only does it make life easy, it makes your life continue. So

next time just let me shoot the bastards when they question us."

"I still don't think your philosophy applies to all situations," Bear

replies.

Just as he says this, a third man crawls from the hatch of the tipped

over vessel. Emmett throws his knife and kills him before throwing his

arms up in frustration at Bear. "Get it together," he groans. "You are the

biggest waste of killing potential I've ever seen. Literally, the biggest! I

bet you've killed a man with a single punch. Hasn't he kid?" he points at

me.

"I mean he has," I say. "But only when he had to."

"Before Jack lost his way we only ever used violence when

necessary," Bear says. "We'd like to keep it that way if we can."

"You people are going to bring me down with you," Emmett says, defeated.

"Doesn't anyone want to know what that explosion was?" I wonder out loud. Partly to interrupt their bickering and partly because I would like to know what had just been blown up.

"It's safe to assume Jack's men have taken out another submarine just as it was about to reach the surface," Bear says. 'Either way, it isn't anything for us to be concerned about right now."

"I say we jump in and take a look around," Emmett suggests. "I was going to recommend that we take their sub, but I doubt even Bear can roll it back into the water." Without another word he walks around the submarine to the windows and splashes into the water as he jumps in.

"Something is broken inside his head," Bear says.

"Maybe his mom dropped him," I reply with a smile.

We both walk over to catch up with him. He's already swimming away when we gather our bearings underwater. It's filled with dust and it isn't possible to see more than a few feet. I never thought we would experience something worse than our journey to the America Tower, but now every time I reach out a hand I fear what it might be touching. Bear flicks on a headlamp attached to his goggles and does the same for me. It's straining to try and catch up to Emmett, but now that I can at least see his feet. Before we can get close enough to him, he disappears from sight behind a slab of the fallen tower. Bear motions for us to each take one way around. When we meet on the other side Emmett is still missing. The floating graveyard we just ran into also doesn't help. I bump into a body, thinking that it's Bear until I realize I'm swimming through dozens of bodies. Each hangs a few feet from the surface, either stuck to parts of the tower or weighed down by weapons and gear.

The tower itself is being held up by a row of others that sit just a few levels below the surface. For the most part the insides are still intact. Tangles of cords float around, some with people wrapped up inside them. We push our way through and enter the belly of the building. The new horizontal layout makes it hard to navigate even though most of it looks the same. We take our time with the immediate area when we see the white walls of Caldwell's level. Hopefully if Dylan is still here, we can find him and take him home. And if we find Jack later on we can leave him here and be glad. Either way I want to get out of this maze before we become part of the graveyard it holds.

As I dig through chairs and rubble I find a corner of what looks like one of our vests. I tug on it, but it doesn't budge. Before moving more pieces of crumbled tower out of the way I prepare myself. When I finally pull the vest free part of Dylan comes with it and I spit out a cloud of puke into the ocean. What remains of his body is charred and mutilated. His face is less than human. I wave away the cloud of vomit as Bear swims over. He produces a large net and gently puts Dylan inside. He grabs me by the back of the head and gently puts his to mine. We leave him there for now as we continue the search.

After three more levels of bodies there is no clear sign that Jack was among them. We give up and head back to where we started. At this point we know we wouldn't find him down here, but it had been nice to think it was possible, even for a moment. When we get back to the outside we run into the lights of seven headlamps sweeping the area. We're too far away to be seen so we click off our lights. Still, one of them shoots straight for us. We grab Dylan and swim behind a large bunch of camera equipment. Emmett appears through the haze. He sees us almost right away and excitedly motions for us to come to him. When we reach him his eyes tell me it isn't a good kind of excited. He madly searches around himself until he finds a piece of dust-covered glass. He rubs a finger across it in an attempt to write. When it comes out as a blob he motions for us to go topside.

We swim through the debris and I pull myself up over the edge of a part of the tower still above the surface. I rip my goggles off and help Emmett up as he tries to scramble onto the concrete. When Bear gets out and finds a spot next him he starts to speak.

"I caught up with Wolf and them," he says quickly. "Something has happened, you need to see it for yourselves."

"Just tell us now," I beg.

"The place, your base," Emmett stammers.

"Yes, the library," Bear interrupts.

"It's gone."

ABOUT THE AUTHOR

Alex Beld lives in Wisconsin. He enjoys beer and time spent out in the snow.

www.ingramcontent.com/pod-product-compliance
Lightning Source LLC
Chambersburg PA
CBHW070641180626
46817CB00006B/2193